Totally Bound Publishing books by A.B. Wilson

The Shellenberg Brothers
The Role
The Game

The Shellenberg Brothers

THE GAME

A.B. WILSON

The Game
ISBN # 978-1-83943-774-8
©Copyright A.B. Wilson 2022
Cover Art by Erin Dameron-Hill ©Copyright March 2022
Interior text design by Claire Siemaszkiewicz
Totally Bound Publishing

THE GAME

Dedication

This one goes out to the members of my mother's book club who can still look me in the eye after reading my sexy scenes.

The author acknowledges that she has utilized artistic license with professional and collegiate sporting schedules to further the plot of this book.

Chapter One

Abby

Air horns, club songs and pile-ons from teammates. Confetti raining down in the drizzle, sticking to our hair and rain-spattered, grass-stained jerseys. I would never forget the moment that the F.C. Chelsea women's soccer team won the Championship. Never, ever in my life had I felt the level of exhilaration that the men's team must feel after the average game, because that's how many people had jammed into Stamford Bridge stadium to watch us win — a sold-out crowd.

All around me my teammates had torn off their jerseys to trade with our opponents and were battling tears with sloppy hugs. Something magical happens at the closing whistle of a hotly competitive match that the average person never feels. The way in which your direst enemy suddenly becomes your friend, happy for you in your happiness. There is that solidarity amongst female athletes where those congratulatory moments mean something, and I'd been dreaming of this one since I was five years old.

Up in the manager's box the entire men's team was cheering us on. And there. Right in the middle of the crowd, if I could be bothered to look, would be my nemesis with his dirty-blond hair trapped in a messy top knot. His nice dress clothes most likely all rumpled and his sleeves rolled up to show off his massive, tattooed forearms.

His electric-blue eyes would be crackling above his stubbly, chiseled cheekbones and jawline. He was probably waving his hands theatrically, acting the fool with everyone loving on him. If he were American instead of German, I'd have bet money on his tie being wrapped around his head. Matti Shellenberg, a man I'd wished a bad case of jock itch on more times than was probably healthy.

Knowing he was up there was enough to make my blood boil. My eyes shot straight to him — like there was a magnetic force between the two of us — even at this distance. To my complete shock, he wasn't in the mix with his teammates. Instead he was sitting all alone in a corner of the box — him, the man who was never still, never at rest, never less than one hundred percent positively on. The center of attention and master instigator. Now he sat slumped in his chair like a puppet with his strings cut, head in hands.

He's probably pissed we're getting all the attention.

One year later, I could still feel the mashed potatoes crusting in my eyebrows and long auburn hair, which I'd curled so carefully the night of the fundraiser for pediatric cancer patients. Those hyper-realistic plastic spiders he'd stuck on my chair that made me scream and flip my plate, launching a shower of food down on top of me and my tablemates.

I could still see him in my mind's eye, doubled over in laughter, wiping tears of hilarity off his flushed cheeks. Could still hear his delighted slow clap and taunt. *"You gonna come after me with that steak knife, Stabby Abby?"* I hated nicknames, but I had to admit that 'Stabby Abby' was one I could get behind. *That clever jerk.*

The confetti storm had finally settled in colorful, sodden clumps and the team's owner and head of operations strode through the tunnel and out onto the pitch for the trophy ceremony. I winced as I wound my way through the crowd. My bad knee was twinging like a motherfucker after a tackle from Porto's defender that had knocked me awkwardly onto my ass. Hopefully I'd only twisted it, nothing more serious.

My co-captain, Teresa, wrapped an arm around my shoulders and started tugging me toward the hastily erected podium at midfield. The team song was still blaring through the stadium speakers and the emotions of the day were catching me. I'd won a gold medal with the U.S. Women's National Team, but this was somehow bigger. Better, because it was unexpected. Times like this reminded me that every sacrifice I'd made to play professionally was worth it.

Tears pricked my eyes as Teresa hugged me close. "We did it, chica. Can you believe it?"

I hugged her back and we wiped each other's tears and laughed. "You get up there first," I encouraged. She hopped up on the stage and pulled me up behind her. Together, we walked to the podium to accept the trophy. The owner and manager were tag-teaming a self-congratulatory speech about how delightful and historic the moment was. Teresa and I exchanged a Look. This moment would have come a lot sooner if the club had bothered to invest in its women's side the way it did in the men's.

The owner handed us the trophy, almost bobbling it as he attempted to kiss our cheeks. The smell of whiskey flowed off of him as he leered at us. Teresa and I did our duty, ignoring the foul, smelly man as we smiled and raised that trophy high above our heads. Not even a lecher could rub the shine off of this one for us. I kissed the cool, damp metal that smelled like blood and fresh grass. That too-brief kiss was, without a doubt, the greatest in my entire history of kisses — not that that history was particularly long or interesting.

I jumped down with the Cup, wincing again as my knee protested the action, and passed it off to my teammates. Teresa and I stood back from them, arm-in-arm as we watched the celebration continue. The men's team would be rushing the field soon because they could never handle the women's team having the lion's share of attention. I had no interest in being out there when Ratty Matti showed and turned to Teresa. "I'm going to the locker room, need to hit the ice baths before we have to get ready for the party. Cover for me?"

"You got it. Guess we all need some extra time to look our best tonight after this, huh?" She winked at me.

"Ugh, totally. But if I don't get in an ice bath soon, I'm not going to be able to stand in high heels." My tone was rueful and she slugged me in the shoulder, jerking her head in the direction of the locker room.

I took one last mental picture of my still-celebrating teammates, and the fans who hadn't stopped singing our song, and started for the bench to scoop my kit. As I maneuvered around the celebrants and the men's team clattering up from the tunnel, I glanced back at the owner's box and got one hell of a shock. Matti was still there, not down with the rest of his team trying to steal our glory. No, he was still in his seat with his head in his hands. *Curiouser and curiouser.*

The locker room was empty, but the training staff were there and ready with congratulations and help getting the tape off from the brace around my knee. I'd suffered an ACL tear not too long ago and coming back had been an excruciating journey.

The physio helped me into the tub and one of his assistants started dumping in the ice. The cold burn of an ice bath was something that athletes supposedly got addicted to. Me, though, I was dreaming about tropical beaches and a solitary walk on white sand with the ocean curling in to tickle my toes as I shivered uncontrollably while buried in the tiny cubes.

"McKinnon, your mobile's ringin', darlin'! Says 'Sylvie'. That's your agent, right?" The head physio shook my shoulder as he showed me the screen of my phone.

I sank back into the tub and managed to get out through my chattering teeth, "It can wait till I'm done here, probably a congratulations."

"I dunno, darlin', this is the third time she's called in five minutes. You're about done, let's get you out of there and you can take the call." He hadn't even really congratulated me. Nor had he asked me if I was okay, given the slight limp I knew he'd seen with his laser-like focus on all of our working extremities. My stomach hollowed out and my shivers got bigger and stronger as I accepted his hand and let him haul me out of the tub.

What does he know?

I grabbed my phone and headed back to the locker room with a newfound sense of foreboding and sent a quick text to Sylvie that I'd call when I was out of the shower. I resolutely ignored the immediate buzz of a reply and the repeated chimes that indicated an incoming call. All I needed was one more moment to bask in the feeling of winning, of being a winner, of finally, *finally* achieving my dream before the real world could intrude again.

The water speared into me and I could barely hear the shouts and laughter of my teammates finally coming off the pitch over its spray. Our ancient locker room was about to turn into a pre-party while we all got ready for the huge end-of-season shindig thrown by the club's owners.

A bunch of us—me included—wanted nothing more than to go home, but one simply did not skip this event. No matter how tired, no matter how injured. You went, you gladhanded the shit out of everyone, and you pretended to have the best time. Every year, I dreaded it. This year, though, things would be different. We were winners and I was trying to shake my salty reputation—my contract was up for renewal in the off-season. I cranked the water to cold to rinse out the last of my conditioner and practiced my biggest, most pleasant smile. My cheeks hurt already.

With my team all around me, their chatter echoing off the cinderblocks that needed a new coat of paint, I felt like I was in my safe space. Safe enough, at any rate, to call Sylvie back. The insulation of their enthusiasm made a little bubble around me as I waited for her to pick up. I snorted when her voicemail kicked in. That was so Sylvie, harass me for hours, then pout when I finally did what she wanted—probably thought she was teaching me a lesson.

Joke was on her, though. I'd grown up in the most passively aggressive toxic home with a mother who knew how to wield silence as a weapon as easily as a backhanded compliment. In a small Midwestern town in southern Wisconsin where everyone knew you and your business.

Shoving thoughts of Sylvie aside, I forced my attention to making myself up to appear as photogenic and approachable as possible. Most of the other girls had completed their transition from sweaty athlete to debutante and were starting to file out to the hired cars that would take us to the Fairmont Hotel for the celebration while I was still winding a final section of hair around my curling iron.

"Want me to make sure there's a car for you when you finally finish?" Teresa asked with a small smile as she appeared in the mirror behind me. She knew how much I hated the schmoozing that went along with our captain's badges.

I waved my curling iron at her and pointed at my freshly made-up face. "Nah, no big deal. Just need to make sure Sam's makeover wasn't in vain. If I miss the last car, I'll cab it."

Teresa shrugged and gave me a tiny finger wave as she pushed through the swinging doors. "Your funeral if you miss it."

"I'll be there, don't worry."

After much overspraying, the last section of my stick-straight dark-auburn hair was obediently wrapped around the hot iron. The big pin curls were fantastic in contrast with my pale, freckled skin and gray eyes. I looked like a dolled-up gladiator in my dark green dress with the black lace overlay and admired the way it hugged the smooth muscles I'd sacrificed so much to build and hone. I was taking a last dab at a slightly overcolored spot on my top lip when my phone finally rang.

And like every time it rang without me immediately being able to see who was calling, my brain shouted hopefully, "Mom?" I castigated myself for still believing in the impossible. She hadn't come around to my profession or my love for the game in twenty-three years. There was no starting now. I flipped my phone over and saw my agent's face with her badass shark grin and tapped the screen.

"Sylvie," I said without further greeting. Sylvie hated what she called "perfunctory nonsense."

"Abigail Jean," she returned grandly. Never mind that that wasn't my middle name. First- and middle-naming me was the way she showed her affection and Sylvie changed it up every time.

I rolled my eyes. "What's up?"

"Did I feel you rolling your eyes at me, young lady? Because I got a *distinct* vibe from that—"

"Sylvie, cut the crap. What's going on that you had to blow me up like this tonight of all nights?" I asked impatiently.

"My dear, I know. I know. While I would love to let you rest on your laurels, I unfortunately can't." She sighed and my stomach knotted again as she continued, laying it out bluntly and with no sugary sweetness to cushion the blow. "The team has decided that they'd like to go a different direction next season. They have some kid from South Korea on scout who is basically you pre-ACL tear on performance-enhancing drugs."

I couldn't speak or breathe. Now? After six years and a championship. Had they seen me limp around after my knee got torqued to hell?

"I know, dear, this is a lot to take in and it feels like it's out of nowhere," she said with no small amount of sympathy. "I was shocked too. Completely taken by surprise. Between you and Matti, Chelsea is — "

"Matti? What happened to Matti?" I asked, my voice higher-pitched than I would have thought possible. Sylvie managed both of us and he was a recent sign for her after his last agent cut him loose. And that had gone down in a spectacular, flaming ball of shame when yet another of his infamous house parties had turned into a drug-and-alcohol-fueled orgy. Management hadn't been fond of those photos when they appeared online.

"He's being cut. Only the team had the grace to actually tell him in person, unlike this fiasco."

"When did you find out about us?" I asked, wondering if they'd already decided they wanted someone else before they'd seen me win the game for the team, before they might have spotted the slight limp.

"Well," she prevaricated. "Here's the thing, they called me right at kick-off. Matti was told at your half-time. I don't want you to worry. There are going to be a lot of teams interested in you after today's win and Matti is always bankable. I've already had a few calls for each of you."

She paused and I could tell she'd popped in a square of nicotine gum as I heard the aggressive chewing noise. "I know how you feel about him, but I need you to do me a favor and keep an eye on him tonight. He's not answering his phone and when he drinks, bad things tend to follow. I need you two to be on your best behavior while I negotiate."

"Sylvie, I'm not his keeper and tonight's going to be crappy enough. You know how badly he embarrassed me back at that fundraiser," I responded through a clenched jaw.

"You don't have to talk to him — although maybe it wouldn't be such a terrible thing if you could pull that stick out of your ass and drop the grudge. I've always thought the two of you would make such a cute couple." She muttered the last part and sighed heavily, like I was the one who made her life difficult and not the eternal man-child. Who, yes, was super hot, but oh my god was he an awful person.

"Please, Abby, get him in a cab if he gets too unruly, I'll text you his address," she begged.

I groaned and felt a headache start to form behind my eyes. "Fine, but I want a cut from his signing bonus for doing you this favor."

Sylvie ignored my sarcastic comment. "I'm flying out from La Guardia tonight, will be at Heathrow tomorrow morning. We'll meet then and can start talking about your options."

I sighed and slumped back onto the bench, feeling completely unmoored. My options. Six years, the peak of my career as an athlete, and they'd "*decided to go a different direction*." The pendulum had swung back and the price I'd already paid to play the sport that I loved, the only thing that had ever mattered to me, now seemed indecently high. *Fuck this beautiful fucking game.*

Who even am I without soccer to define me?

Chapter Two

Matti

My phone wouldn't stop buzzing, Sylvie's surprised face beaming up at me every five minutes. Surely she'd back off eventually. At least she knew enough not to text. Given my literacy challenges, she'd quickly figured out that was futile unless she wanted to end up trading GIFs and emojis like preteens.

"Oy! Shellenberg! Matti, get your arse over here!" Connor was bellowing at me again.

I shook my head and slid my empty glass back to the bartender for a refill. I appreciated Connor's effort, but I wasn't going anywhere. Despite firing me during the game, the owner and team manager still expected me to show up and play my part—the merry prankster keeping everyone amused—until the story dropped. Nik and Silas were assholes, but they knew how to manage the message. After all, they'd been doing it on my behalf for the last two years.

So, nah. Playing my part didn't sound super fun. I was here, holding up the corner of the bar at this fancy hotel for everyone to gawk at and that was going to have to be enough for the night. The famous soccer player who couldn't hold down a contract to save his life. I raised a glass to my own idiocy — fit for nothing but being an athlete, yet couldn't keep a job.

"Well, well. Ratty Matti Shellenberg." The voice behind me morphed into a real person as Abby McKinnon dropped heavily onto the bar stool next to me.

Wonderful. The woman of my dreams who utterly hates me, here to rip me a new one once again for taking — yes, I admit it — a very juvenile dare.

"Ratty Matti, eh? I didn't know you cared, Stabby Abby. How's tricks? Loving that winning feeling? Don't worry, the shine will wear off soon enough." I took a genteel sip from my fresh drink. My usual sparkling banter seemed to have gone AWOL on me. Too bad because I'd fallen for her the first time I met her — the steely determination and drive to be the best I'd seen in those Ice-Queen eyes had knocked me on my ass.

"Oh, shut up, Matti. You know Sylvie's my agent too?" she asked.

"Yeah, of course." No, I'd completely forgotten, actually.

"I'm supposed to keep an eye on you tonight," she said with a sigh.

"Don't need a minder. I'm just sitting here, doing nothing to get in trouble. I'm sorry about the spiders too, all right? Leave me alone," I grumbled as I rolled my half-full drink back and forth between my palms.

"It's okay. Let's forget about it for tonight. Instead of a babysitter, maybe you'll take a drinking buddy?" She met my eyes for the first time in over a year. Their arctic color warmed slightly, melting the iceberg that had settled solidly in my chest after the "it's definitely you, not us, we have to let you go" conversation with Nik.

"Why? I don't need anyone to feel bad for me. What did Sylvie offer you for this?" I couldn't help but doubt her intentions. I'd messed up big-time with that prank designed to get her attention. I'd wanted her to see me, but all she'd ever see was the guy who dumped spiders on her chair.

"What? I mean, nothing. Obviously she cares —"

I shook my head and felt the knot in my hair start to loosen. "This is bullshit. Even if she does, you don't need to do anything." Before my hair could truly go haywire, I grabbed the elastic and yanked it out. Frantically scraped the tangled blond mess back and tossed it into a new knot with an even tighter band I'd had in my back pocket.

Her gaze softened further and went a little glassy as I went through my hair routine. She shook her head in a daze and reached for the drink menu. "I'll take a Manhattan," she said to the bartender, and he gave her an appreciative once-over and turned to do her bidding. I snorted. Yeah, she was gorgeous with her curvy, muscular body poured into that green dress. Those legs, shit. And, while I longed for her, she hated me — the sex would be off the charts.

She turned back to me with the usual fire and ice in her stare. "Excuse me?"

I had a real problem with internal monologues staying internal. Insomuch as they never did. Stay internal, that is. I waved a hand at her and sighed. "Sorry. It's been a real bastard of a day."

"Matti, that's why I came over and asked if you wanted a drinking buddy. It's only partially because of

Sylvie. I'm not getting renewed either. Seems like we're both on the job market." She dropped her eyes to her lap where she shredded a bar napkin, barely noticing when her drink was brought over by the bartender.

"Say what?" I asked more gently than I'd thought possible, and nudged the highball glass toward her. She took it gratefully and tossed half of it back immediately, choking and flushing a delicious red as she coughed and waved a hand in front of her face.

"You're supposed to sip it, Abby," I said.

"I know," she gasped. "Can't stand whiskey but there's no way I'm staying sober tonight."

"They're seriously not renewing you? After today?" I glanced around, convinced that a camera was hiding somewhere. This was a perfect prank scenario for her to exact retribution. "You're the golden girl of the team. Captain and all that shit. I don't get it." I pulled her drink away as she tried to reach for it again. "Nuh-uh. Explain."

She gave me a dirty look that somehow didn't have as much heat in it as I would have expected of her. "There's nothing to explain. They decided to 'go a different direction', with a teenage phenom who is, as Sylvie says, 'me from five years ago on steroids'."

"Ouch." I grimaced at her.

"Yeah," she said and finished her drink.

I waved the bartender over. "Two more, please."

"Thanks. Anyways, Sylvie wanted me to find you, she's flying over tomorrow. Apparently she has a few options for each of us, but she hasn't been able to get a hold of you." The last statement was really more of a question.

"I'm not taking calls right now," I said. To my surprise, she started to laugh. It was a really pretty laugh. Warm and open, friendly. Like honey bubbles in the chamomile tea my grandmother used to make me whenever I visited her as a kid.

Our drinks came and I slid hers over, raised my own, and we clinked our glasses together. "So, what are we doing to fuck them all over?" I asked.

She closed one eye and stared at me. "Why would we do that? It's a game. Just a business to them."

"Because it's bullshit? You don't deserve this at all. Me, I mean, maybe I do. But you definitely don't," I tried to explain.

"Bah," she muttered. "I'm no good at revenge."

"We should join forces then, because I am very good at revenge."

"I bet you are." She smiled at me and her whole face changed while something in my chest rumbled to life. Like a clogged engine turning over for the first time in years.

"Does the team know you got cut?" she asked.

"Connor does," I said with a shrug, referring to our rookie goalkeeper and the closest thing I had to an actual friend on the team. "Why?"

"What if we were to do something ridiculous? And get in trouble. Would they use that as their reason for letting us go?" she wondered.

"I have no idea what your brain is doing right now, but I like it. Continue."

She turned toward me, gray eyes glittering like manic crystals above the two red spots high on her perfectly rounded cheekbones. "We should definitely kiss," she declared so certainly that I started laughing.

The glitter dulled. "What?"

"You're not kidding?" I asked slowly.

"No, it's perfect. Players from the men's and women's teams aren't allowed to have intra-club relationships. What if we pretended we were together and then, when we were busted and inevitably fired, we could go to the press with our — *sob* — love story, and the cruel, cruel club who kicked us out for our tragic affair," she explained feverishly.

Holy shit, she wasn't kidding. And it was actually kind of — dare I say it — a brilliant idea. Like taking back control of the story. Shutting down the inevitable conjecture that we'd secretly been injured or anything else that would make it harder for us to get new jobs.

"I *could* kiss you. I guess you're kind of pretty," I teased as I leaned toward her and willed my very excited dick to remain chill. I might have jerked it a time or twelve over my top-secret crush who was now offering to kiss me, but that didn't mean that he had permission to go buck wild.

"And I *could* kiss you, I guess. You're pretty fucking hot. Even if you are a complete jerk and I hate you," she said with a very slight slur.

Huh. I'd take that. She thought I was hot, no, scratch that, *"pretty fucking hot."* From Abby McKinnon, no less. *Be cool, man.*

"So, how should we do this, boss-lady?" I reached out to wind one of her bouncy curls around my finger. I stretched it out slowly and we both watched, fascinated, as it *boinged* back into place.

"Hmm." She looked around. A few people were staring at us curiously. Then she leaned closer, trailing her fingers up my forearm and sending little zing of heat straight to my cock, and hooked my bow tie, pulling me in. "I was thinking I could whisper sweet nothings in your ear, like this. Now, laugh."

I did. I couldn't help it, her whiskey breath tickled. She seemed pleased with my response and leaned closer. "Do you see how many people are looking at us?"

Her lips brushed the shell of my ear and I shuddered. Whether she intended to or not, she was turning me on. But we were playing a game and attracting a lot of attention—which I guess was the entire point. I placed a hand on her thigh and she jumped. My fingers tightened and she whimpered. *Whimpered. Be still my beating cock.*

"Shh, Abby. Maybe we should tone it down a notch? This is going to get me in a lot of trouble," I managed to whisper in her ear, and she shivered as goosebumps broke out all over her exposed arms and legs.

"Isn't that the point?" she whispered back as she swiped my earlobe with the very tip of her tongue, then nipped it.

My mind went completely blank. "The point?" I reached for her and she leaned back.

"Nuh-uh." Her turn to wave a finger at me playfully.

"Abby, stop messing around," I ground out as she stood up. Her legs were a little wobbly, like a newborn colt's, and she tapped each of my thighs with one of her long fingers, the nails buffed and shaped into perfect half-moons but still short and practical. Polish-free. My legs parted almost of their own volition and she stepped into the void. "You really want to do this? Play this game?" I asked in a hoarse voice and, when she nodded, asked the most relevant question. "With me? You want to do this with *me*?"

She stared up at me, still so much smaller than my own six feet six inches. Her eyes were bright with mischief and something else, excitement, maybe, as she trailed her fingers up my thighs and clutched the lapels of my suit coat. "Oh, I really, really want this. Let's fuck 'em up, Matti."

"*Give the ladies what they want*" had always been the advice of my father. I gave him a mental tip of the hat as I pulled her toward me by the hips and kissed her, my hands moving to cradle the back of her head. She let go of my jacket lapels and cupped my jaw as her tongue slid into my mouth, dueling with my own. I liked the way she wasn't content to let me take charge of the situation.

It had started out as something funny, something petty to hurt other people the way we'd been hurt. A bargain between two consenting adults, only one of whom probably had any respect for the other—only one of whom actually liked the other. Somewhere along the line, maybe fifteen seconds in when she nipped my lower lip playfully and I groaned like I hadn't come in months, everything changed and we both turned to devour each other.

She tipped her head back and I pulled away to kiss down her jawline and neck, across her exposed collarbone. Her eyes opened slowly and she slid her fingers into my long hair, loosening it again from the knot on top of my head and pulling me closer. I wanted her pulling my hair all night, naked in a hotel suite, anywhere but here.

Abby hovered closer and whispered, "Why do you have to feel so good—" She cut off with a moan as I covered her mouth again with my own.

My hands tightened on her hips and she gasped. A tiny puff of air that made me growl like a caveman against her lips. "I'm sorry, are you okay? Did I hurt you?"

She shook her head and grabbed for one of my hands, squeezed it in reassurance, before dragging her fingers across my stomach and skating over my chest to wrap around my neck. "Do it again, I liked it. Want more."

A hard smack to my shoulder distracted me and she jolted away, staring at me with dazed eyes and a kiss-swollen mouth. I slowly twisted around on my stool and saw Connor glowering at us. I turned back to Abby and my stomach dropped as I watched her eyes dart past me. She dropped her arms from where they'd encircled my neck and I felt that loss of warmth like a bucket of cold water dumped on my head. I turned back to the crowded room. All of our teammates and the operations leads were staring, jaws on the floor. At least half a dozen phones were pointed directly at us.

"Crap," she breathed. Her eyebrows were scrunched up in confusion and she shook her head like she was emerging from a pool and trying to shake the water out of her ears.

Wasn't this what she'd wanted to happen? I shrugged and took her hand, trying to telepathically remind her that it was okay and that we were in this together. As the silence stretched longer, she started to tremble. Ultimately, it became too much and she broke, tearing her hand from mine and fleeing the ballroom.

"What are you waiting for?" growled Connor as he slapped me again, this time upside the head. "Go after her, you arsehole!"

I nodded, still dazed from the power she'd packed into her kiss, and lurched to my feet to chase after the first woman to make my heart pound like a teenager since I actually was one. My thoughts were scattered as I dashed through the hallways. All I knew was that I had to find her before it was too late to apologize.

As I pushed through the front doors of the Fairmont, time seemed to slow down. I spied Abby taking a half step off the curb, her foot hovering in mid-air before she disappeared amidst loud car horns, shrieking and finally the crunch of metal on something infinitely more breakable. A sick, meaty thud.

The numbers on my phone were incomprehensible in that horrific moment as I pushed onlookers aside and raced toward the small figure in the green dress who now lay crumpled in the gutter. For the millionth time, I cursed every teacher who'd ever given up on me. I stabbed at the digits' placement roughly, hoping I'd hit the right ones to call emergency services.

Other than a few scrapes from meeting the concrete curb, there were no injuries on her face, but from the neck down she was a mess. As I watched, a small trickle of blood started to flow out from behind her head. I swore furiously. "Get back, everyone, get back."

Sirens erupted as I tore off my suit coat and laid it across her legs to cover her from any eyes that might try to peek. "Abby, baby, it's gonna be okay. An ambulance will be here soon. Hang in there." I was barely able to choke out the words and my hands were shaking so badly that my jacket kept sliding off of her.

"Lad, you have to let us work. We need to transfer her immediately. Are you together?" A man with a strong Scottish brogue wrapped an arm around me and heaved me to my feet.

I nodded wordlessly as he led me back a few steps.

"Girlfriend?" he asked and I shook my head.

"Wife?" He frowned, more impatient as they loaded her into the ambulance. I made a move to join her.

"Lad, you can't go with unless you're related and if she's not your wife—"

"My fiancée! She's my fiancée! I have to go," I practically shouted in desperation, and I heard the murmur of the crowd grow behind me as they realized who we were. The dots started to connect for the EMS tech and he ushered me into the ambulance.

"All right, Matthias, she's in good hands, but you need to come with us now. Figure out who else to call and they can meet us at the hospital." He handed me the iPhone with a big crack in the screen that he'd pried out of Abby's hand.

I nodded silently, cursing the unfamiliar phone that the medic had handed me after holding it to her unconscious face to unlock it. I scrolled through the contacts, but it was useless without the photos I relied on and I threw it down, hissing in anger. I grabbed my own phone and asked Siri to call Sylvie stat. When she didn't pick up, I left a message.

"Sylvie, there's been an accident. Abby was hit by a car. When you get in you need to come to —" I turned, helplessly, to the medic. "Where are we going?"

"St. Vincent's," he grunted as he continued to work the bag delivering oxygen to her lungs.

" —St. Vincent's. Get here as quickly as you can, Sylvie."

"Come on, Abby. Open your eyes, please, baby, open them." I didn't realize I'd said it out loud until one of the other EMS guys gave me a soft smile.

"We've got her. Don't worry about a thing," he promised and clapped me on the shoulder.

I didn't care if she was in the best hands possible. This was my fault. If she couldn't play anymore after this, I would never, ever forgive myself.

Chapter Three

Abby

Sweat drips down my legs and pools behind my too-big shin guards that are hand-me-downs from my older brother. I'm eight and standing in the middle of my hometown's scraggly field that's mostly clay with scattered spots of crabgrass. One of the goalposts is slightly crooked and the crossbar is tinged with rust spots. There are tiny divots from cleats baked into the hard ground, grass a distant memory on this hazy August afternoon.

This is the day that I realize that all I ever want is to feel the excitement of winning, scoring the final goal for my team, forever. This beautiful game.

Beep, beep, beep…

My mother is cutting my hair at the kitchen table because we can't afford to go to the one salon in town. There's a single light swinging over the table and her agitation and tears seem to make it sway faster. I'm sixteen and she's trying desperately to salvage my long red hair, but the gum spit into *it by the homecoming queen has hardened and it's not coming out.*

I don't really care if there's a bald spot, my ponytail will cover it up on the field, but my mother is bereft – realizing that I will never be one of the popular girls sitting on the Homecoming Court while my football-playing boyfriend wins the game under the blazing Friday night lights in our little farming town in southwestern Wisconsin. I will never be invited to the church youth group's parties or the not-so-secret bonfires that the other kids go to in the Anderson's back field, where they get wasted on beer stolen from their parents.

But I do not care. All I want is my ninety minutes on the field, where I am the best and the rest of this pissant town can disappear. And she will never understand, never bridge this gap, this widening chasm between us.

Beep, beep, beep…

"Abby, can you hear me? I'm so sorry this happened, please come back to us."

"Matti, the doctors say she's going to be fine. We should let them do their work."

"I'm not leaving her. She's my fiancée!"

Fiancée?

The crowd is cheering and there are unfamiliar songs blaring out of the loudspeakers in a gigantic stadium in a foreign country that I'll never get to see outside the Olympic Village. I'm twenty and the Women's National Team has won the gold medal, my teammates are all around me and we're hugging and crying like war heroes returning home from deployment.

I sat the bench for most of the game, but was put in when our star midfielder was injured and played the final minutes of regulation. I scored the equalizer that led us to overtime. In the closing seconds, it was my left foot that made the assist that our striker smashed into the upper-right corner, the ball making a beautiful, textbook-perfect curve to skim between the crossbar and post. Beautiful, just like this game I love so much that I've given up everything – my family, social life, academics – to play.

Beep, beep, beep…

"C'mon, Stabby Abby, please wake up. God, I can't wait for you to open those gorgeous gray eyes of yours and gut me with the Ice-Queen daggers. I know this is my fault, but…"

Matti Shellenberg? Why is Matti Shellenberg talking to me? Where am I?

"Aw, Abby. I see your eyes moving beneath your eyelids. Come on, baby, you can do it."

Baby? The audacity of that man.

The confetti rains down on the pitch, mixing with the gray drizzle and sticking to our dirt- and grass-stained uniforms. I'm twenty-eight and F.C. Chelsea's women's team has won the Cup. After the trophy ceremony, I head to the locker room, where my agent delivers the worst news of my life. Then I'm at a fancy party in an even fancier hotel, pretending that these people around me haven't shattered my heart. And there's a man, someone I've always been aware of, someone I've never liked, but he's there for me in this dark moment and maybe we have more in common than I thought. Then he kisses me, and every part of me that used to only care about soccer is now lit up and pulsing for something, no, someone, new.

Matti Shellenberg.

Beep, beep, beep…

"She's waking up! I swear, she squeezed my hand and look, her eyelids are fluttering."

"Sir, step back. You'll need to step away from your fiancée for a moment."

"No! I can't leave—"

"Matti, come with me. Let's get a coffee—"

"Sylvie—"

"No, Matti, come on. Let the doctors do their jobs."

The door swung shut as my eyes fluttered open. My hand, which until thirty seconds before had been clutched tightly by someone else, was slightly sweaty and unnervingly empty.

I'm twenty-eight, in the hospital, surrounded by doctors, when I'm told that it's very likely I will never play soccer again. This heartbreakingly beautiful game.

Chapter Four

Matti

"Sylvie, I really don't think this is a great idea," I said as I paced up and down the hallway outside Abby's room while the doctors did their thing. Sylvie sat in the single chair by the door, knitting away like someone's auntie, not the badass agent I knew her to be.

"Matthias, you honestly only have yourself to blame, you know," she said as she smiled down at her knitting with satisfaction.

"Maybe I started it, but you're the one who's finishing it," I grumbled. "She's going to kill me when she wakes up."

"Perhaps," Sylvie allowed. She peered over her glasses at me. "You know, this accident is a terrible thing that happened to Abby, but our plan for the two of you might be the best possible outcome. I need you to have some faith."

I nodded and continued my pacing, still not completely convinced in any way, shape or form that Sylvie's grand plan for us to continue a fake engagement was "*the best possible outcome*." Nor was I thrilled that she was now calling it "our" plan.

The door to the hospital room opened and one of Abby's doctors, the fairy-tale prince good-looking one, popped his head out. "You can go in now," he authorized with a warning glare. "She's tired. Don't wear her out."

Sylvie and I nodded and trooped in, the indomitable agent leading the way with her knitting tucked neatly into the tote bag under her arm. I wasn't certain what I was expecting, but it wasn't Abby's piercing stare to stab me right in the forehead as she craned her head to peer around Sylvie. I supposed I'd imagined her to be woozy, uncertain, and we'd take care of her. Instead she appeared alert, albeit slightly confused, and...angry.

Sylvie gave me an encouraging smile and motioned toward the bed where Abby was sitting up, her auburn hair sticking out between the bandages in little tufts of copper, deep red and blonde. I swallowed hard and stepped forward until I reached the chair next to her bed — the chair I'd barely left over the last four days. Her glare made my palms sweat as I dropped a folded newspaper on the bed and sat down, reaching for her hand. She pulled back abruptly and I was left hanging, my fingers closing on nothing in mid-air. It seemed that we were back to our Abby Hates Matti starting point.

"What happened? What are you two doing here? Why does everyone think we're...engaged?" Her voice continued to get louder and more shrill until the last word, when it dropped to a whisper.

I opened the paper, folded it back carefully and handed it over. "It's like this. I don't know how much you remember from the other night—"

"Other night? What day is it? The last thing I remember is that party at the Fairmont after…after the Championship." She blinked, clearly remembering the party and that she'd been fired.

"Yes, the Cup, which you won, and then the party. You and I got to talking at the Fairmont about…all of the things we have in common," I said slowly, distracted by the fact that I could still faintly smell her light, fresh perfume—something tropical without being cloying—through the antiseptic atmosphere of the hospital.

"Things we have in common? Like both of us getting fired on the same day? That we hate the club more than anything else? Yeah, I vaguely recollect," she said sarcastically and closed her eyes. "My head hurts. Finish the story. Engaged. Please, explain."

"What happened is we kissed, then we stopped, everyone was staring, and you took off running. I chased after you and followed you outside. You tripped off the curb and got hit by a drunk driver. I didn't know who to call other than Sylvie and she wasn't in town yet, so I told the paramedics you were my fiancée. I know it sounds ridiculous, but it was the only way I could ride in the ambulance with you. You may not like me very much, but I didn't want you waking up alone."

She winced, struggled to swallow and started to reach out with her eyes still closed for the water bottle on the side table. I slid it over to her groping fingers and helped her bring it to her mouth.

"Thanks," she muttered. "Now, finish the story."

"You sure you're okay?" I asked as I took the bottle back from her before she dropped it.

When she nodded, I continued. "Anyways, yeah, I got in the ambulance with you and I've been here ever since. The medics told the journalists that I was quite the doting fiancé, their statements got paired with ones from the people who photographed us kissing at the party and the story has kind of taken off. Check it out." I gestured at the cheap tabloid sitting in her lap.

She opened one gray eye and winced at the light. "Can't read right now." The bruise high on her cheekbone was blue and purple. Her forehead wrinkled slightly as she directed her questions at Sylvie. "And why, in your infinite agent wisdom, did you allow this story to continue? Why didn't you, and-or Matti here, not deny the story and set the record straight?"

Oh, Abby sounded dangerous, but Sylvie simply smiled. Her silver pageboy bob was never less than perfectly coiffed, and her makeup and clothes were still fresh despite the fact that, like me, she'd barely left Abby's side for the last three days.

"Abby, Abby. Have I not always looked out for you? Been your surrogate parent? Do you not trust that I have your best interest at heart?" Sylvie purred.

"Sure. When it aligns with your own best interests." Abby frowned at her. She was slightly frightening in her assertiveness after waking up from four days in a coma. The boss-lady voice also had a detrimental effect on the tightness of my pants, which was absolutely not ideal given the circumstances.

"Fine, let's put it this way. Have the doctors told you what happened? How badly you're injured?" Sylvie asked in a brisk voice as she pulled her knitting out from the tote, wielding the long needles as a pointer.

"Of course. Bruised ribs, concussion, laceration on my scalp and my bad knee got blown out again. Although that was likely helped by the fall I took during the game." Abby recited it all in a dead voice and I winced in sympathy. For an athlete, those injuries were tantamount to a death-row sentencing.

"Right, it's very bad. Bad enough that all of the teams that were interested in you have withdrawn their offers," said Sylvie, not making eye contact as she counted stitches.

Abby sat back, her eyes closed, and her breath left her all at once in a *whoosh*. This time she didn't pull away when I took her hand in between both of mine and squeezed. Her fingers wrapped around my palm and she gripped me tightly.

"Bottom line is that you are going to need significant care and rehabilitation before we can start looking around for a new team for you. In the meantime, Matthias here" — she pointed one of those wicked needles at me — "has been offered a one-year contract in the States. The Chicago Rebels professional team to be exact. They want him in town and ready for practice as soon as humanly possible, but they also had a number of concerns that they've worked to address with stipulations in his contract."

"Poor guy," Abby said sarcastically, but she squeezed my hand at the same time — like maybe she didn't mean it and sarcasm was her default communication style. I felt guilty all over again and took a deep breath as Sylvie got to the big bad, the favor we were going to ask. Abby's arms were covered in goosebumps and I pulled one of my hands free to stroke her arm in a weak attempt to soothe her, the tiny hairs tickling my palms.

"One of those stipulations," Sylvie continued, "is that he must either be in a committed relationship or remain celibate for the entirety of the season. The team had already passed on him when the news of your 'engagement' broke and him doting on his injured fiancée changed their minds. Plus the idea that Chelsea was cutting you because of your forbidden romance has made the two of you quite the hot topic."

We both blinked at that. Sylvie hadn't told me that the deal had almost been torpedoed before negotiations had even gotten under way.

"So," she said with a finality that, I think, scared both of us. "He can join the team in Chicago if he's in a relationship, and everyone assumes, for the moment, that you're together. You, Abby, need significant rehab, and Northwestern has one of the best sports medicine programs in the country. It's also your alma mater, which means you'll know people and be close to your—"

"Shut up, Sylvie, don't you dare say another—" The venom in her voice was startling.

"Estranged family. It is in both of your best interests to double down with this fake engagement and move to Chicago together. You need each other." She stopped to recount stitches, but she must have dropped one because she shook her head and muttered something about knitting being a pointless hobby and repacked her tote. "In the meantime, I'll keep an eye out for teams for you, Abby—stay in the news with Matthias and hype your rehab process. Remember, this is only for a year."

"One year, Sylvie? That's it, right? And you promise to keep looking for me?"

Sylvie nodded.

I'd stayed quiet this entire time, but knew I needed to commit too. "I promise to do whatever it takes to get you back on the field where you belong. I'll cover all of your costs—moving, medical care, everything."

"I need to think about this. It's a lot to ask of both of us. How does a fiancée behave anyways?"

"You don't have much time. I'm going to assume you're saying yes unless I hear otherwise by midnight." Sylvie pulled her jacket off the coat tree in the corner and walked to the door. "I'm on a morning flight out of Heathrow and need to find you a place in Chicago. Be ready to move within the week. I'll leave the two of you to hammer out the fine print."

She was gone so quickly that Abby and I were left with our jaws hanging open, still holding hands. As the door shut, we turned to each other. She glanced down and pulled her hand free, opening and closing it like she was restoring the circulation. Her eyebrows were knit together in confusion. Maybe it was her concussion, but I had a sneaking suspicion her uncertainty was due to the fact that she couldn't get over the fact that she'd been clinging to me, of all people.

"Sorry," I muttered. "Didn't mean to hurt you."

She tapped my wrist. "It's okay. You were quiet back there. How do you feel about all of this?"

"I don't know, to be honest. I mean, I'm grateful to be getting another shot, but I feel bad for you getting caught up in it. I know you don't like me very much—although, you have to admit that the spider trick was pretty funny." I gripped the back of my neck and tried to smile at her, my fake fiancée.

She gave me a half-smirk and tried to scratch under her bandages. "Promise I'll get you back for that someday."

"Here." I handed her a pencil. "Use that."

"Thank god," she muttered, and slid the pencil underneath her bandages.

"Will you do it, then? Move to Chicago with me? I'm serious, I'll cover all of the moving costs, housing, food, rent and your medical bills."

Abby stopped scratching and dropped the pencil. The long stare she threw my way stabbed into me with its intensity. "I don't know. With the exception of the night of the party, we don't get along. This sucks."

"I know I haven't done much to make you think otherwise, but take a look at my phone if you can handle the light. You should see what people are saying." I opened one of my social media accounts and scrolled down the timeline, searching for the right image. I tapped on a picture we'd been tagged in from the party, right before our big ol' kiss.

She glanced down at it and winced. "Ah, bad decisions."

"Check out the comments."

Her eyebrows climbed her forehead until they were so high they could hide beneath her bandages. I knew what she was seeing. I'd had the same reaction. Comment after comment talking about how adorable we were, how glad people were that we were together, a modern-day Romeo and Juliet—but with soccer. How hot our babies would be, support for her injury, offers to help pay for our wedding and more.

"They love us?" Her voice cracked. "*Us?*"

"Big-time. It's the only reason I haven't put a stop to it. I know you hate me, but people like us together and I can help you. If we keep up this ruse—isn't that a great word? Ruse?—anyway, if we keep up the story, both of us can benefit." Seeing the indomitable Abby seem so vulnerable brought out a tenderness in me that I hadn't known existed. It had me squeezing her hand again, trying to imprint my sincerity through my palm.

"You make me look good, a reformed bad boy, and you get tons of support to heal and rest, plus plenty of PR for when you're ready to make your comeback. I promise I won't be a dick. I'll be whatever you need me to be. Just…please, let me help you."

"You really need an answer right now?"

"Unfortunately."

"Be quiet for a second."

She dropped my hand and started tapping her fingers on the scratchy sheets. Her eyes were closed, but I could see them moving back and forth like she was reading something behind her eyelids.

I started to vibrate with the need to move around, work off the excess energy and dread that being in the hospital tended to cause professional athletes. We refused to admit that our careers could one day be cut short if our bodies gave out. Being here was a terrible reminder of how quickly I could lose everything that mattered.

"Fine," she said as she slowly opened her eyes. "Fine. I can't even begin to afford the PT and surgery I'm going to need to get through this. But I still don't like you and only trust you as far as I can throw you. That hasn't changed. If we do this, I want everything in writing and I want you to agree that this is a business relationship. No more kissing unless it's scheduled and agreed upon by both of us. For publicity only."

"No problem. I'll get Sylvie to write it up. Even the no-kissing part, although I think you're being a bit hasty given how hot our first one was." I tried to grin at her, sort of-kind of half-joking.

She glared at me.

"Fine, fine, even the no-kissing clause. You've got it."

"All right, you've got yourself a fake fiancée, then."

"Fair enough." We shook on it, her a lot harder than I expected given the extent of her injuries. I gripped her hand tightly in return and used my thumb to tickle her wrist. She flushed and glanced at her hand, frowning as if it had betrayed her. Her gray eyes seemed to X-ray my entire body and soul, cataloguing every fault, every immature action, every one of my secrets. I felt like I was coming up short, but she nodded and grabbed the remote without another word.

"Want to watch a game or something?" she asked as she laid her head back.

"Sure. I don't have anywhere to be and I've got new clothes over there. This recliner is actually pretty comfy to sleep on. Whatever you want." *Is this our first date?*

She smiled and I realized that it was slightly lopsided, only one side of her mouth twisted upward and one cheek dimpled while the other seemed to hold itself back, more reserved, the wait-and-see type. The freckles on her nose wrinkled.

"It's not a date, you know." Either she was a mind reader or I'd said that last thing out loud. My bad habit of losing any minimal filter that existed between my brain and mouth seemed worse around her.

"Whatever you say, Stabby, whatever you say." I grinned and she flicked on the TV, resolutely ignoring me. But she didn't stop me as I snuck out a hand to wrap around hers, and her fingers pressed gently back into mine as they intertwined.

Chapter Five

Abby

"Dammit, dammit, dammit, Matti," I whisper-shrieked at my helpful assistant whose long strides outpaced my slow crutching by a mile.

"Sorry, what?" He turned back with his hands on his hips, shirt sleeves pushed up to show off the colorful, complex tattoos that covered his arms. The pose called out how devastating his body was. Broad shoulders, lean hips, ropy quadriceps and calves. He also hadn't tied the drawstrings of his joggers and they sagged a bit, showing off the waistband of his Calvins and a smooth swath of skin.

I shuddered and forced my eyes back up to meet his, which were twinkling knowingly at me like little blue stars. "My eyes are up here, sweet cheeks," he said as he tapped the corner of one of them. "What's up?"

It would totally be my luck to have the hottest, most annoying fake fiancé on the planet. "It's these crutches.

They're harder to maneuver than I thought with the broken collarbone and taped-up ribs." I winced in pain.

"Should have listened to the doctor about taking your pain meds and the wheelchair," he reminded me in an entirely unsympathetic tone. "Now, where did Sylvie park my baby?"

I snorted, because of course he was the type of guy who called his car "baby." It was probably some ridiculous red sports car that could *zoom zoom* every woman on the planet out of her panties.

"Ah-ha!" Matti shouted and took off running toward a distant flashing light and beep while I slowly crutched along behind him, trying to hold back my whimpers. I caught up with him as he was popping the tiniest little hatch on the tiniest little car I'd ever seen. At least I'd been right about the size. Not much else, though.

"*This* is your car?" I asked in complete disbelief. It was miniature, it was turquoise and it had a vanity license plate. FUS-STUD. "What's a fussy stud?" I asked trying, and failing, not to laugh.

"Fußball stud," he proclaimed with pride. "Because I play fußball and I am, obviously, a stud."

"You're ridiculous, you know that, right? Do you take anything seriously?"

"Of course I do, don't be absurd," he snapped, more offended than I'd expected.

"I'm just surprised this is your car, had you figured as a supercar kind of guy not a—" I squinted at the name plate and insignia. "A hybrid Fiat 500?"

"I'm environmentally conscious," he huffed as he slung my backpack in the hatch, helped me slide into the front seat and laid my crutches in the back.

"Sorry. I'm grumpy, hungry and hurting. While I'm usually grumpy, it's not always this bad. I guess we're still getting to know each other." It was the understatement of the century.

He sighed and clenched his fingers around the steering wheel. "Yeah, early days," he said with his eyes downcast. "Which is why I've planned something very exciting for us."

"Can't you take me home? I feel and look like garbage," I complained.

"You *are* always grumpy, aren't you? No, I'm sorry, but Sylvie wanted us to be seen today with you leaving the hospital and all. So I made a little plan, and we don't have to be there long, but we need to get photographed as part of our reputation rehab." He seemed genuinely contrite. "I know it's not going to be fun with your injuries."

"Fine, fine. I get it," I grumbled and slumped down in my seat. My knee and ribs were screaming at me. "Where are we going?"

"A little park near my apartment," he muttered as he checked his mirrors before signaling and turning out of the parking garage. We pulled out into traffic as the clouds moved in and a gentle rain started. The windshield wipers thunked back and forth like a metronome.

"A park?" I asked, not sure I'd heard correctly,

"Yeah, I'd planned a picnic," he said sheepishly. "But London weather…"

I couldn't help it. I laughed harder than the situation called for. Because of course the consummate good-time guy with the environmentally friendly mini-car, this prankster extraordinaire, would have planned a picnic in a park with London's dicey weather.

"Fine," I managed to splutter. "Let's have a damn picnic."

* * * *

I wasn't laughing thirty minutes later as I surveyed the scene. The park had been a no-go due to weather and we'd ended up sitting in one of the parking lots at Stamford Bridge stadium because we couldn't figure out anywhere else to go.

"What do you mean this isn't romantic?" He gestured impatiently at the blanket across the hood of the car, which was slowly getting soaked in the drizzle, and the adorable wicker picnic basket that looked like it was wilting. We remained inside, in our seats, waiting for the photographer to show.

"To start, Matti, we're pretending to have a picnic in the stadium parking lot of a club that fired both of us. Our picnic blanket is emblazoned with the emblem of that same club and it's raining," I answered. "What about this strikes you as romantic?"

"I'm really sorry. The park would have been better," he said with a frown.

"Yes, the park would have been better." I sighed. "Come on, the photographer is here."

There was no way I could sit on that blanket given my injuries. We figured we'd do a quick photo of us standing in front of it in a fake clinch. "I'm sorry. I've never even had a girlfriend before, much less a fiancée. I'm going to do stuff wrong. Going to screw this up, I know it." He looked worried, like really and truly worried. I reached out without thinking and took his hand. The crease between his eyes flattened as my fingers pressed into his palm.

"We'll be okay," I tried to reassure him, even though I highly doubted it. The dislike between us was too strong for this thing to go anywhere but down.

"I'm going to hold you to that." He let go of my hand and wrapped an arm loosely around my waist. "Is this where we make all of our promises of devotion?" he asked, and there was a wicked twinkle in his eyes. I'd never met anyone who could change moods on a dime the way quicksilver Matti seemed to be able to, and it drove me nuts trying to predict his reactions.

"Sure…" I said slowly.

"Okay. I promise that I will maintain this fake exclusive relationship for as long as you want to be in it. I'll handle all of the care, costs, everything that you need for the duration. How about you?" His voice was serious, but a little nervous. There seemed to be a hitch in his breath as he asked me the last.

"I promise that I'll do whatever it takes to be the best fake fiancée in the world. That if I want out, for whatever reason, I'll talk to you about it first. And exclusivity. I promise that, okay? I've never been one for dating and I can't see myself being interested in anyone for the time being."

Matti let out a relieved-sounding sigh and pulled me closer — more gently than I would have imagined for such a big guy with a bull-in-a-china-shop personality — taking care not to jostle my bandages and injuries. I ignored the sharp pain in my ribs as I reached up to drape my arms over his shoulders.

He twitched as my cold, damp hands clutched his neck. "Sorry, that tickles. Can we seal this deal with a kiss? For the cameras, of course."

"This is one of those times, scheduled and approved, I guess." I glanced over at the photographer who'd popped out of her car with a jacket over her head to protect her camera from the rain. Her long-distance lens pointed right at us as we stood next to his silly car and the sodden blanket. "Fine, but I want the sickest ring you can imagine for all of this and I'm keeping it when we're done, too."

"Deal," he said quickly and leaned in, stopping right before our lips brushed, waiting for me.

"Deal," I said softly in an echo of his certainty and closed the distance between us to press my lips against his. I pulled back before either of us let our tongues get involved in the fake kiss and rested my forehead against him. "Just, please, please talk to me about stuff, okay? We've got to communicate or this whole thing is going to go up in flames."

His nostrils flared and his eyes opened wide. Those guileless blue eyes met my own with an honesty that I so wanted to believe, but still wasn't completely ready to trust. "I promise."

* * * *

It had turned out to be an excellent Thursday evening. Matti had taken off after helping me up the stairs to my apartment. My jammies were on backwards and I was talking a blue streak to my cat while high on pain meds. Somehow, I managed to blast a mostly coherent text to my teammates explaining that I needed help packing since I was moving to the States in less than a week.

"*Merow*," whined Spock, plaintively, as he jumped on my bed to perch his furry butt on my pillow. The little bugger had been hiding when Matti had carried me through the door and this was his first foray out from the closet. Teresa had been taking care of him while I was in the hospital, but he was still pissed at my abandonment. I set my crutches carefully aside and plopped back on my bed as my phone started pinging with responses.

Everyone wanted to bust my lady balls for not telling them about my secret engagement and express their support and outrage over the team cutting us because of our relationship. I felt guilty for continuing the lie, but I'd already told Teresa the truth about Matti and she'd sworn herself to secrecy. No one else could know. I gave up on responding after I sent an incomprehensible emoji stream that even I couldn't translate.

"Are you ready for a big move? My little fuzzy guy?" I scratched behind his ears and Spock purred while butting his head against me. "There's going to be a new man in our lives, buddy. His name is Matti. It's okay if you hate him. I do. In fact, if you could give him a good shredding at least once to pay him back for that mean trick he played on me, I'd really appreciate it."

The consummate cat, Spock spat out a disgruntled-sounding *meow* and leaped off the bed. Noted — my cat already liked my fake fiancé more than me. Just like everyone else in the world. I sighed, wallowing in the gloom of my one-woman pity party.

Matti would be the first guy I'd ever brought home to…meet my cat? How pathetic. I'd never really dated, only barely lost my virginity, and since then it had pretty much been a small army of battery-operated boyfriends that took care of everything I might need a man for.

Like any professional sport, soccer was a limited-time gig and I had to make the most of it. Grab the most sponsorships, hustle the hardest, save the most. Because I was damned if I was moving back to the U.S. with nothing to show for it. Damned if I'd listen to my parents ask me if I was ever going to do anything with my degree in sports management from that fancy-shmancy Northwestern University. Couldn't I have at least gone to Madison? Met a nice guy from Fox Point if I wasn't going to stick to my hometown like my sainted brother?

"Spock, am I doing the right thing? I'm scared. What if I won't ever be able to play again?" I awkwardly curled up on my side, my sore ribs supported by soft pillows, and he hopped back up and marched over my legs, turning himself into a furry comma against my stomach. His purrs rattled my battered body, but the meds were kicking in and that reassuring rusty engine sound soothed me.

"Hmm. You're right, one thing at a time — rehab first, then sorting out Matti Shellenberg." I yawned, my jaw cracking loudly. "Prepare yourself, my friend, the team is coming over tomorrow to help me with packing. Buddy, we're heading home."

* * * *

Three days later, my cat almost killed me as he wound around my legs and crutches as I hobbled toward the door, trying to navigate the narrow path between shipping crates. "Dammit, Spock, asshole cat," I muttered.

The bell buzzed again, three short bursts then three long ones. "One second," I shouted. I was within five steps when the knocking began, two steps when the singing started in time with the knocks.

"It's me, here to help." Matti's voice was muffled by the door but completely unmistakable in its golden retriever-like enthusiasm.

My heart rate picked up and matched the staccato pace of his song. He was like a bad case of poison ivy — absolutely everywhere.

"Stabby Abby, let me in. I'm bringing you breakfast so you'll like me. Let me in, let me in."

I opened the door and he tumbled in, hand still raised in a fist. He righted himself with the reflexes of a professional athlete and casually leaned against my doorframe. "Hey," he said, as nonchalantly as if we'd simply run into each other at the corner shop.

"Hey," I said more cautiously, trying to hide my annoyance. "What's up?"

"I'm here to help you pack." He grinned and waved a bakery bag and a coffee carrier that was looped over the middle finger of his right hand. "I heard you like sweet things, so I come bearing gifts." He pushed past me and, almost as an afterthought, yanked something out of the pocket of his joggers and tossed it to me. A small velvet-covered box.

I snagged it out of mid-air without dropping my crutch and watched him waltz into my apartment like he owned the place. He stuck his nose and obnoxiously large head into every corner and lifted the flaps on a few packing boxes. "Oh, hello there," he murmured at Spock, who was perched on top of one of them, before plopping on the bar stool in my breakfast nook. He pulled a chocolate éclair out of the bag and shoved half of it in his mouth. As his eyes bulged and he struggled to keep the food from flying out, he managed to garble, "Are you going to open that?"

Following him much more slowly, I nudged Spock off the cardboard that was sagging beneath his furry weight and limped toward the kitchen, thumbing the soft blue velvet. "I was kidding about the sick ring," I said.

"Only the best for my lady." His voice was still mangled by the éclair and crumbs were shooting out of his face. "Sorry, please sit down. You need to get off your feet," he said more clearly as swallowed.

A little pantomime played out as I handed him a paper towel to clean up his mess and he tidily scooped all of his crumbs and wrapped them up in the toweling. He jumped up to toss it in my trash can and glanced around for another chair. When one didn't magically appear, he beckoned me over, held out his hand for my crutches and guided me into the seat. The crutches got leaned up next to me so I could grab them and run — or smack him, I supposed. He plated a second éclair and handed me one of the coffees from his carrier. I gratefully took my first sip and he waved an impatient hand toward the box.

"Come on, open it." He promptly started gnawing on a thumbnail without meeting my eye and shifted back and forth on his feet like he was about to start dribbling an imaginary ball around my microscopic kitchen. I recognized that energy. A ball bouncing at my feet was where I was happiest, where my mind was clearest too.

The soft blue box was worn in places, the velvet rubbed away by what must have been years of handling. "Where is this from?" I asked as I popped the tarnished clasp.

The lid opened to a quilted bed of aged ivory satin. And there, resting gently in the slot that appeared to be made for it, was the most beautiful ring I'd ever seen in my life. A thin, gleaming platinum band that split into four delicate prongs holding a single enormous Asscher-cut diamond surrounded by a framework of smaller brilliant pavé diamonds. It was old, in that Gilded-Age style that looked like it belonged on the hand of Daisy Buchanan, and now it was mine. I simultaneously wanted to toss it into the nearest volcano for everything it represented and never, ever take it off. My eye twitched as I considered how to respond.

Chapter Six

Matti

"Do you like it?" I asked as I switched over to my right thumbnail. Abby was staring at my grandmother's ring with huge eyes, the icy gray melted to the shade of a dove's wings. One hand with its short, squared-off nails was covering her mouth.

Leaving the ring in its bed, she snapped the box shut and set it on the counter. With one finger, she poked it across the smooth surface toward me while keeping a wary eye on it as if it were a ticking time bomb. She started to reach for the box again, but snatched her hand back at the last second. "I can't accept this," she said softly.

"What? Why?" Hadn't she asked for, and I quote, *"the sickest ring"*? I stopped jittering around the kitchen and slid the box back toward her. She pushed it back with equal assurance.

"Where did you get that?" she asked again.

"What does that matter? You wanted a sick ring. I believe that qualifies." If she was going to be stubborn, she'd find out very quickly that I could be equally tenacious. I had skin in the game here. That ring was gorgeous, my only inheritance, and it was royally pissing me off that she would try to reject it. "It's mine, all right? Before my grandmother died, she gave it to me. I didn't want to get caught shopping for something new since we've supposedly been hiding this engagement and I had this sitting in my top drawer. So..."

"So it's too much, Matti. I can't keep it," she said, and her voice was low, husky, like honey on rocks. I liked it when she said my name in that voice. Would have liked to have heard it again while she rode my cock in my bed with all of the sheets twisted around us, maybe while tying my wrists to the wrought-iron spindles on my headboard. *A man can dream, no?*

I shook myself out of the brief slutty daydream. "Fine, let's make a deal. It's yours till we get to the States and then we'll get you something that's only for you, okay?" I didn't know why her response affected me that badly. We weren't real.

She nodded slowly and the acid burn of disappointment knifed up my throat. I cleared it and said, "Put it on and let's get on with packing."

Abby reopened the box and stopped again to admire the antique ring before plucking it from the slot and sliding it onto the third finger on her left hand. My own twitched with the compulsion to yank it from her hand and put it on her myself.

"Good, looks lovely on you. We should take a picture and post it on our social media accounts. Sylvie can do it. Do you mind?" I asked as I slid over next to her, held my phone out and a little above us as I picked up her be-ringed hand and kissed it, clicking a few times to capture the moment. "This okay?" I showed her the pictures.

She laughed as she thumbed through them. I glanced over her shoulder at the very candid shots where I looked my usual handsome self. Her eyes were bright and glowing, but she also had an exasperated pinch to her lips—like she wasn't sure if she was wanted to kiss or kick me. Which was a fairly common reaction for women, to be honest.

"Perfect. I look like I want to kick you in the nuts. Can you text those to Sylvie?" As she shifted slightly away from me, she grabbed for a piece of toweling to wipe up some stray éclair crumbs.

"Sure, sure." I sent the pictures and jammed my hands into my pockets with my phone. "Is there anything you need me to do around here?"

"Thanks, but I'm pretty much packed. Going to sell all of my furniture. I wouldn't mind a little help getting the books off my top shelf, I guess."

"Ah, I was hoping your undergarments might need some special attention. What do you think?" I gave her my infamous smirk, which was met by an eye-roll. She was immune to my persistent charm and it left me feeling completely at sea. If I couldn't get her to loosen up and join Team Matti, this was going to be the shortest fake engagement in all of history.

"Clothes are packed, dickhead. Focus on the books, please. The team's been over the last few days taking care of most of this." She pointed a crutch in the direction of her cramped living room and the single open shipping crate.

I spent the next hour putting books into the crate while Abby directed and Spock, the adorable little kitty, attempted to distract me. "You know your cat is going to be half mine, right?"

"Never. Spock is no man's cat," she said definitively.

I scooped up the cat and he rubbed his head under my chin, then reached out a tiny, white-socked paw to bat at the strands of hair that had fallen from my top knot. I blew them out of his reach and glanced over at Abby, who was watching me with her jaw open and eyes glazed.

"Hot guys and cats, no?" I teased.

"We could do a calendar," she mumbled. "Every month, you and some adorable kitten. Make a fortune."

Ping! My phone chimed with a text from a contact I'd tagged with glasses and a computer— Sylvie. I glanced down and saw multiple lines of text that I knew would take me hours to try to read. I tossed it to Abby. "My phone doesn't have a passcode. Can you check that for me? It's from Sylvie."

"Sure?" She seemed surprised that I was giving her access, but she *was* my wife, or the next best thing. "Yeah, Sylvie loves the pictures. They're already getting massive engagement from fans."

I snorted as I continued to pet the cat. "Of course they are. We're hot and everyone loves a reformed bad boy."

She hummed in agreement as she tapped a message back to Sylvie. "Are you really?" she asked with a wry twist of her eyebrow. "Reformed, that is?"

"Of course." I put Spock down and tugged the elastic band out of my hair, then re-tied it more securely. "I haven't slept with anyone for almost six months. That latest orgy scandal? I wasn't even home during that party. Connor threw it while I was in Germany visiting my family."

"What about the mad bar hopping?"

"I mean, I still enjoy a fun night out here and there, but I haven't been to a club in almost a year, and the only thing I do in bars is have a drink or two. I haven't even gotten a group singalong going in ages!" My outrage wasn't even slightly faked when I realized how long it had been since I'd done anything fun.

"I'm twenty-eight. Half of the crap people say about me is based on who I was three or more years ago. Since moving to England I've only done a few boneheaded things. And of course I've gotten caught every time. People expect that of me, it's part of my useless, pointless brand." I tied off the knot firmly.

"I'm sorry, my only real knowledge of you comes from the tabloids and that one fundraiser—"

"And I'm sorry about that too, okay? I'm done with pranks and stuff. It was funny at the time, but it was also the last one I pulled—aside from crap I've done to my brothers," I added. I closed the box with a great deal of finality and whipped the packing tape gun across it multiple times. I twirled the gun with a flourish and tossed it on the sofa.

"It's fine," she muttered. "I'm sorry too. I didn't mean to upset you."

"You didn't. It's not like you know me." The little cat batted a ball of tape my way and I kicked it back, trying not to put too much stock in this conversation. I liked her more than she liked me and that fact wasn't going to change any time soon.

"No, but I should know better than to believe everything I read in the tabloids and on social media.

You really took the fall for a party that Connor threw at your house?"

"Yeah, he's a kid and still on trial. People expect me to pull crap like that, but he wouldn't recover as easily."

She frowned as she re-evaluated me. "I can't believe you did that. No one has any idea, do they?"

I shrugged. "It's not that big of a deal. He's a friend."

"Matti, you got *fired* over it. It's a huge deal. I hope Connor knows he owes you big. Dammit, hold still," she said as she limped over. I stood like a statue as she brushed something off my face. "There, smudge."

I caught her hand and flipped it over, kissed her palm without thinking. She gasped quietly and her fingers closed around my own. We watched each other, both a little warily, with our hands clasped. "That's everything, I think?" I asked.

She dropped my hand like it was a hot coal. "Yeah, pretty much."

"Do you want to order pizza or something? Hang out?" My own house was totally packed, waiting for the movers to come the next day to pick up the cartons. Our flight was later in the afternoon.

"I think I'm going to heat up some soup, take a pain pill and go to bed, if that's all right with you." Her eyes darted back and forth as she shifted awkwardly. "It's been a rough couple of days and I'm peopled out."

"Oh, okay." I grabbed my hoodie off the counter and tried to hide my disappointment. "Glad you like the ring. I'll pick you up around noon then, to go to the airport? You, me, Spock?"

"We'll be ready. Promise."

"Good. You better not leave me hanging, Stabby Abby," I joked.

"Wouldn't dream of it, future hubby." She grinned and smacked my ass as I crossed the threshold.

Before I could do more than yelp, the door closed behind me and her brilliant, perfect American smile seemed to accompany me out into the night. It was one of the first times she'd actually directed that particular weapon at me, and I felt it burn deep in my bones.

* * * *

"Maaarkus," I hollered into my phone, which I'd clenched between my chin and shoulder as I attempted to pry off the bottle cap on my beer by slamming it against my marble-topped island.

"Matti?" my oldest brother asked with that very special tone that only barely humored me. "To what do I owe this honor? Need more advice on how to break up with your girlfriend who sold a torrid secret baby story to the tabloids?"

"Screw you, Markus. That was one time," I said and spat the cap into the sink after yanking the rest of the stubborn bitch off with my teeth. *Goddammit, why did I already pack my bottle openers?*

I set my phone down on the counter and hit the little speaker icon. *Much better.* Until Markus' amused voice echoed through my apartment again. "If it's not about that, what do you want? Are you calling to make fun of my last film?"

"No, get over yourself, Mister 'I'm a movie star living the high life in L.A. with my hot as fuck baller wife.'" I grumbled as I yanked the tie out of my hair and scrubbed a hand through it. Maybe it was time for a new style. Or a new tattoo. There was a spot on the back of my left hand that was crying out for the tender attention of needle and ink. I flipped open my tablet, muted myself and voice searched for open tattoo shops.

"Matti? Seriously, what's going on? Is everything okay?" Now he sounded concerned. "You're not doing the thing where you're contemplating rash haircuts and random tattoos again are you?"

He knew me altogether too well. I turned off my iPad, shoved it out of reach, and unmuted myself.

"Noo...what? Why would you say that?" I asked, backing slowly away from the counter.

"You've got that weird warble in your voice and I know how you get when you're stressed," he responded, and I could practically see him grab the back of his neck and start to pace — his tell when he was agitated.

"Fine, yes. Fine. Okay, I'm calling for advice, all right?" I slammed the rest of my beer and tossed the bottle into the open recycling bin. It clanged musically against the other empty from earlier in the night.

"You don't need to sound so annoyed about it." His voice had relaxed and thinly veiled amusement was peeking through. "Can you either take me off speaker or quit throwing glass bottles near the phone?"

"Sorry, sorry," I apologized immediately. "I guess you could say I'm calling with good news and bad news. Good news, I'll be moving closer to you very soon — like, tomorrow. Got traded to the football team in Chicago."

"You got fired or something? And you're moving here?" That very unwelcome, judgmental older brother tone was back.

"Not exactly. Not to L.A. Like I said, Chicago. And no, before you ask, I didn't actually *do* anything to get fired. It's not like I asked Connor to host a party at my place and then leave me with the dirty receipts. Jesus." Rather than grab another beer, I scooped a kiddie training ball that had somehow escaped the eagle eyes of the packers and started juggling it from foot to foot.

"Okay, Matti, okay. Calm down. I'm sorry it came out like that," he apologized. Then, more gently, "What happened?"

I jogged the ball from left foot to right foot, where I stalled it before flipping it up to my chest and letting it drop back down. "What I said. Connor threw a party at my place the last time I was in Germany and it got a little out of hand. Took a while before the pictures leaked, but when they did I ended up taking the heat."

"That's awful, I'm sorry. Didn't the team listen?" He somehow managed to sound both apologetic and angry.

"I never bothered to deny it. He's a kid and it would end his career before he even got started." I shrugged and pulled a third beer out of the fridge, managed to slam it open with a firm slap on the top against the counter, and took a fortifying drink. "Anywho, as they say, I'll be moving stateside tomorrow—"

"*Tomorrow?*"

"Yeah, tomorrow. Me and my wife-to-be will be hitting up the...what do they call it? The 'Windy City'?" I tossed the cap into the bin with the others, where it clinked gently on the glass.

"*Wife-to-be?*"

"Keep up, Markus, yes. The woman wearing Grandmother's ring even as we speak. Sylvie found me a new gig, but I have to either be celibate or in a relationship." I scrabbled around my cabinets trying to find some leftover sustenance. Nothing. I reached for my iPad, intending to call up a takeout menu, but realized my brother had been silent for way too long. "Markus? Hello?"

"I-I'm sorry. You. A fiancée," he sputtered.

"Yeah, fiancée—that thing you do before you get married. Abby, she's my fiancée. I mean, fake fiancée, if you want to get really picky about the whole thing."

"And you gave her Grandmother's ring?" Oh, now he sounded angry.

"It's not like I had any others lying around and I couldn't exactly go shopping, you know?" I tapped on the icons for the food I wanted to order and hit the checkout button. Bless the delivery service that translated all menus into pictographs.

"No, I don't exactly know," he said slowly.

"The club cut her for a younger player and Sylvie is her manager too. This all kind of came together at the last second." I summed it up while avoiding the whole we kissed, it went a little haywire, she got hit by a car, I was dumb and told people we were engaged, everyone believes it so I gave her Grandmother's ring and I sort of wish it were real, but it's not and now we're stuck thing. No one needed to know all of that.

"Oh, brother." Markus's tone was somehow both sympathetic and exasperated.

"I know, right?" I sighed.

"A fake engagement? It's like a romcom. You know how those end, right?"

"It does seem a bit ridiculous when you put it that way." I finished my beer and set it down in the bin, topping off a happy little pyramid made of its fellow empties.

"Matti, we love you. Always and no matter what. Is there anything we can do to help with the move?"

I wondered at what point in a relationship people lost track of their individuality. When it turned from "I" and "me" to "we." Abby would never use the royal "we" when it came to us, but I knew it was right around the corner for me. I'd liked her for way too long and needed to keep my head straight—she didn't feel the same.

"No, but I'll call you when we get in, figure out a time for a visit." My doorbell buzzed and I started for the door, focused on the takeout. "I have to go, but we'll see you soon, yeah?"

"Sure, Matti, sure, but tell me this before you go—are you truly okay? Happy? Can you do this with this Abby?" His concern touched me.

"I think so. I actually do like her quite a bit and she needs me right now. I'm... I don't know, actually. I think I like the ring on her a little too much," I admitted.

"Oh, *that's* your problem. You actually like your fake fiancée. Oh, this is going to be precious. Best of luck, baby brother. Call us when you get in." He was still laughing when I hung up on him.

Bastard.

I scarfed down my Indian takeout and dragged myself to the balcony off the master bedroom. London had been good to me, but it wasn't home. Maybe Chicago would be closer. I was tired of feeling restless all the time, tired of feeling like I didn't fit anywhere, like I was always on stage. I wanted what Markus and my other siblings had, that bone-deep assurance that they were where—and with whom—they were always meant to be. When would it be my turn?

Chapter Seven

Abby

Snoring. The big lunk next to me was snoring, slumped over in his cushy business-class seat with his head pushed up against the window and mouth slightly agape. Unfortunately it wasn't a loud, annoying chainsaw of a snore. No, instead it was the most adorable little snuffly rumble of a snore, like one I would have expected to hear from a floofy Bernese Mountain dog puppy, not a jacked and tatted-up playboy with a man bun. The doofus had a baby smirk on his face as he turned his head toward me — almost as if he couldn't resist responding to my grouchy mental sarcasm even in his sleep.

Matti mumbled something as he curled into the window while I slowly stood up and flexed my leg in its heavy brace in a vain attempt to maintain some limited mobility. My knee was screaming at me and the rest of my body ached like a car had run me down—oh, wait. It had.

As if he could sense my distress, Spock *meowed* plaintively from his carrier. I sat back down with a groan and nudged his plastic prison with my toe. "It's all good, little man. I'm still here," I murmured. He gave me one unhappy chirp, as if he'd needed that reassurance, and twisted his body around so all I could see was a black furry cat butt pressed up against the grate of the carrier's door. I swear he sighed and a low rumble started to emanate from the cat to join in chorus with his new daddy.

I pulled out my tablet from the seat pocket in front of me and tapped my reading app. There was no way I'd be sleeping on this flight, even if I reclined. The awkward brace kept my knee from being able to fully straighten or bend and its bulk made me have to sit crosswise in our row. Even now it was intruding into Matti's space, but somehow he was aware enough to curve his body away from it.

This whole situation was incredibly surreal and sometimes I was positive that it was all the pain medicine's fault that my erstwhile nemesis had become such an accepted part of my life. In fact, it shook me to realize that I could no longer consider him my nemesis at all. We were something else now, not necessarily friends and definitely not lovers, but maybe uneasy allies—teammates.

Sylvie had been right that we needed each other. I'd spent a lot of time researching my new fiancé over the last few days. My head had been so deep in the game, in my own little world, that very little but the biggest stories had permeated the walls I'd built around myself.

While I'd heard the worst over the years — the fake pregnancies, orgies, cheating scandals — I'd missed the small stuff. Apparently my fiancé had once made a habit of getting drunk and streaking London — he'd been caught multiple times. There were videos of him egging on his friends and teammates to do ridiculous things while out at clubs, stealing towels and stuff from rival team's clubhouses. Nothing that was misogynistic or super sketchy, but signs of an immature man-child who brought everyone down to his level. No wonder people had doubts about him.

Yet in the time that I'd actually come to know him, it had become clear that that behavior was an exaggerated front, part of a carefully curated image he'd constructed to divert attention from the real him. But who Matthias Shellenberg really was seemed to be anyone's guess.

He was never photographed with the same women twice, nor the same group of friends, other than teammates. In fact, the only people he was repeatedly photographed with were his family members. His mom or sister came to most of his events as his date and he was with his brothers constantly in the off-season — and those pictures, *whew*. I fanned myself discreetly and felt the blush creeping up my neck as I remembered some of those pictures I'd honestly devoured on social media. It was probably illegal for three brothers to be as stunningly attractive as the Shellenbergs.

There was a mystery to my fake fiancé that I wasn't sure I wanted to solve. I'd always been introverted, single-mindedly focused on playing soccer, while he had the supportive closely knit family and raucous social life I sometimes daydreamed about.

Here I was, twenty-eight with no family or friends to speak of, no money because London was hugely expensive and female professional athletes were paid in free shoes and clothes from endorsements and a small salary that was no better than a stipend. There was a reason I'd lived in a musty shoebox in a crappy part of town while Matti had lived in a plush townhouse a mere walk away from Chemist's Park and the stadium in the very tony neighborhood around the club.

I sighed and shifted again. We had one year together and the deal would be up, I needed to keep focused on that—one year to get back on the field where I belonged. Nothing could get in the way of my recovery. We could be allies, maybe even friends, but getting sucked deeper into his charismatic whirlpool would have a bad ending for both of us.

Another plaintive chirp from Spock's carrier had me murmuring something nonsensical and Matti seemed to smirk at me from his seat again. I laid my head back and shut my eyes. We'd be home soon. Our fake, temporary home.

* * * *

Our apartment building was a blinding monstrosity of pre-fab minimalism on Lake Shore Drive, one of the newer buildings that stuck out like a sore thumb among a host of stately, pre-War gray- and brownstones. Matti and I glanced at each other as we stood on the curb sweating in the hot and humid August afternoon, gawking at our new home. He made a face and rolled his eyes. "Sorry, not much character," he said. "I think Sylvie said it has an elevator. The lease is month-to-month too. We can always move once we get the lay of the land a little more."

Mind reader. I intensely disliked the fact that he could read me so clearly, and touched my cheeks surreptitiously to make sure my resting bitch face was still locked in. "It's cool for now. I'm not a huge fan of modern architecture either, but it's furnished and I'm sure the view is stunning."

He grinned and gave me a friendly shoulder nudge. "Look at you, all ready to—what is that saying? Bury the hatchet? Where does that come from, anyway? I remember hearing it on an episode of *Friends* and being super confused by it. Of course that was when I was a kid, living in Barcelona at soccer boarding school, and the dialogue was dubbed in and even more messed up." He blinked his big blue eyes at my incredulous face. "You know what? Never mind."

The driver finished unloading our bags onto the pavement and a doorman rushed over to us with a cart. "Need a hand, folks?" he asked breathlessly as he waved over a younger man sitting at the front desk to start loading the cart.

We nodded and Matti cleared his throat while I clutched his arm, trying to stay upright. My knee was killing me. "We're moving in today and someone else arranged all of this. I'm actually not completely sure which apartment is ours," he said in a charmingly apologetic tone.

I frowned. Sylvie had sent both of us an email with details for arriving. "It's 1404, Matti. Didn't you read Sylvie's email?"

He shrugged and the doorman nodded, smacking the automatic door button with his left hip to open the sliding glass panels. We followed him in, me leaning heavily on Matti in the absence of my crutches, which were buried beneath the luggage pile on the sidewalk. We all smushed together in the elevator and no one spoke as we started our ascension to the fourteenth floor.

Matti's arm was a tight band of warmth where it wrapped around me and I caught a confusing whiff of cedar and salty beach air from his shirt as he tugged me close to make room for the doorman. His breath tickled the small hairs on the back of my neck and goosebumps slowly rose on my arms. I shivered as he started to whistle along with a jazzy EDM cover of *The Girl from Ipanema*. *Plink plink* went the electronic piano and I leaned into his warmth as the air conditioning blasted us from an open vent on the ceiling.

"Here we are, folks. We'll bring your luggage up shortly."

The two mirrored panels opened and I caught a glimpse of our reflections as they separated. I was flushed and a little wobbly, flustered. Matti was the picture of cool, casual jock swagger with an arm looped around my waist, his head tilted toward me with a barely perceptible smirk as if to say, "Sure, she's mine, and isn't she cute when she blushes?"

Sylvie opened the door to 1404 and came rushing out to help us inside. Me she ushered over to a plush leather couch that was so new it crackled as she helped me to sit. Matti wandered around on his own, checking out the view and disappearing down the hall. Sylvie thanked the doorman as he held open the door for the guy from the front desk to wheel in our luggage cart. After tipping them both and sending them on their way, she came and sat on the armchair opposite me.

"Matthias, come unload this cart!" she said loudly.

Matti slunk into the room like a leopard after moving our suitcases to the bedrooms, and propped my crouches against the coffee table. He gracefully lowered himself down to sit next to me and threw an arm across the back of the couch. Sylvie raised a curious eyebrow. My cheeks blazed and I shook my head as subtly as possible.

"Excellent. Matthias, Abigail Susan—" she started to say.

"Wait, that's your middle name?" Matti asked incredulously. "Susan?"

"No, you ass, she likes to first-middle name me because she thinks it's cute. I don't actually have a middle name," I said and waved a hand at him, hoping to cut off the questions.

"Really?" he asked. "That's so fascinating. What else—"

"Children," Sylvie intoned. Matti pouted and she continued, "I'll assume that your flight was fine and that London is still standing in one piece on the other side of the pond. No claw marks on Matthias here, and Abby still seems to have all her hair and eyebrows."

"Sylvie, come now. That was one time," Matti said with a frown.

"It was the captain of your team, who you knew would be making a speech. It wasn't funny then, young man, and it still isn't funny now. I was a little worried, haven't heard or seen anything in the news from either—or both—of you since that impromptu engagement ring photo," she said as she fussed with the hem of her pencil skirt. She pulled out a tube of nicotine gum, popped one in her mouth and sighed deeply. Then she reached back for her needles and yarn.

"Matti, would you mind checking the cupboards, see if there's any tea or anything?" I asked. Sylvie's skill at wielding silence was a power move that I was used to, but Matti appeared to be edging closer to explosion.

"Sure, sweet potato," he said as he bounced to his feet and headed to the open kitchen, where he started banging open cupboards and rifling through drawers. Sylvie continued to count.

"It's Abby, dickhead. Not sweet potato, not sweet cheeks, nothing else — nada, you got that?" I called out to him, and he flipped me the bird behind his back as he dropped the kettle on a burner and lit it up with a *whoosh*. He brought a tea bag he'd discovered up to his nose and inhaled deeply. Then coughed.

"Is peppermint okay, cutie pie? I was hoping for chamomile, but you haven't brushed your teeth in a while anyway," he said matter-of-factly, and I was reminded of my very strong desire to punch him in the nuts.

"Of course, cuddly boo, that would be delightful," I managed to grit out.

Sylvie snorted quietly but kept counting, ignoring both of us. The smell of peppermint wafted over from the kitchen as Matti poured the hot water over the tea bag, carefully covered it with a trivet and brought it to me.

"Thanks."

"No problem." He smiled at me, one of his special ones where the little flecks of gold in his eyes seemed to wink at me, the lines in the corners of his eyes deepening and his sharp left incisor catching on his full lower lip. I had learned quickly that that particular smile was devastating to my lady parts, and my ovaries started to hum as he caught me staring at him with my mouth open. He tapped my chin to close it and grinned even harder.

Sylvie cleared her throat and I tore my eyes away from that tractor beam of a smile and glanced at her. "Now that that's settled," she said with an acerbic tone, "we need to discuss what's going to happen over the next week or so and how you two are going to establish yourselves as the sweetest, most wholesome couple in all of Chicago."

We both nodded obediently like children.

"First, I'm staying here for at least the next week before heading back to New York. I want to make sure you're both settled, get a feel for Abby's doctors and see how these first few workouts go for you, Matthias."

"Fine, Sylvie, you'll stay here for a while and help us get settled. Do you have anything lined up for us? Endorsement stuff, PR?" I yawned hugely. "Maybe you could write it down and email it to us? Because I really need a shower and maybe some pizza before crashing. Anyone else want anything?" I pulled out my phone and tapped an app for delivery services, scrolling to the pizza options.

Sylvie and Matti ignored me, locked in a stare down. He adamantly shook his head, clearly understanding whatever she was trying to telegraph. She glanced at me. "Pizza sounds good, dear. Why don't you pick something out and order it, then take a shower. I have a few things to go over with Matthias. After, we can all eat and get some rest."

I tapped a few more icons and checked out, secure for once in the knowledge that the shared debit card in my wallet had enough money to afford the veritable feast that would be arriving at our door in thirty minutes. "Fine. Chicago's finest coming our way, along with a growler from a local brewery." I heaved myself to my feet. Matti was up in a flash to help me get my crutches situated solidly beneath my arms, but I shook him off.

He sighed and sat back down to face Sylvie. I heard her start in on him in a hushed voice as I hobbled toward the hallway, "Matthias, you have to tell her. She can help you."

"Absolutely not, Sylvie. It's not part of the deal—"

I paused and glanced back. He was staring at me almost angrily and gestured for me to keep moving. Sylvie was giving him one of her patented "you will do what I say, young man" looks. I stuck my tongue out him and he crossed his eyes back at me and shooed me away again. I'd let it slide for now, but if I was supposed to help him, this was one secret I was going to be prying out of his annoyingly attractive clenched jaw.

Chapter Eight

Matti

"Ahem." Sylvie cleared her throat meaningfully. "What was that all about?"

"Nothing," I muttered. "We're getting along, all right?"

Sylvie hummed noncommittally and turned back to her knitting before harrumphing and setting it aside. She leaned toward me and the sharky agent expression disappeared, replaced with concern. "I mean it, Matthias. Tell her about your reading issues. She can help and you're going to need it."

"I'll figure it out, I always have," I grumped.

"Yes," Sylvie said quietly. "You always have. But the stakes are higher now and you don't have anyone here to cover for you. She has her secrets too, you know."

"Fine," I said. "I'll consider it."

"Fine," said Sylvie. "This will be tough for both of you, but she'll need your help and support to heal. I've got a lot of events for the two of you and a few ideas that I want you to think about for publicity."

I growled but didn't say anything. I felt like I was trapped. A prisoner of other people's expectations and juggling a million tiny balls trying to keep up the façade. I got up and walked over to the sliding glass door between the living room and balcony, staring out over the busy road that separated us from the lake. The leaves were starting to turn, even though it was warm in the early August sun. My brain felt like it was short-circuiting with all the changes and pressure.

A door opened and the tropical smell of coconut and plumeria wafted out of the bathroom, followed by the sound of another door opening and shutting. Abby was done in the shower, probably rifling through her things trying to find new clothes, maybe wrapped in a towel as she carefully balanced on her crutches. Maybe she needed my help…not that she'd ever admit to it.

Abby's halting limp as she came down the hallway toward us distracted me from the view. She had thrown on warm-up pants and a long-sleeved T-shirt to guard against the chill of the air conditioning and her hair was damp, leaving wet trails on her white shirt. A buzz of the intercom indicated the arrival of dinner and she hobbled over to the island, where she plopped on a high stool. Sylvie busied herself by pulling out glassware, plates and paper towels. The strange mood that Abby had walked in on dispersed as we ate and Sylvie started to list off the things she had planned for us.

I was to start working with the club's main philanthropic organization, running free camps for inner-city schools and guest coaching at their teams' practices, and she wanted Abby to help out with them somehow as well. It would be good for us to be working together in the public eye, she claimed. *Bah*. I tuned out and focused on eating.

Abby's laugh pealing out like bells interspersed with a completely unexpected delicate snort pulled me out of my ferocious concentration on the best pizza I'd ever had in my life. The beer wasn't bad either.

"Sylvie, you can't be serious," she managed to say in between adorable little snorts. "A morning show appearance? Sue? The Bean?"

"Dead serious. You two are a couple and you need to be out and about in the public eye. That means learning the town, checking out the sights. Getting your photos taken and meeting fans," she said with growing excitement. "I can see it—you ask a tourist to take your picture, we make it seem like Matti's proposing again. It would be adorable."

"I can barely walk," said Abby as she calmed down a bit.

"What's the Bean? And Sue? And we're doing a game show?" I asked, completely confused.

"Sylvie wants us to go check out this sculpture in Millennium Park—it looks like a big, mirrored bean. Sue is the name of the massive Tyrannosaurs Rex skeleton at the Field Museum, another major Chicago landmark," Abby explained and snorted again. Her hand flew to her mouth as if she'd realized the noises she was making were less than—well, ladylike.

I swatted her hand away. "And I'm supposed to pretend to propose, again?" I asked and started to grin. This could be fun. Abby smacked me in the arm as I leaned over to steal her pizza. She pinched my thigh and I howled. "That hurt, you monster." I leaned toward her and she started laughing and ducked away, throwing her other pizza crust at me, which I managed to catch and shove in my mouth.

"Yes," Sylvie interrupted and glanced back and forth between us with an eyebrow raised. "I want you out in the public as soon as Abby is more mobile, becoming part of the city, being recognized and raising your profiles. Can you do that?"

I checked Abby out from the corner of my eye. The flush from her cheekbones traveled down to her chest beneath the loose collar of her shirt as she nodded along with me.

"Good, because it starts tomorrow morning bright and early with Abby's first doctor appointment.

"Then, Matti," Sylvie continued, "you have to check in with the team for your first workout. Abby, while you're at Northwestern, maybe you could drop in and say hi to Coach Williams if there's time. He knows you're in town and would probably love to see you."

Abby nodded silently and finished her pizza. Her fingers twisted the paper towel into a rope and she started to wrap it around her fingers—something I'd learned she did when she was nervous. I reached over and covered her hand with my own.

"And maybe your family?" Sylvie asked

Abby's fingers tightened beneath mine on the towel and her arm muscles tensed. I squeezed and she slowly released her hold. "No, Sylvie, I think I'll be okay without talking to them," she said evenly.

"Oh, fine. If you change your mind, let me know," Sylvie said after a brief pause. "I'm glad we're all in agreement on how to handle the next few weeks. Now, this old lady is ready for bed. You two can handle clean-up and I'll see you bright and early for your first appointment— Abby, eight o'clock."

The door to the guest room shut behind her.

"I guess that takes care of the sleeping arrangement question." I got up and started to load the dishes into the dishwasher.

"I can move into the guest room when she leaves. Since she'll only be here for a few days."

I changed the subject, not wanting to admit that I would totally be okay with maintaining a shared sleeping arrangement. She clearly still found me unworthy. "What did Sylvie mean about your family? Are they nearby?" Her face changed in an instant, from open and laughing to shuttered and dull.

"Yes," she said quietly, and began to twist that paper towel again. "I don't speak to them, we're not close and, no offense, but I'm really not interested in talking about it."

"Fair enough. I didn't mean to offend you. My family is really close. They'll probably want to adopt you by the end of this," I joked and was rewarded with a faint smile.

I finished the dishes and wiped down the counter. "Come on." I offered her my arm. "Let's head to bed."

We slowly moved down the hall and I could see the pain on her face. "Have you taken any pain meds today?" I asked, and she shook her head. "Why not?"

"I don't want to get dependent on them," she said with a wince.

"Abby, you've got to take this seriously. You need the meds."

"Let it go." Her voice was sharp. "You're not my mother."

I shrugged and opened the door to the master bedroom. Our suitcases were lined up against the very far wall of the large space that was dominated by a huge modern platform bed. It was high enough that it would be easy for Abby to get in and out and big enough for both of us to have plenty of space. It was covered in a pristine, fluffy white duvet and the pillows puffed up like clouds. Abby's suitcase was open and a small trail of clothes draped out of it. *Already making her mark on our shared space. I like it.*

"This is nice. Plenty of space for both of us."

She nodded. "Yeah, the bed is huge. Mind if I take the bathroom first? I only need to brush my teeth and stuff." It wasn't really a question as she was already rummaging through her suitcase. She pulled out a small red leather case.

Sleeping in long sleeves and warm-up pants? This had disaster written all over it—I slept warm, and usually naked. Hopefully this would prove to be a matter of modesty in an unfamiliar situation because she was going to be hot if we were sleeping together. I shut the blackout curtains over the floor-to-ceiling windows and dropped my dirty clothes in a pile with hers. Barely managed to pull on clean underwear and a pair of old team shorts as she came back into the room. The elastic on the shorts was shot and they sagged over my hips. Her jaw dropped when she caught sight of me, and I smirked.

"Is that what you're wearing to bed?" she managed to squeak out.

"I've been told I'm like a furnace when I sleep, so I'm usually naked. Take your pick — short-shorts or nada." I shrugged and walked into the bathroom.

By the time I came back out she was sitting up against the backboard reading, her lower half under the covers, right leg elevated on a pile of pillows. She made eye contact and quickly returned her attention to her book. Her eyes darted back toward me again a moment later and snagged.

"What?" I asked as I slipped beneath the covers.

"Um, nothing?" she said uncertainly, but she wouldn't stop staring at me. "You have a lot of tattoos. I didn't realize there were more than the ones on your arms and legs."

Hmm, was my little fake fiancée a fan of ink? I smiled internally. "Yeah, I do." In fact, I was pretty much completely inked. Arms, shoulders, chest, back, a few on my thighs and one on my left calf. Mostly traditional American designs, all chosen in one-off sessions. "Do you like tattoos?" I asked curiously as I attempted to scan her body without looking like I was ogling her.

"I guess? I mean, I don't have any, but I've always kind of wanted to get one."

"Then you should. Who's stopping you?" I yawned and stretched, lying down and turning toward her.

"No one, I guess. My family raised me pretty strictly. It was never an option and I'm a little scared of needles. But these—" She reached out as if her hand were a moth drawn to the open flame above a candle burning at two ends inked on my bicep. "These I like."

My arm sizzled where she touched me lightly and she snatched her hand back as if the candle's flame had physically burned her. We stared at each other for a moment, the clean smell of her tropical shampoo wrapping around me, practically strangling me. I wanted to touch her, draw something on her that would be as indelible as the ink on my own arms.

She turned down the corner of a page, closing her book with a snap. "Good night," she murmured as she leaned over and clicked off the reading lamp, cloaking the room in complete darkness.

"Night," I said and closed my eyes, fighting the desire to roll into her and pull her against me. A security blanket against the unknowns of the next day. If I were to tattoo something to remind me of her and this night, it would be an anchor, maybe a bird cage. Something grounding, but entrapping at the same time.

Chapter Nine

Matti

That night, I dreamed of peaches — peach pie to be exact. Once upon a time I'd played on a team with an American whose mom used to ship him pies made with peaches from his grandmother's orchards in Georgia. How she had gotten them to Cologne still fresh was a mystery that probably cost an outrageous amount of money. But they had always been fresh and cloying, tasting like summer. Sometimes he would make vanilla bean whipped cream the way his grandmother had taught him to put on top. When he was in a generous mood, he'd share and, up to that moment, I was sure it was the greatest thing I'd ever tasted.

Up to that moment only because I had my tongue buried in Abby's pussy and it tasted better than that perfect, summer golden honey-syrup that had drenched the peach slices in the filling. Her hands were knotted tightly in my hair, pulling me so deeply into her that I could barely breathe as I held her thighs down and spread wide to allow my broad shoulders between them.

I alternated smooth decisive licks of her slit, delving in and out for more of that delicious flavor, and twirling lightly around her clit before sucking hard while she cried out for more. My name was a broken curse that tumbled from her lips as I slid one then two fingers inside her and curled them toward where my tongue nibbled on the sensitive nub. Abby screamed and shattered around me, her walls fluttering and gripping my fingers tightly as she came.

As her shudders subsided, I kissed my way up her body. Those icy gray eyes, now softened like molten silver, stared up at me in surprise. Her eyelids were heavy but her hands were still tangled in my long hair and she pulled me down for a kiss. I settled above her, caging her in with my forearms and nipping at her chin, jawline, and up to the delicate shell of her ear. I whispered, "God, Abby. I love you so much."

She shivered and pulled me down to blanket her completely and whispered back—

"What? Matti, what the hell? Wake up!"

My eyes opened slowly, and the warm little package that had been curled into me had turned into a shrieking ball of arms and legs all trying to extricate themselves from my embrace. A cat meowed above my head and I felt little claws and toe beans kneading away at my loose hair and scalp. Abby's flailing arm caught me in a very unfortunate place and I doubled over in the fetal position. She rolled upright with a face as red as a traffic sign.

"What did you say back there?" she asked in a deadly calm voice.

I stared at her wordlessly, still able to taste the phantom peach pie of my dream, smell the scent of her tropical bath products as they heated up with her arousal.

"Because I heard something that I'm really not sure I ever want to hear again." She paused and inhaled. "Also, if you're dreaming about fucking someone, could you at least have the courtesy to not give me a sleep-talking play-by-play?"

"Uh, yup. I'm sorry. Did I say something offensive?" I asked more than a little nervously, hoping against hope that my declarations of love had been completely garbled or silent.

"No, some mumbles that sounded like 'pussy tasting like peach pie,' and you were snuggling me like it was your life's mission—I literally *couldn't* breathe."

She stared down at me, her eyes fixed on my crotch, where I'd pitched a tent. Truly impressive, given the confines of my underwear. The head of my cock twitched under her beady eye and I nearly bucked toward her. I wanted her hands, her mouth, anything, all over me.

"Peach pie," I said with my eyes closed again. "It's my favorite, my absolute favorite."

"Mmhmm," she murmured, and maybe it was my imagination, but that hum seemed closer and the smell of plumeria or hibiscus seemed to be tickling my nose more strongly, as if maybe—just maybe—she'd been dreaming the same dream as me and wanted to see it through to the end.

"Kiddos!" Sylvie's grating voice cut through the thick air and I opened my eyes in time to see Abby pulling back, flushed and breathless, the whites clearly showing around her gray, now stormy, eyes. She grabbed for her crutches, heaved herself off the bed and limped to the bathroom. The door shut behind her with a decisive crack as our agent's fist pounded on our bedroom door. "Abby Belinda, Matthias, get your asses out of bed. We're going to be late to the first appointments!"

"Relax, Sylvie. Abby Belinda is up and in the bathroom and I'm getting dressed," I shouted back to reassure her.

"Gonna make the coffee. Meet me in the kitchen when you're decent." She clattered off down the hallway. We were going to need some rugs or Sylvie's spike heels were going to destroy the hardwoods.

The covers pooled in my lap as I sat up and scrubbed my hands through my hair, catching in a rat's nest of tangles while I listened to Abby tunelessly humming in the shower. I frowned at my still twitching cock, which was perking back up as a picture of a rosy and deliciously wet Abby rubbing herself down with a sudsy washcloth invaded my mind. "Down, boy," I said as I pressed my left hand, hard, on my crotch. *Jesus*.

* * * *

Abby's first appointment was with an orthopedic surgeon and trainer at Northwestern University. Sylvie left us in the waiting room and bowed out, saying she'd had enough of hospitals and medical professionals since Abby's accident and wanted to go grocery shopping for us. Abby had my hand in a death grip, her face was white, jaw clenched, as we waited for the team to assemble in the private room we'd been ushered into by a set of fluttering nurses.

"It's going to be okay, Abby—" I tried to promise, but the door swung open and interrupted me. I felt Abby stiffen further and her grip somehow tightened, cutting off the circulation in my hands. One look at the wildness and fear in her eyes and I stopped trying to wriggle my fingers loose. I shifted closer and she leaned into me.

"Abby, great to meet you. I'm Doctor Mitchell, lead on your care team," said the young, jocular doctor with the receding hairline. It was incredibly immature, but I was relieved that this team of doctors didn't have any fairy-tale princes or superhero types.

She nodded and cocked her head at me. What did she—oh.

"Hi, I'm Matti—the fiancé," I said and extended my hand to the doctor.

"Yes, another famous soccer star! Delighted to have you both here. Let's dive right in." He was all business as an intern bustled in and put up some scans on the light box and flipped the switch. A mangled leg, knee bent at an impossible angle, glowed from the screen. I winced.

"As you can see," he said, "we have a tear in the ACL—definitely your second if not third—and the meniscus is badly damaged too. Surgery is the first step toward recovery, then extensive physical therapy. Luckily, you're in the right place here. In the last year our team has reconstructed the ligaments and knees of over five hundred athletes, from high school to professional."

"How long till I can play again?" Abby asked quietly when the big braggart stopped to draw breath.

The medical team glanced at one another, then a young woman with a bouncy ponytail stepped forward, clipboard crushed to her chest. "That's up to you. Your knee will feel almost normal after surgery, but full recovery to active playing status is a different animal altogether. It will ultimately depend on how much you're willing to invest in your therapy. I'm Angela, and I'll be your physical therapist, by the way." She shot a toothy white American smile at us.

A little more medical mumbo jumbo, surgery scheduling and we were done. Very efficient, almost German. We hobbled out and found Sylvie sitting in the waiting room. She looked at me with raised eyebrows. I shook my head slightly, hoping that Abby wasn't paying attention. Sylvie grimly smiled to the nurse over our shoulders and hustled us back out to the car, one of my hands still clutched tightly in Abby's iron grip and the other around her waist, holding her upright.

Abby's face remained set, her eyes remote and staring into the middle distance as our agent pulled out of the parking spot and sped towards the exit.

"Hey," I said, "that wasn't terrible news. They've scheduled your surgery for next week and, depending on how your rehab goes, you have a great chance at getting back to playing."

She dropped my hand like it was red hot. "Then you do all of this. You get your knee wrecked, reconstructed, and force yourself through agonizing therapy for months. For the hope that *maybe* you'll get better." Her words were venomous.

We all lapsed into silence until we pulled up at a massive athletic campus. My new home, but I didn't want to get out of the car yet. Abby seemed to be holding herself together by a thread as she stared out at the people in practice uniforms dodging and weaving around cones. I tapped her chin and she glanced up at me with narrowed, glassy eyes that were threatening to spill. "I mean it, Abby. I promise, say the word and anything you need to get back on the field will be yours. If you need me to work out with you every day, be your lifting partner, your cheerleader, whatever — I'll do it. Anything."

She nodded and hurled herself against me. Less of an embrace and more of a drowning person clinging to a buoy. From the front, Sylvie cleared her throat again and Abby drew back, wiping her eyes with the back of her hand. Her tears had dampened my shirt and I could feel the moisture clammy on my skin. It was both a brand and a promise sealed with tears. She *would* get better.

* * * *

"Shellenberg? Matthias?"

"That's me," I said to the lady at the desk as I slid my passport over to her.

"No, no need for that. You're pretty recognizable," she said and shot a flirtatious grin at me. I smiled reflexively back. It felt fake, like my smiles were stuck in a dark SUV heading toward Lake Shore Drive when they should have been in my back pocket, ready if needed.

"I'll call Coach Sherman, then, shall I?" she asked.

"Please." I turned away from the desk. Started to pace back and forth. As always when I got nervous or stressed, my thoughts fractured into a million little slivers that seemed to slip through my fingers as I desperately tried to corral them back into place. What if everyone hated me, what if they found out that I was barely a functional adult? Could barely read, write or think straight unless I was moving with a ball attached to some part of my body.

"Matthias," boomed a man's voice that would carry across the pitch through a thunderstorm.

A short man with a barrel chest and impressive mustache that almost hid a wide grin hustled over.

"Good to meet you, man. We're glad you're here!" he said in a slightly quieter voice.

"Coach Sherman, hey." I held out my hand for him to shake. He clasped it and held tight as he charged back through the hallway behind the desk, dragging me along with him. In quick succession he took me through the massive complex, showing me the locker rooms, training rooms and cafeteria before opening a small door into a room with windows that overlooked a practice field.

"Have a seat, son," he said in a stern voice. I'd wondered when the other shoe would drop. Sherman had a reputation as a hard-ass, someone who played by the rules and despised showboats and off-pitch "problems." Both of which were things that I was guilty of at some point in time.

"Thanks, Coach. Can I say how excited I am to be here? And thank you for the opportunity?" I said as sincerely as I could.

"You should be. I understand that you were almost in for an early retirement if our ownership group hadn't made a stink about signing you," he said.

"That's my understanding too, yes," I said and dropped my eyes. My foot was drumming and I could feel his desk start to vibrate.

"Son, here's the deal. I don't like you and didn't want you on my team. You're a brilliant defender, absolutely fucking brilliant, but a shit human from what I've seen. I don't tolerate your brand of assholery here, got it?" He stared me dead in the eye and the desk started to vibrate more quickly.

"I understand, and thank you for this chance. I'm not going to say that all of that shit about me was a lie, but there's a pretty big proportion that was either outright untrue or highly exaggerated. But I'm not here to make excuses. I recognize this is my last chance and I only want to be left in peace to play," I said as I clasped my knees to try to stop them from drumming.

"One chance, son. One. That's all you get from me. We're a family-friendly club here, got that? Traditional values and all that other bullshit." He stared at me, all joking gone. "Do we have a deal?"

"Absolutely, sir," I muttered and held out my hand again. Sherman looked at me for a long moment before taking it.

"Don't let me down," he said as he yanked my hand back and forth. "Don't let your club down."

"I won't, Coach, really. I'm here to play, don't want any trouble," I said as earnestly as I could, even though he was pissing me off. Who cared what I did in my own time?

He ushered me out the door. "Let's go meet your team."

Introductions to a handful of guys, other coaching staff and a few members of operations were a blur. Everyone seemed cool, a bunch of them invited me out for a drink and, when I laughed and declined, the coaches seemed to relax. Maybe it had been a test.

One guy stepped forward at the end and introduced himself. "Daniel Lopez, striker. I'm your co-captain, man. Come with me, we'll get you outfitted and ready for practice." We walked down the hall, his sandals slapping against the tile, and he showed me into the locker room, pointing out where the spare uniforms and towels were. "Listen, bro, Coach is out to get you. He didn't want you here, so you're on thin ice, got it?"

"I know, but seriously, hardly any of that crap was true," I defended myself.

"Sure, sure. But you gotta be a changed man, okay? Keep everything on the downlow, right? You got a girlfriend or wife or something?" he asked.

"Fiancée," I said, and the word tasted strange in my mouth, half a lie, half the truth.

Daniel grunted. "Good, stick with her and keep everything in public on the straight and narrow. Sherman can be a real dick. You're brilliant, played against you back when you were on Cologne and I was on Bonn, not that we faced off—I rode the bench—but I saw you. You're one of the best. Maybe you and your lady could come over sometime? My wife and I have a daughter, a house, like to host parties. Get settled and we'll have you over. Yeah?"

"Yeah," I said and grinned. "I'd like that."

"And don't let the kids try to drag you down. Those young guys? They're hungry. And cut-throat. Watch your back around a few of them." He shook his head and bent to tie his shoes.

"I will, man. Thanks for the heads-up," I said.

"Bueno, let's roll. Get kitted up and I'll see you on the pitch." He finished lacing up his shoes and strolled off, his cleats crunching on the cement floor.

* * * *

I drove home with a spinning head after a day of meeting too many new people and holding together the lies about me and Abby. Loads of handshakes and back slaps, little *wink winks, nudge nudges* about how hot she was, how talented our "little kickers" would be. It had been tiresome and had only underscored how horribly chauvinistic professional sports could be — and we had been talking about one of our own.

"Stabby? You around?" I hollered to be heard over the poppy instrumental music playing in the apartment as I dropped my keys on the table by the door and kicked off my slides.

"Yeah, in the living room."

"I'm gonna grab a snack. You want anything while I'm up?"

"No, I'm good. Already ate. There's leftover Thai in the fridge. You don't have a peanut allergy or anything do you?

"Nah, but thanks for checking."

Sylvie had outdone herself this morning and the fridge and cupboards were stuffed full of food. I snaked out the leftover Pad Thai that Abby had mentioned and grabbed some napkins and a fork before wandering into the living room.

"Dis is goov." I really had no manners to speak of.

"It is. Surprised you're home already, kind of thought you'd be going out with the team."

"Saving that for later, Stabs. I'm still jet-lagged. Plus I figured that Sylvie would want to grill us on something."

"Didn't you check your texts? She's heading back to New York early, something about a client crisis."

"Oh. She left us on our own?" I must have sounded mildly panicked. Abby started to laugh.

"You're gonna be okay, buddy, I promise. Want to watch a movie or something tonight? We've got a bunch of beer and I purposefully haven't taken any pain meds so I can have one too."

"Sure…"

"Cool. Just so you know, we're watching *School Ties*. I love my early nineties Brendan Fraser and will die on this hill."

"Whoa, noted. Strong feelings about Brendan Fraser," I teased.

"I'm going to marry him some day," she said with one hand over her heart.

I rolled my eyes at her. "I'll have my brother put in a good word for you. I think they worked together on something a while back."

Abby shot upright. "No. He didn't. He knows Brendan Fraser?" She squealed and I winced. *My eardrums.*

"Want me to call and ask?"

"Yes! I mean no. Oh fine. Can you text him?" She clasped her hands beneath her chin and gave me the big eyes.

I tossed her my phone. "Text him yourself. He's saved under the movie camera emoji."

She snagged it out of mid-air and started thumbing through my contacts. "Why aren't there any names in here? Only emojis or photos?"

"Um. It's how I remember things better," I hedged.

She put the phone down on her lap and took a deep breath. Her eyes were curious, a little cautious. "Matti, can I ask you something really personal?"

"Uh, sure? I mean, we're stuck together for a year…"

"Okay, and I'm sorry if this is offensive, but I noticed that you work off of pictures most of the time and never read anything that Sylvie sends us." She paused for a second, like she was steeling herself for a fight. "Can you read?"

It was so out-of-nowhere shocking that someone who barely knew me had even noticed. In twenty-some years, I'd never been called on it by anyone but Sylvie.

I exhaled hard, feeling my nostrils flare, and shook my head. "Not really." That small admittance was like a tiny hole in a dam ready to blow wide open. "I mean, I can read — and write — if I absolutely have to. If I really force myself to concentrate and take my time."

"How did you get by?" Her face was astonished. Sympathy was hiding in those soft gray eyes too. I swear it. "How does no one know?"

"Eh, people will generally do anything for you if you charm them enough," I said with a shrug. "And if you're funny, or attractive."

"But...you went to school and your teachers never tried to get you help?" She clearly had never heard about the farm systems for the major clubs in Europe. The teachers were basically chaperones and their only job had been to teach us enough to get by.

"Nah, they never cared. Told me I was too stupid to learn, yelled at me for not picking it up quickly enough, but kept passing me because the coaches wanted me playing League when I hit sixteen or seventeen. There's a lot of pressure on the clubs to turn out players, you know."

"Have you ever gotten help as an adult? There are tons of teachers and therapists out there who specialize in —"

"I've been tested for dyslexia and ADHD, but I don't have anything. My brain didn't click right away with letters and words and all of a sudden it was too late. I'm fine. I get by."

"Not even your family? I mean, I'm assuming Sylvie knows."

"She does," I said with a grimace. I hated that even one person knew my weakness. "But no one else and it doesn't leave this room."

"But…" she spluttered. "Your family?"

"We're super close and I love them, but my oldest brother — the world-famous actor? Reads and memorizes lines for a living? My middle brother — CEO of a multimillion-euro wine business? Or maybe his twin sister — the award-winning green architect?" I couldn't sit still anymore and jumped to my feet, pacing in tighter and tighter circles.

"And my parents, right? The ones who roll their eyes at me, the big dumb jock. The oops baby. I mean, I know they love me, but they don't *know* me — they pushed me out the door when I was ten and that was that. Home once a year for Christmas, then right back to Spain."

"Oh my god, Matti. I'm sorry. I had no idea." She started to put her feet down and tried to reach for me.

I rushed over to sit her back down and plopped next to her. My knee wouldn't stop bouncing and I wanted nothing more than to run screaming from this conversation. "It's fine. Like I said, I get by." I repeated myself one more time to reassure her.

"It's not, though. That's a huge amount of mental effort you're expending to keep people from seeing — and knowing — who you really are."

I couldn't meet her eye. "It is what it is." I tried to play it off with a grin. Redirect, that was my top skill as a player. "What do I have to do to make sure you keep my secret?"

"You are ridiculous."

"I know. I'm told it's my most charming quality."

She snorted. "It's not, but if you want to talk more about this, I'm here. I can help, find a teacher, work with you myself — even though you'd probably want to kill me. I don't know that I'm any good at teaching another human being anything other than how to kick a ball or tackle an opponent."

I laughed too, relieved to have the discussion over, and nudged her with my elbow. "Shut up, it's fine. Let's watch this movie — and don't forget to bug Markus. He'll love it. Everyone in my family is dying to meet you."

She snorted again. "Okay, Matti. Have it your way." She flipped on the TV and started scrolling through my phone, searching for my brother's contact information. "But if you think I'm going to let this go forever, you've got another thing coming. You're helping me so much, I want to help you too."

Her voice sounded reluctant, a tad bit grumpy, like she didn't really want to want to help me but she was going to, goddammit, because she owed me. And with that single grudging comment, Stabby Abby McKinnon stole whatever was left of my heart that I'd been trying to keep away from her. She might never be mine for real, but having someone finally in my corner felt amazing.

Chapter Ten

Abby

"Abby, do you know where my new cleats disappeared to?" The boisterous shout rang through our still-too-empty and too-loud apartment.

"No and, daily reminder, I'm not your mom or your keeper. Where did you leave them?" I shouted back and rubbed at the crease between my eyebrows. Living with Matthias Shellenberg was like living with a twelve-year-old tornado. He never stopped moving and was constantly leaving his crap everywhere. A small trail of equipment, cat toys and food wrappers seemed to follow him wherever he went.

"Meow," chirped Spock from his perch on one of our bookshelves. Next to him were the missing cleats.

"Matti, Spock found them," I yelled.

Matti came dashing down the hall in a bespoke suit, clutching his backpack. Home exhibition game today, no traveling required, thank god. "That lovely little pussy. Come here, buddy, I wanna kiss you. You take such good care of your daddy, don't you?"

Spock purred and delicately knocked one then the other shoe to the ground, and I groaned. Matti swooped him up and danced him around while the little traitor rumbled contentedly. He loved, *loved*, his daddy, who never got tired of doting on the furry little bugger. Since we'd moved in together, Spock had started enjoying fancy food and treats, tons of toys, dedicated catnip time and walking on a leash. The press and public loved that—Matti proudly walking behind the little black cat, me usually limping along in their wake, trying not to laugh.

I wanted to hate him for how easily he'd won my notoriously nasty cat's loyalty, but I couldn't. Matti had burrowed himself into our lives so thoroughly that I couldn't imagine it any other way.

We hadn't even moved into separate bedrooms after Sylvie left, both of us nodding and saying how we'd probably have guests soon and it would be a total pain in the ass for our housekeeper to keep re-washing bedding. Plus that big bed was much more comfortable and my stuff was already in the dresser. Spock liked it better there too, and I wasn't going to leave my formerly feral cat in the hands of a first-time pet daddy.

We'd been in Chicago for a month and things were going okay. My surgery had been successful and I was in physical therapy four days a week, which was going less smoothly. It was hard, it hurt, and it was a constant stop-start with progress. I was scared shitless that this was it, that I'd never come back even though I had the best care and a constant cheerleader in Matti, who would drop everything to take me out to the field or the weight room in our building for an abbreviated workout.

Every night I went to bed praying that the next day would be my breakthrough, but it never seemed to happen. I would lie awake, my thoughts running a million miles a minute while Matti slept, snoring softly next to me. Inevitably, he'd roll toward me and wrap me up in those big inked arms and hold me tightly against his chest. The only way I could sleep was with the slow, steady *da-dum* of Matti's heart beating beneath my cheek. Not that either of us would admit to it.

In addition to the surgery and therapy, I was working with the Rebels' philanthropy wing to handle logistics for all of the camps Matti was running during the fall and spring. On top of that, during my last appointment at Northwestern I'd run into Coach Williams, who'd been the women's coach when I'd played. He was now coaching the men's team and had asked me to come speak to his athletes and help with conditioning for the midfielders.

It was a lot, and Matti was starting to piss me off with his probably well-intentioned concern for me. He was constantly harping on me to relax, slow down, take things easier—but he didn't understand how my brain worked. I had to stay busy or I would sink. Drown in the what ifs of what it would mean if I could never play again.

"You're coming to the game, right?" Matti's question broke me from my downward spiral. He stared at me expectantly, still clutching a very smug-looking Spock beneath his chin, and waggled the cat's paws.

"Yeah, yeah. Sorry. I'm coming, just have to finish up that paperwork for the new school you'll be working with next week, but then I'll be there," I apologized.

"Cool," he said, and grinned at me exuberantly.

I blinked. The energy that Matti expended merely living was baffling, and before every game he seemed to vibrate at a super-high frequency that was almost imperceptible. How could he keep it up twenty-four-seven?

"And afterward? We have that karaoke showdown team bonding event later tonight, but maybe we should try to check off some of Sylvie's list. What do you think?" he asked. "It's an afternoon game and still nice out. Maybe we could go down to that Bean thing before dinner?"

Ugh. The "Bean thing" — it was the lowest on my list of priorities for Sylvie's photo ops and reminded me of a trip to Chicago that my family had taken right before my senior year in high school. My brother had graduated with his degree, joined the fire department in our small town and recently proposed to his childhood sweetheart.

We'd done all of the touristy things, including scarfing down Chicago dogs from a street vendor and the requisite trip to the Bean, where some other tourist had taken a photo of the five of us, me standing slightly apart with a pained smile. The four of them had seemed to be the family unit and me the stranger.

"Stabby Abby? You okay?" Matti asked with a strange expression on his face. "You look like you're contemplating homicide and trying not to fart at the same time."

"For heaven's sake, Matti, I'm just thinking."

"Ookay, sweetums, want to make sure you don't live up to your namesake. I know I test you unbearably," he said with a sassy grin. He thrust the cat at me. "Here, he wants his mommy. So the game then the Bean thing?"

"Thanks, yeah. Game and Bean thing," I said with a grumpy frown.

"Aw, come here, it's not that bad," he said and pulled me and Spock into a big Matti hug. The long ends of his hair that he hadn't pulled back yet tickled my cheeks as I leaned into him. His arms were almost hot as they wrapped around me and he smelled faintly of my shampoo and body wash since he'd run out of his own the other day and refused to buy more. I had plenty, he'd reasoned. Why waste money?

"Stabby Abby, baby girl," he murmured as he started to sway with us in his arms, then surprised me as he dropped a kiss on the top of my head. He let go and stepped back, eyeing me up and down with a concerned tilt to his mouth. "You're okay, though? No pain?"

"No, no pain. You know I'm not the biggest fan of some of the WAGS in the box lately and I really don't want to do the Bean thing," I muttered.

While I didn't mind a few of the older players' wives, the girlfriends of some of the younger ones were not my favorite people. No one except Mercedes, Daniel Lopez's wife, seemed to know how to relate to a wife or girlfriend who wasn't a professional model or influencer. But all of that paled next to how badly I did not want to do the bean thing.

He pulled me back in and this time kissed me on the forehead as he said, "We'll make it quick then—game,

Bean and back home. You want to cook tonight, or should we order?"

"Order, please," I said with some relief. We'd started cooking together lately and it was a surprising amount of fun, but I wasn't going to be in the mood after the day.

"You got it," he said and, to my surprise, kissed my forehead again. His hands were tight on my shoulders and it felt like his lips lingered on my skin.

He'd always been very comfortable being physical with me. The man was a hugger and a cuddler to the point where it was almost annoying in its cuteness, but these kisses were new. I hated how much I liked them. Wanted more. And now he was staring back at me, pupils dilated with a rising warmth in his eyes that rivaled the blush traveling from my chest to my cheeks. My ears started to burn.

"You better go," I blurted as he stepped closer to me.

He blinked, spell broken. "Yeah, yeah," he muttered, and his outstretched hands seamlessly rose to pull back his hair into a high knot with the elastic around his wrist. "See you," he called out as he swept up the cleats Spock had found for him and headed for the door.

"See you," I whispered as the door shut. I needed to cut him off.

* * * *

"You play too?" a voice that sounded like claws sliding on quartz countertops asked me a few hours later in the family and friends box at the Rebels' stadium. "Is that, like, how you met?"

"Sort of. Matti was on the men's team, I was on the women's, but we've known each other for a while longer — we have the same agent," I answered. I'd done this song and dance with various wives and girlfriends during each of the games and events I'd attended.

"Ooh, and didn't you both get fired because you were together?" This time her voice went soft and she had big red hearts blazing out of her eyes. "That's so romantic!"

She was a sweetheart, truly. One of the nice ones who was an actual fan of the game in addition to being the requisite young and beautiful, but she was there for Christian James, an asshole and one of the young guns who was always trying to get Matti to go out when he wasn't supposed to.

"Yeah, I guess," I answered. "Listen, I need to go to the bathroom and get a water. I'll see you around?"

"Absolutely!" She glowed with enthusiasm and my tired, cynical soul wanted to smack her. Shove her face in the fact that the guy she was "dating" probably didn't see their relationship the same way she did, that all he ever did was dog other players' wives and girlfriends. And cause trouble for my fake fiancé, the absolute wanker.

"Abby, come sit over here!" Mercedes' lightly accented voice was a welcome sound after the squawking from the various birds of prey I'd had to navigate through after going to the bathroom and snagging a bottled water.

"Mercedes, good to see you!"

"Mer, silly. How many times do I have to tell you?" She tut-tutted and went to work smoothing back some stray hairs that had pulled free from my ponytail. "Sorry, I'm a mother and can't stop meddling."

"It's sweet, Mer. Thanks. You might want to give some of them similar treatment," I murmured as I jerked my head in the direction of the girlfriends, the new accessory to Christian appearing a little lost among the glittering crew.

"Oh, that Michelle, right? Dating Christian?" Mer asked and I nodded. "Michelle!" she immediately called out. "Come sit by us!"

We could see Michelle's relieved sigh from across the box. She excused herself from the crowd to squeeze into the empty seat on the other side of Mer.

"Thanks." She laughed nervously. "Are they always like that? So...scary?"

Christian was going to eat this sweetheart for dinner. He'd slept with at least three or four of the girls she'd been talking to.

"Sometimes, sweetie," Mer said gently. "Christian has dated a few of them."

Michelle dropped her eyes to her lap. "I didn't know that."

I sighed, wondering where Mer was going to take this. She'd probably be all gentle and whatnot, whereas I lacked that delicate touch. "Listen, he's not worth it. You seem really nice and smart. Don't let him play with you—he's a fuckboy. Try dating Bryce—he's the real sweetheart on this team and completely single right now."

Mer started to laugh as I harrumphed.

"What? She'd figure it out soon enough. And Bryce is cool." I shrugged. "Whatever, it's your life. Do what you want."

Mer nodded, tears streaming from her eyes. "Bryce is a good guy," she managed to choke out as she wiped away the moisture with the tip of her pinkie finger.

Michelle's giggles cut off. "And he's super cute," she said dreamily. "I don't really like Christian, we've only been out once. He doesn't deserve a call back."

"Nope, he totally does not. Mer, can you invite Michelle to your daughter's party? Get her hooked in with Bryce?" Mer nodded and continued to laugh at us. My bluntness tempered by the nice manners of the sweet young thing next to me.

"There, settled. Now, can you two shut up so I can watch the game?" I was never going to lose the grump reputation. They'd have to pry that one out of my cold dead hands.

Out on the field, the team was being announced. Matti was one of the last names called and when he came out of the tunnel he looked straight up at the box where I was sitting and made an entirely goofy heart shape with his hands, then pointed at me.

"Oh my god! That's sooo cute," cooed Michelle next to me.

I grunted. All for show, I tried to remind myself. It wasn't sticking though, and I felt the warmth of his eyes even when I turned away to talk to Mer.

The whistle sounded and they were off.

* * * *

"Stabby Abby! How was I? Super genius?" Matti's voice boomed out over the heads of the rest of his team and their families.

I rolled my eyes and headed over to him, ignoring the glances—curious, envious and otherwise.

He was back in street clothes, wearing fitted gray jeans, a black T-shirt and an army green bomber jacket. Regardless of how hot he'd appeared in that bespoke suit this morning, this was how I preferred him. Hair styled back and showing off the buzzed undercut beneath the long hair, casual swagger with an undeniable edge. I wondered what people thought when they saw us, me almost a foot shorter than this tatted-up sex god, wearing trainers and a plain old T-shirt and jeans next to his trendier version of the same outfit.

"Great game, Captain. I especially dug that wicked tackle of Rodrigo charging up the middle. You literally made him flip over in mid-air—and no card," I murmured as I hugged him tightly, nose buried in his chest. His arms reflexively wrapped around me and the jacket rustled in my ear.

"Thanks, Abby." Like this morning, he lowered his head to brush his lips across my forehead. I sighed and leaned into him. He slid his hand beneath my hoodie to rub my back and my skin heated up beneath my thin T-shirt.

"Get it, old man!" A loud catcall and whistle had both of us springing apart and looking for the source of the noise—Christian James, who seemed to be partnerless at the moment. He grinned at us like a shark and I stiffened. Matti tightened his arms around me imperceptibly—a warning.

"Jealous, James?" Matti asked genially. Teammates and WAGs laughed as they also saw that Christian was alone. He flushed red and stomped away.

"You shouldn't have done that, Matti. He's going to cause trouble."

"What? I asked him if he was jealous," he said, and smiled innocently at me with wide eyes that watered as I punched him hard in the arm. "He can't do anything and you know it. Coach will have his ass off the team and, unlike moi, he doesn't have the talent to balance his bad-boy nonsense."

"Ooh, is that what you are?" I said and poked him in the chest. "A bad boy?"

"You know it, baby. You're the one who tamed me." He winked and I heard a few of the wives and girlfriends titter in the background as they overheard our exchange.

I grabbed him by the shoulders and pulled him down to my level. The laugh left him and he eyed me questioningly, but I didn't give him a chance to ask what I was doing. I was tired of denying everything. Tired of pretending that I didn't appreciate everything he did for me, that I wasn't incredibly attracted to him, that him standing up for me didn't mean anything. I cupped his sharp jaw in my hands and went up in my toes to quickly kiss him softly on the lips, then dropped back on my heels.

Matti's hands had gone reflexively to my shoulders to steady me as I rose up on my toes and they stayed there as he stared at me. I winked at him, and it was my turn to smirk. "Get your tongue off the floor, old man. Let's go check out a bean."

I twirled around and grabbed one of his hands. Started tugging him toward the door.

"I'll check out your bean, baby," I heard him mutter behind me as we rolled out.

* * * *

I turned as I heard my name called, still in Matti's arms. We'd had our picture taken at the Bean and were now wandering around the sculpture, pushing and pulling each other like a couple of horny middle school kids who need physical contact with their crush but absolutely don't know what kind of touch is appropriate yet.

"Abby McKinnon? Is that really you?"

"Yes?" I said to a bouncy, curvy blonde who darted up to us. She was vaguely familiar, maybe from college?

"Oh my stars, I knew it had to be you! That hair! I'm glad it recovered after the gum incident." She laughed suddenly and it clicked. Cynthia Morris, pastor's daughter, homecoming queen and overall bane of my existence growing up.

"Cynthia," I replied stiffly.

"You do remember me! How cool! What are you doing here? This is so funny!"

Sure, it's funny. If you have a crap sense of humor.

"I live here with my fiancé," I said and pulled Matti next to me. He nodded at her and went back to people-watching, his feet starting to shuffle. "He plays for the soccer team here. I'm rehabbing."

"Oh, that's right. I can't believe you're still playing that game. Anyway. We're" — she gestured over at a guy with a paunch and receding hairline and a bored preteen who was the exact replica of Cynthia at age twelve or thirteen — "here looking for a special middle school dance dress for Dara. You remember Phil, don't you?"

Oh, yes, I remembered Phil. Former football star, now managing his family's used car dealership. He'd made my life miserable, along with Cynthia.

I nodded at him. "We should go," I said.

"Nice to meet you," interjected Matti as I started to tug him away from Mr. and Mrs. Evil.

"Abby! Don't you want us to tell anyone hello back home? Your family maybe?"

Like in high school, Cynthia's voice sliced through the crowd, past my carefully constructed walls. I shuddered and Matti glanced down at me in concern. I shook my head, picking up the pace to re-establish the distance between my old life and new.

Neither of us said a word until we walked into our apartment. Matti headed straight for the wine rack, grabbed a bottle that I could see had his family's name on it and twisted off the screw top. "Here. Thank god I talked Max into using screw tops, am I right? Finding an opener in this place is impossible."

I gulped straight from the bottle and a little overflowed. I wiped my mouth with the back of my hand as I handed the bottle back to him. He took a swig, swished it in his mouth like it was mouthwash and passed the bottle over again. Another deep drink and the level of the liquid dropped to the halfway mark. I set it down on the counter with a sharp clink.

"Thanks," I said and rolled out my shoulders, shrugging off my hoodie and rain jacket.

"No problem?" he answered quizzically. "Now, do you want to tell me what that was all about?"

"Not really," I said, and threw my coat over a chair and walked toward the sliding door. The glass was chilly in the September evening and I pressed my flushed forehead against it.

Matti slipped up behind me and put his arms around my waist. "Please," he whispered and I closed my eyes as his breath tickled my ear.

"Fine, will you start a fire and I'll order dinner?" I stalled for time.

"Sure..." he said slowly, and walked over to the wall, where he flicked a light switch. The gas fire in the fake fireplace roared up.

I backed up into the kitchen and, with shaking fingers, tapped in an order for our favorite pizza place. Then I scooped up the wine bottle, grabbed a couple of glasses by the stems, and brought them over to where Matti sat leaning against the fireplace.

"So...?" he prompted as I plopped down next to him and poured each of us a glass.

I sighed as we silently clinked our glasses together. Was it endearing to anyone else that Matti was incapable of drinking anything without a toast? "As I'm sure you gathered, that was someone I grew up with."

"Mmhmm," he hummed noncommittally.

"And that's really it," I said.

He made that tuneless humming noise again, a sound I'd come to realize was a stand-in for "I don't believe you," and I wondered if his mother had ever pulled that crap with him. *So annoying.*

"Fine, we didn't get along, and one time she stuck gum in my hair. I didn't care, but it made my mom cry. And her husband was really mean to me too."

Yet again he hummed.

"And she was messing with me about my family. I haven't talked to them since I was nineteen and I have no interest in starting now. I'm sure she knows that, it's a small town. My family doesn't know me. They've never understood me—never even tried—and I can't handle even thinking about them."

"Nineteen?" he asked incredulously. "You're twenty-eight!"

"I am?" I said sarcastically. "I mean, I am. Yeah, it's been a while."

"I barely go a day without talking to someone in my family," he said.

"I know," I muttered. I loved and hated that fact about him. Loved hearing him stomp in circles or dribble a ball around our apartment while barking in German at one of his family members. Hated feeling jealous when I knew that I'd been responsible for cutting my family off. "I don't really want to talk about it. Can we leave it at the fact that we're estranged and that it's better if we remain separated?"

He was quiet for a long time, but finally nodded solemnly. "If that's how you want it to be," he said and held up his glass for a refill.

I leaned against him, craving his warmth. "Do we have to do this karaoke thing tonight? I really hate it unless I'm drunk."

"Hmm, if it's drunk you want to be, we've got a good start going right now."

Yes, wine drunk and emotional from regurgitating my trauma and now we're supposed to go sing karaoke in a bar? But I had made a promise, and I always followed through on my promises.

"This is awkward, but how can you do karaoke with the lines running so fast on the screen? I know you need extra time to work through reading usually."

"Oh, I figured we'd sing something I know already. Want to know which song I'm thinking of?" He grinned and I knew I was stuck. I couldn't out him.

"Maybe you should surprise me?" I asked weakly as I took another sip.

His shoulders shook with laughter. "You're gonna love it. It's a duet."

I was going to need *all* the drinks for what was to follow.

Chapter Eleven

Matti

The slight smell of nicotine seeped out of the walls of the bar even though smoking in bars had been banned in Chicago for years. I might not have been out much since we moved, but I dug this bar. Old-school German beer hall that was near the Rebels' practice facility. It was the team's regular watering hole and I tried to stop by for any team events. Abby had never been and her nose was wrinkled as she stared around the crowded space.

"Please tell me you're joking."

"I would never joke about something as serious as karaoke." I did the whole crisscross over my heart with my index finger and gave Abby my best puppy-dog eyes look.

She blew a strand of hair out of her face and glared at the ceiling of the dingy bar as if someone would come down and spirit her away from the hell she found herself in. "We have to do this?"

"If you want me to fit in with the rest of the team, we sure do. It's tradition." I grinned at her as she stole another sip from my beer stein. The drizzle that had started on our way over to the bar made the little wisps of hair that had escaped her ponytail curl wildly. I put my arm around her and hoped no one saw her go stiff as I leaned in to whisper in her ear. "It'll be fun, I'm a horrible singer, and think how hard everyone's gonna laugh if they see a clip on social media."

"Promise me we'll only post a clip of your part?" she begged and reached for one of the shot glasses I'd lined up in preparation for us.

"Swear." Again I did the cross-my-heart sign and, to further underscore the seriousness of the situation, I held out my pinkie finger.

"Fine, but you owe me, and I'm gonna need a little more liquid courage before this happens." She slammed the shot and dropped the glass back on the bar while I wordlessly handed her the next one. Tossed that one back with a grimace and reached for the third one, which was supposed to be for me.

"You sure you need that one too?"

"Yup, most definitely." She snorted. "Dolly Parton and Kenny Rogers? *Islands in the Stream*? Absolutely."

I shrugged. The woman had a point. She snagged the glass and tossed it back like a champ, but came up with a gasp and watering eyes that she carelessly wiped with the back of her hand.

"Tell you what, you go get this set up and I'll meet you up there." She waved at the bartender and held out her shot glass.

"Okay." I backed away slowly. She was starting to get that glint in her eye that I hadn't seen since the end-of-year party at Chelsea. *Looks like I'll be the one getting us home.*

I carefully threaded my way through the crowd toward the DJ, nodding at my teammates who heckled me along the way, and told him what we needed to have queued up. His enormous smile and nod made me feel marginally better as he announced us and I watched Abby toss back her last one, do a full body shudder and start to weave her unsteady way over to the stage. The DJ handed me two mics and the opening bars started to play as Abby hopped up and snagged one of them from me.

"You ready for this, Chicago?" she yelled into the mic, and I watched my teammates holler and whistle for her. Her natural showmanship rose to the surface as she started to theatrically sway back and forth. She smiled at me, gesturing for me to take the lead.

We traded off the lines while doing a campy set of dance moves as we continued through the peppy love song about two misfits standing strong against the world. Our terrible voices were only offset by the horrific dancing we were playing at, but the fire and the smile in her eyes were electric. For the last verse, Abby shook off all her inhibitions and joined me in really tearing it up, pulling off Stevie Nicks-level dips and growls as I sang my final lines.

The lyrics had me by the balls, but her grin grabbed my heart and held on tight. *I'm such a goner for this woman.* Confused desire seemed to waft from her flushed skin. Maybe she didn't have beating hearts jumping out of her eyes, but I swear that, for the first time ever, there were some tiny ones hovering in the corners. She was losing her struggle to jam me into the fake fiancé box.

Join the club, missy. Welcome to my box of unrequited, uncomfortable feelings.

The music cut off and we were treated to thunderous applause and whistles from the other team members. She threw her arms around me and whispered in my ear, "We make a pretty good team, huh?"

"We sure do, Stabby, we sure do."

As we made our way back to the tables the team had commandeered, she stumbled a little and I could see the shots had hit her hard. I grabbed a beer for both of us. "Here. Hold onto it, drink a few sips, and I'll go get you a water too. We can get the hell out of here after a few more minutes of chitchat."

She raised her eyebrows and clinked her bottle against mine, a little too hard. "Oh, no, Shellenberg. You dragged me out here, you made me sing karaoke, we're not going anywhere now." She punctuated her sentence by leaning in and giving me a big smacking kiss on the lips that tasted like bourbon, bad decisions and everything grand in the world. "Like that, huh?" She tried to wink, failed miserably and twirled off to talk to someone who was pulling on her sleeve.

Stabby Abby, life of the party after four shots.

Probably a half-hour later, I was mid-conversation with Daniel Lopez when she dropped heavily into my lap and wrapped her arms around my neck. "Matti, let's get out of here," she slurred into my ear, and followed it up with a nip that made my dick jump in my jeans.

"Um, Abby, this is Daniel —"

"S'up, Danny boy? I know your wife. You better treat her right or I'm gonna cut off your balls."

"Pretty sure she can handle that on her own. But thank you, Abby." Daniel struggled to keep a straight face.

"Yeah, you're probably right... So, you need my guy here anymore? Because he owes me a dance and then we need to G.T.F.O., if you know what I mean."

Daniel, the traitor, started laughing and gestured for her to take me away as she leaped up and started yanking me toward the tiny square dance floor by the DJ booth. It was some trap song that had a deep beat and we started to move carelessly together. Her arms wrapped around me, she tipped her head back and shouted up at me, "So fun, this is the best night ever."

"Glad you're enjoying it. How's your knee?"

"*Psh*, what knee? You know what would make it even better?"

"What's that?"

"We should definitely kiss again. I don't know if people think we're actually together."

"Uh, Abby, I don't know..."

She stopped grinding on me and took a step back, her eyes all big and glassy, lower lip quivering, and I quickly pulled her back to me and dropped a kiss on her upturned lips.

"Gotcha!" She grinned triumphantly.

The little sneak.

I was laughing as she pulled my face down to her level and kissed me, hard. A real one this time. I tried to pull back again. "Hey, what are you doing?"

"Kissing my fiancé." She reached down and groped my ass. "Mmm, this is nice, you know? I like seeing it in my bedroom, in the bathroom, in the kitchen. It's a good ass."

"Abby!"

"What? It's really nice and you should be proud of it. Now get down here and kiss me again."

I gave her a quick kiss to pacify her but this wasn't happening with her so messed up. "Come on, we need to get out of here."

"Ooh, can we keep doing this at home?"

"Sure, sure, let's go." She hung on me as I dragged her through the crowd, and waved at my team, who all cheered as they watched her try to grope my ass and kiss my chest.

I had an Uber arrive within two minutes and shoveled her in. The guy confirmed our destination and she jumped onto my lap, straddling me as she squished my cheeks between her palms. "I like this face too. It's very good-looking." She dropped a kiss on my nose and her hands went to my hair. "This is very nice too. Although I hate how good it always looks in the morning when mine looks like shit." A tug on the ponytail interspersed with increasingly passionate, open-mouthed kisses and I felt like she was drugging me, passing along her inebriation via kissing. She ground down on me and my traitorous dick liked it, perking up like "finally, bitch!"

"Mmph, Abby, stop. What're you doing?"

"Taking advantage of a situation. We should do this more often," she slurred and kissed me harder and, god help me, I went with it. Until the car stopped and I managed to pull away from her lamprey lips. I thanked the driver, scooped her up and carried her into the building while she kissed up and down my neck muttering about the things she had planned for me.

I plopped her down on the kitchen counter and avoided her octopus-like arms and legs while I got us each a glass of water. "Drink this, Stabby."

"And then can we get it on?" she whined as she gulped, sloshing half of the liquid down her front.

"Oh, my darling Stabby, not tonight, okay?"

"No?"

"No, not tonight. You're drunk, I'm a little buzzed. We can't."

She pouted and wrapped her legs around me to pull me closer. "Soon?"

"I tell you what, Stabs. When you're sober, we can have another talk on this subject, okay? Remember that contract about not kissing?"

"We should burn that." Her eyes were drooping and she *pew-pewed* little finger guns at me. "Gonna hold you to that talk."

"Come on, let's get you to bed," I murmured, my heart in my throat as she nuzzled in close to me while I scooped her dead weight up.

She brushed her teeth with her eyes already closed like a mechanical doll and obediently raised her hands to help me get her undressed and ready for bed. I tugged a shirt over her head and she flopped back onto the bed, already snoring.

"Night, Abby," I murmured, giving up trying to wrestle a pair of shorts onto her wet noodle body. I tossed them on the floor and went about my own nighttime routine.

As I slid into bed, she wiggled her ass closer to me and I heard her mumble something about hearts and hot dance moves. I fell asleep with a smile on my face. Things were taking a turn and maybe we weren't as far apart as I'd thought we were.

Chapter Twelve

Abby

Finding out Matti's secret and giving him access to my own had started a shift, transforming the distance between us into an ever-shrinking ribbon that pulled us closer and closer. And whatever had happened during the karaoke night—even though we both avoided talking about it—had only tied us tighter together.

We were past allies, past uneasy roommates reckoning with strong attraction. I didn't know where he was at, but my head was a mess. My brain kept screaming for boundaries, but my heart and ovaries were starting to be in direct competition. No matter how hard I tried to maintain the slightest distance, I kept getting sucked back in.

We were now a "we" whenever I talked to people on my own. Our linked future no longer glowed radioactively in my mind's eye. And, oh my god, I had not thought it was possible to *want* someone so voraciously. If we were in the same room, we'd be in contact—even if it was only the occasional brush of a shoulder or finger. It was always present, this desire to press nearer, push harder. The constant touching had me wound tighter than a new yo-yo.

Whenever his finger swept a loose hair from out of my eyes, I shuddered. If I tapped his shoulder, he broke out in goosebumps on the back of his neck. I think we both liked the one-upmanship to see whose touch could elicit the strongest response. He seemed to be winning—if the guttural moan that slid out of my mouth when he nipped my earlobe as he reached around me to pour his coffee and whisper, "Good morning," in my ear had anything to say about it.

Or maybe it was a tie considering the hard-on I'd felt as I arched back into his chest and ground my ass into him while he nibbled from my earlobe, down my jaw to my collarbone. It was a dangerous game we were playing.

But it wasn't just the ever-burning physical attraction that simmered between us. Sharing our pasts with each other had tweaked my entire perception of him. I no longer saw the annoying playboy who would never grow up and tried to bring everyone down to his level. Instead I saw a man who had forced the world to work for him, despite his limitations. His strength of will and stubbornness were equal to my own, and that was hard to comprehend.

Slowly, I'd started to convince him to seek help for his reading issues, and he'd agreed that maybe, just maybe it was time to face that particular bogeyman. For his part, he'd assured me that I didn't have to see my family if they really were that toxic. Although I could tell he didn't quite believe me—despite his very real gripes about his own, they loved him dearly. While mine? Mine were the stuff of passive-aggressive nightmares. What they didn't understand, they rejected. What they rejected ceased to exist. I imagined that's what had happened when I'd stopped going home, stopped calling. To them, they no longer had a daughter, a sister.

* * * *

"Abby? I'm taking the first shower, cool?"

"Yeah, I'm good, showered at the gym," I replied from the cozy window seat where I was reading a book, still in my warm-ups from a morning PT session.

"I'll try to be quick," he called out as the shower turned on.

Right, quick. I snorted. The man took longer showers than a sixteen-year-old. Of course, I'd only recently discovered why they were so long and, as the shower door opened and shut, I felt a faint buzz of anticipation.

Carefully, I hopped off the window seat and inched nearer to the open door. Maybe I should have felt some sort of shame about peeping in on his personal time, but I couldn't help it, the allure of him naked and wet was too much for me. I licked my lips, my throat suddenly parched with anticipation, and knew that the temperature in the room was from more than the hot shower that he'd turned on.

Sitting on the floor in front of the dresser gave me the perfect view of the bathroom mirror that faced the shower and I could see the muscles in Matti's back and ass tighten and release as he quickly ran a sudsy loofah over his body, hung it back on the hook and leaned his forehead against the tile on top of a brightly colored forearm.

My skin felt too tight as I watched him slowly run a wet hand down his lower abs to his perfectly cut cock. He shuddered as he wrapped his hand around it and gave a sharp tug, then twisted his wrist on the downstroke. My breathing picked up into a series of jagged pants as his mouth opened and a very quiet groan echoed through our silent room.

The pace of his stroking increased and he ran his thumb across the head, pressing on the underside. His ass clenched as he bucked into his hand again and again, grunting and finally growling out my name as he came. *My* name. It had me hot and wet, practically screaming for a touch. The water shut off and I startled.

While he toweled off, I quickly threw on new underwear and clothes and went and waited for him in the living room. He grinned at me, all smooth and relaxed after his shower, and held out an arm to guide me out of the apartment to the elevator to the parking garage. "You okay?" he asked. "You seem kind of flustered."

I shrugged and blushed in response. He hummed tunelessly—*Islands in the Stream*—as we rode down, and shot me a side-eyed grin. *If he knew I watched him...*

"Did you grab the gift?" I asked with one hand on the SUV's passenger door handle in case I needed to run back for it.

"Of course. It's in the back seat." he said impatiently as he drummed his fingers on the steering wheel. "Get in."

"Fine." I snorted. "Keep your shirt on, I'm coming."

"Oh, Stabby Abby, you know if my shirt was off...you'd be coming in seconds," he said and grinned at my shocked face. "Like that? Got a bunch more if you want me to dig into that corner of the vault."

I buckled my seatbelt, willing the flush to die down, and leaned my hot cheek against the window. "Drive, you jackass," I muttered.

"Abby, that's weak. Come on, lay it on me." He giggled, clearly proud of himself for winning that battle.

We were on our way to Daniel and Mercedes Lopez's house for their daughter Daniela's birthday. She was turning five and was a tomboy-princess who loved playing her dad's sport as much as she adored dancing around pretending to zap people with her ice princess powers. Matti had picked out her gift himself and we were both looking forward to her opening it.

"How many people did Mer say she'd invited?" Matti asked as we approached the Lopezes' long driveway.

"The whole team, her family, Daniel's family, some of her friends from work," I answered as we drove past car after car. "I'm guessing maybe around three hundred?"

"Holy shit, can you imagine that many people at your fifth birthday?" Matti asked incredulously.

"What's this? The life of the party, center of attention, doesn't want a big birthday party?" I teased him. "Noted. I hate parties."

"Oh, Stabby, that's because I've never thrown you a party before. I promise your birthday is going to be...what do the kids say? Epic? Yes, I'm going to throw you an *epic* birthday party, baby. And you're going to love it."

I rolled my eyes as we approached a valet stand. I stepped out of the car and slid my sunglasses back on my head, my forehead starting to break out in an unseasonable sweat. It was October and Chicago was in the midst of an unusual heat wave, that last gasp of summer before the long, dark Midwestern winter kicked in. I glanced around at the fairy lights faintly glowing in the late afternoon sun, the music and barbecue smoke wafting from the backyard. A live band and a valet — how extra.

Matti tossed the keys to our car to the valet and wrapped an arm around my neck and shoulders, pulling me in for a forehead kiss as I pretended to choke. He held me there and I squirmed, finally sinking my teeth into his forearm to get him to release. He yelped and jumped away, rubbing his arm resentfully. "That hurt."

"You totally deserved that, don't even play." We walked through the silent house toward the sliding doors in the kitchen that poured out onto an enormous patio and deck that were crawling with people. The wall of noise slapped us both upside the head and we each took an involuntary step back.

"Come on, Stabby, let's go party," he said and took my hand to lead me out into the madness.

"Hey, I'm going to go find Mer. You go find Daniel. Maybe we can head out in like a half hour? This is kind of overwhelming," I asked nervously.

"Sure, sounds good. Other than the guys from the team, I don't know anyone and, honestly, if my old teammates or my brothers could see me today, they would never let me hear the end of it."

I frowned as I eyed him up and down. "Why? You look hot." He was adorably handsome with his hair pulled half back, white tennis shorts that cut above his knees and a summer-weight plaid linen shirt with the top two buttons undone. His preppy leather boat shoes were the crowning touch on his perfect early-nineties, trust-fund, Nantucket-kid outfit. His aviators were tucked into his breast pocket.

He laughed. "Oh, hot? Hmm? I'll take that for now, but you're going to need to elaborate later when we get back to the apartment."

I blushed and punched him. "Ugh, get out of here, you animal. See you in a half hour or so?"

He grinned. "Anything you say, darling sweet cheeks. Anything."

* * * *

I'd been talking to Mer and her sister for twenty minutes or so, keeping a half ear and eye out for Matti's boisterous laugh and flying hair, but he'd disappeared. The last time I'd clocked him, he'd been holding the girlfriend of one of the younger guys at arm's distance as she'd tried to get to his hair. Maybe she was a hairdresser?

There wasn't a huge crowd of so-called "jersey chasers" that ran with the team and I didn't begrudge or judge them in the slightest. They had their thing and as long as it was mutually consensual and beneficial, more power to them. How they made themselves happy was none of my business — unless one of them tried to move in on Matti.

Our half hour was pretty much up and I murmured an excuse to Mer, who was trapped in a conversation with her aunt. She rolled her eyes at me over the woman's head and I went inside to find the restroom before searching for the MIA Matti.

I hummed as I washed my hands, thinking about what we could order for dinner—or maybe we could go out. Or maybe something else. I was starving and the last few weeks had been fraught with sexual tension between the two of us. It was an intense distraction from my feelings of despair over the lack of progress in my therapy, and I was down to eat my feelings—all of them.

The air between us had become combustible, our mornings full of lazy stretching and rubbing up against each other, pretending that nothing, of course nothing, was happening. That neither of us were feeling a draw that was almost painful to keep denying. I would watch him the shower, then see him getting out with a low-slung towel wrapped around his waist and had to literally bite my knuckle to keep from launching myself at him.

The mere memory of his earlier shower, what he'd said when he came, made me blush, my legs clenching as I shifted from foot to foot while I tried to tempt the little flyaways back into my ponytail. Giving up, I opened the door and saw Matti struggling to get away from a woman draped across his chest as she attempted to twirl a strand of hair that had come loose. My redhead temper started to rise—we might have been fake, but he sure as hell was *my* fake fiancé, and I didn't see him doing nearly enough to get away.

In retrospect, charging over, throwing her hand off him, grabbing him by the shirt collar to lower his surprised face to mine and slamming my mouth against his might not have been my most suave move. Our eyes were open and his wide-eyed terrified expression made me giggle—yes, giggle—against him.

I started to shift back, but his hand wrapped around my hip and held me captive against his warm, hard body.

"Really, Stabby? Is this how you restart that conversation we tabled after karaoke?" he murmured against my lips, his breath tickling my chin.

"Don't be a jerk. From where I was sitting, you weren't trying nearly hard enough to get away from Ms. Octopus Arms over there." My mouth was still pressed against his and when he stuck his tongue out to wet his lips, he tagged mine as well.

"You missed the part where I tried to explain that I had a territorial wifey-type around somewhere who would beat both of our asses if she thought anything was happening. I don't think you're giving me enough credit here." His low voice was practically a whisper. A horny, tense whisper. "Jealous?"

"Nope, not in the slightest," I replied and nipped his full lower lip perhaps a little harder than I'd intended.

His eyes narrowed to sky-blue slits. "Mmhmm. Really?"

"Mmhmm." The hall disappeared and the woman slunk away, already forgotten as we stared at each other.

"I like you when you're territorial, Stabby. Gets me ten kinds of hot and bothered."

My hands clenched his collar and I pulled him closer, my mouth so dry I could barely whisper. "I don't know if I believe you. You already turned me down once."

"Because you were drunk and it would have been wrong to take advantage of that fact. Maybe now I could show you?" It came out as a question and he licked his lips again, the feather-light tip of his tongue skating across my own. He spun us around and now it was me backed against the wall, one of his forearms next to my head as he reached out and tugged the tip of my ponytail.

"S-show me?" The situation was rapidly moving beyond my control, and we were at a kid's birthday party, for heaven's sake.

His eyes gleamed as he pressed his lower body closer and I could feel him harden against me. I squirmed as he stroked down my ribcage and my hip knocked into a hallway table. The vase of fresh flowers wobbled and sweet-smelling petals drifted down. He picked one up, rubbing it between his thumb and forefinger. As he swept it down my nose and across my cheek, it filled the air with the scent of late summer roses.

For the rest of my life, I knew I'd remember this — the smell of roses would be inextricably tied to this decision. I closed my eyes, reveling in the cloying smell and the crisp feel of his linen shirt still clenched in my hand.

"Yes, show me," I whispered as I opened my eyes wide, staring into his slightly worried ones. Had he thought I'd live up to his annoying nickname for me and stab him for asking?

His breath left him in a sigh of relief and now it was his turn to close his eyes as he rested his forehead against my own. "Not here, Abby. Let's go home."

I nodded and he stepped away from me as he scrubbed his hands through his hair to yank out the elastic and re-secure it. I trailed them up and rubbed the short bristly hair of his undercut. He shivered and leaned into my hands.

"No, seriously, Abby. Home, now, or *things* will happen here, against this wall, at this children's party."

"Mmm, *things*. I like *things*, especially when they're yours." I giggled again. This was completely unlike me.

He groaned. "You'll be the death of me yet, woman," he said and gently extricated my hands from his hair. We stared at each other then, only inches apart, our hands clasped between us like we were standing at an altar about to make a momentous declaration.

"You said something about leaving? I'm ready," I murmured and circled my thumbs on top of his hands.

"You're sure?" he asked hesitantly. "We go now and whatever happens, you're sure?"

I grinned at him and pulled away, started sauntering toward the entryway. "It's only sex, Matti. We'll update the contract if you're worried about it. Let's roll, daddy-o."

He frowned for a half second and I saw a flash of hurt fly through his eyes at my mention of our contract. "Yeah. I guess we do need to update the contract, then." It was a little sarcastic and I watched him shake it off as he bounded past me, threw open the door and tossed the card at the valet, who was messing around on his phone.

The ride home was suffocating, even with the SUV's windows open and the smells of early autumn filling the car. Matti kept one hand on my knee the entire way, shooting me little looks like he was questioning me, making sure I was okay and still with him. Every time I smiled back at him, his fingers tightened, until I covered his hand with my own, interlacing my fingers with his.

We pulled into the garage beneath our building and parked. He rolled up the windows, unbuckled his seatbelt and turned off the car. We sat there for a moment, listening to the engine tick down. The tension rose in waves between us and when finally he turned to me, it felt like his eyes lit up the car the way the illuminated dash broke through the twilight, and there was something so vulnerable in them. He reached over to me and touched my cheek. "I like you, Stabby Abby." His voice shook a little with the vulnerability of admitting there might be some real feelings to contend with now.

I took a deep breath. "I know. I think you're pretty great too. Best fake fiancé ever."

That hurt expression flashed across his face again as he opened the car door and he blew out a harsh breath.

"Matti—"

He shook his head and leaped out of the car, then dashed around to my door, pulling it open. "Forget it, Abby. You sure this is okay?"

"More than okay," I reassured him and leaned down and kissed him. My legs wrapped around his narrow waist and he clutched me tight against him.

In one smooth motion, he pulled me out of the car and slammed the door. I felt him fumble for the key fob in his pockets until the car beeped and the headlights flashed. He took off in an awkward run for the elevator and used my hip to hit the call button while I dropped little butterfly kisses all over his face.

As the doors slid open, he kissed me back, harder, and we stumbled in with our lips melded and my legs locked tightly around him. He stabbed at the button panel and hit our floor. We were panting and I writhed against him as his tongue slipped through my lips to wrap around mine. Still carrying me and never stopping his voracious kiss, we arrived at our floor and staggered down the hall, ping-ponging off the walls until we got to our door.

We tumbled inside and I slid out of his arms, taking a few steps away from him until my back hit the cool marble countertop. His hair was falling out from its hopeless bun and hung in disarray to frame his sharp cheekbones. He nibbled his lip and his hands stilled where they'd been busy unbuttoning his shirt. It gaped open to his belly button, all of that colorful ink peeking out. I ate him up with my eyes. The shadowy ridges of his abdominal muscles flexed as he fought to control his breath after our hurried ascent.

"You're really sure? Do you want to get this in writing before it goes any further?" His voice was low, the uncertainty clear in the wrinkles that suddenly appeared on his forehead.

The apartment was absolutely still, the air humid with the anticipation of the moment.

I fiddled with the hem of my T-shirt and slowly drew it up over my head and tossed it to the side, then dropped my shorts next to it. I stood in front of him in a light pink bra and matching underwear with my staticky hair rising from my own messed-up ponytail. "Positive. We'll update the contract tomorrow — casual sex is now on the table," I answered and he rushed toward me with a growl, sweeping me off my feet and carrying me back to our bedroom, where he gently deposited me on our bed.

The cool linen sheets floofed up around me, smelling like brand-name detergent and fresh ocean breezes as he stood at the foot of the bed watching me with hooded eyes. I raised my hips to peel off my underwear and bra. His eyes were heavy-lidded while his hands fiddled with the button at the top of his shorts.

"Come here," I whispered, and the room was so quiet that my words seemed to echo in the empty space.

A small smile crept over his face as he undid the button, snicked down the zipper and shimmied his narrow hips till the shorts dropped to the floor. I couldn't help but laugh, a laugh that cut off quickly as I noticed how hard he was, straining the elasticity of the tight boxer briefs that Calvin Klein paid him to wear.

He prowled over to the bed, then knelt at the foot, palming his cock through his briefs. I watched as his head dropped back and he pressed his hand against himself. As he lifted his head back up, I spread my legs and beckoned him closer, then used that curled finger to stroke myself, showing him how wet I was, how worked up kissing him had made me.

"Your tits, Abby, touch them," he ordered in a husky voice as he slowly slid a hand beneath the waistband of his briefs. He closed his eyes as he squeezed himself and I moved my hand from my slit to my chest before he stopped me. "Not that hand, that hand stays right where it was. Fuck yourself, Abby. Show me what you want me to do."

Almost in a trance, I began to stroke first one of my breasts then the other, squeezing the pebbled tips until my back arched off the bed with the intersection of pain and pleasure. I brought my other hand back to my pussy, my index finger slipping up to circle my clit, then stroke the inside of my channel.

"Lick it, Abby. Taste yourself."

"Fuck," he moaned as he watched me dip two fingers back into my pussy, pushing them deep and pulling them out, an offering to him. He pressed hard against his cock and knelt down to take my fingers in his mouth. His eyes shut as his tongue wrapped around them. I fucked his mouth with my hand as he sucked my fingers clean.

The shot of power that raged through me as I watched him lose his shit almost undid me.

"Goddamn peach pie, I fucking knew it," he muttered as he rose up on his knees enough to yank off his briefs and toss them aside. Matti settled over me, his weight comforting as his burning eyes focused on mine. "Good?" he asked as I bucked my hips up to rub against his hard cock.

"So good," I murmured again, and he lowered his face to kiss me. He tasted of me, birthday cake and breath mints. When his tongue slid into my mouth to tangle with my own, I wanted to devour him over and over again.

His hands were everywhere, cupping my breasts, curving around my hips as he mindlessly ground against me, every movement bringing the head of his cock closer and closer to sliding deep. "Abby," he gasped as we pulled apart. "I need to be inside you. Next time I'll make it sweet, but right now I need to fuck you hard." He buried his head against my chest, sucking and biting my nipples, first one then the other. Then alternated laving my breasts with his tongue and peppering them with kisses.

My breath was coming out in jagged gasps as he pushed one, then two fingers deep inside me. "Yes, there, Matti. There!"

"Do you have any condoms?" he managed to pant out.

"No, do you?"

"Motherfucker, no."

"I'm on the shot and haven't been with anyone since my last check-up."

"Me either," he ground out. "Seriously? Bare?"

I nodded, but I was trembling. Not completely certain until I saw how bowled over he was. He got it. This was an enormous deal. His face hardened in resolve and he nodded like he was grateful for my trust. Like he'd rather die than let me down.

Slowly, he started a torturous push inside me. His jaw was tight, the muscles and tendons in his neck corded as his eyes screwed shut. I'd never been with someone as big as him and could feel every single vein, every twitch of his cock as he began to slowly slide home. He paused and stared down at me as if he could stay there forever, worshiping me with his body.

"Baby, you're so tight, I don't even know if—"

I wriggled my hips and he groaned as he sank an inch deeper.

"Baby, please, I don't want to hurt you—"

My legs came up and wrapped around his waist and I dug my heels into his perfect ass, forcing him in to the hilt. "Fuck me, Matti."

He shuddered and I felt him settle inside me. I squeezed him tentatively and he jerked back convulsively, groaning. "Jesus, Abby," he growled. "Topping from the bottom?"

I hissed and arched my back again as he surged into me, my senses on overdrive—feeling everything, the fine hairs on his chest rubbing against my over sensitized breasts, the restraint he was attempting to show when he clearly wanted nothing more than to pummel me into oblivion. I smiled at him, taunting him, and kissed his nose. "I don't know, what would you do if I tried?"

"Let you do it, then fuck you harder." He pulled out so only the tip of his dick stayed inside me and he settled one of my legs up over his shoulders. We paused, both of us shaking with need. As he thrust back inside, he slid his thumb between us to push hard on my clit while he attacked me with his mouth and tongue. A shockwave went through me as his tongue and cock fucked me aggressively, his thumb maintaining an ungodly pressure on my clit, extending my orgasm beyond what I thought was possible as he slammed again and again into me. His own orgasm crashed into him and he dragged his mouth from mine and rested his sweaty forehead on my own.

"Fucking hell," he muttered, and his eyes opened as I stroked his jaw.

"*Mmhmm,*" I managed to murmur.

"Next time, Abby... Next time we're making this slow and sweet," he said as he rolled off and collapsed next to me.

"Yeah? What makes you think there's gonna be a next time?" I propped myself up on an arm and started to trace the tattoos on his chest. He immediately caught my hand and brought it to his mouth for a kiss.

"Abby, my dear, we're redoing this contract. I've never in my life fucked a girl without protection and I'll tell you what—I'm never not doing that with you ever again. It's gonna happen a lot. You better prepare yourself for more A-plus quality sex and a lot of it in the near future."

"Hmm. I guess I can handle that." I gave him my version of his infamous smirk and he tackled me down, the vulnerability we were both feeling pushed to the side as we sought to return to our teasing equilibrium. This was fake, sexy fake, but it wasn't forever.

"It's gonna be more than you can handle, I promise." He held my wrists over my head and kissed me gently on the lips, then my nose, then my forehead. "Let's take a shower. I feel like I ran a sexy marathon. Round two, madam?"

He rolled off and extended a hand to me. I placed my hand in his.

"Rounds two and three if you're lucky, old man."

"Psh, why not go for four? It's my lucky number."

I giggled as he picked me up and threw me over his shoulder to carry me into the bathroom. I caught a glimpse of us in the mirror, my red hair everywhere, pale skin blotchy, but my eyes were glittering and almost blue with their softness. I may have had some misgivings, but the tenderness I felt for him in that moment scared me. Hopefully we'd be able to stay friends after our year was up.

He set me down and reached in to turn on the shower and we waited for it to get hot. "Just an FYI, but our contract now says that we must bang at least once a day and twice on Sundays, plus every time we argue."

"Hmm. Lots of fighting in our future?"

"Tons, Stabby, tons."

Then he pulled me into the shower and set about proving every point regarding four being his lucky number.

Chapter Thirteen

Matti

Two glorious months after what had to be the most earth-shatteringly, mind-meltingly, exquisitely orgasmic sex of my life, things reached a very happy equilibrium — at least from my perspective. My team still kind of sucked, but we were gelling and getting better every day. I learned that I could actually handle the responsibility of being a captain. Abby's advice from her experience at Chelsea helped.

Abby and I danced around each other, flirted more, she got pissed at me for minor irritations and we kissed and made up. Maybe we weren't really together in her mind. Just messing around or whatever. I fully recognized that I was going to be the one who got hurt when this ended. She'd walk away fine — maybe a little sore from all the orgasms, but probably fine. I could take the pain. I was a grown-up. We were partners and, same as she had helped me with my issues, I was working out with her, going to her PT appointments whenever I could, trying to lift her up the way she did for me.

A day came when Abby suddenly cut me off from attending any more PT appointments and started phasing herself out of our morning workouts. She was tired, her knee hurt, she had things to do for the camps now that everything was transitioning to indoors, Christmas was coming. Then the phone calls started from Northwestern. They wanted her to come in to help with conditioning training for the men's and women's teams. Asking her to speak to the players. It was all good stuff, but she was overcommitting and her recovery was tanking because of it.

My little teammate was flailing and wouldn't accept help. I got it, really I did. I'd fought her equally hard about finding a reading teacher, but she'd made me see that I was more than a dumb good-time guy. Or I could be more if I pulled my head out of my own ass and faced my fears. I wasn't sure what to do, but she was sinking and refusing anyone who tried to extend a hand. It was time for me to bring in the big guns and make her accept the help that she desperately needed.

Markus called me back a few hours after my rambling voicemail and immediately railed me out for not considering time-zone differences. Fine, it had been six in the morning his time, but really, he should have been awake. His wife was pregnant and maybe I didn't know much about babies, but I was pretty sure that they were cute little early birds.

Babies, aw. Wonder how many Abby wants? Enough for a mini-team? That would be —

"Matti? You still there?" Markus' deep voice boomed out of the phone where I'd left it on the counter on speaker.

"Yeah, yeah. I'm here," I replied and finished loading the dishwasher.

"Okay, what did you want? Something about women? Is this about you getting out of your fake engagement?"

"No! Why would I want out of it when we added face-melting sex as a clause to it?" I was genuinely concerned about my brother. Clearly he hadn't been paying attention the last few times we'd talked.

"What? When did sex enter this equation?" he asked in that type of stern father voice that made me fear for his and Alina's future children.

"I don't know, a while ago. Why does it matter?"

"*Uff*, Matti. Really? It matters because it isn't real, you moron," he said and I could imagine him stalking around his fancy L.A. house scrubbing his hands through his hair.

"Hey—" I was over being called a moron by my family.

"Markus," a faint voice called out in the background, "stop calling your brother a moron." The voice got closer until I could hear a brief tussle, then my sister-in-law's voice came through clearly. "Matthias, what have you gotten yourself into this time?"

"Nothing! Screw you guys. I'm calling because I'm worried about Abby and wanted your advice about how to help her out. She's shutting me out of her training and everything else." I sighed. "I'll let you go, I'm not in it today for the judgment." I was about to click the red "end call" button when Markus' voice cut through the rising, angry static in my head.

"Matti, wait!" Markus said urgently.

"No, I'm serious. I've had it with everyone in our family calling me stupid, acting like I'm nothing but a dumb athlete. Markus, you were sixteen when I left for Barcelona. Did you never wonder why your ten-year-old brother always wanted you, Max or Ella to read me menus?"

"What's this about, Matti?" Markus asked, this time more softly.

"I can't read or write any better than the average six- or seven-year-old, you ass. Teachers and coaches figured out I was freakishly good at sports when I was about that age and, rather than deal with the fact that I was a little slower to pick up on letters than numbers, they told me to concentrate on what I was good at, since it was pretty clear that I didn't have the brains to learn." I was breathing hard by the time I finished. I hadn't planned on ever telling them this—it hadn't seemed worth it—but now I was on a roll and there was no stopping this train.

"At Barça, the teachers didn't bother with us much. They basically kept us contained and semiliterate because everyone knew we were going to be pros and could hire people to do this shit for us if we didn't pick it up quickly. I've thought I was broken my *entire* fucking life until Abby helped me see that I could be much more than what I was pretending to be—the dumb athlete party guy." I blew out another stressed breath.

"Matti, I—" Markus tried to say, but I wasn't having it.

"I'm not done yet, Markus. It turns out I'm not stupid. I just had a really crap bunch of teachers and role models, plus a family that was too busy with their own lives to pay a single bit of attention to their 'whoops' kiddo.

"Must have been a relief to Mother and Father when Barça called and they could ship me out to be someone else's problem. Abby is the only one who noticed, besides my current agent, and the only one who's pushed me to get help. So, fuck you guys if I want to help the one person who has bothered to actually see me. *Fuck. You.*"

My finger hovered over the red button again to disconnect the call as I waited for a response. My teacher and therapist had told me that I needed to confront my family at some point, but I'd never thought it mattered that much. I figured I was over it all. Apparently not. I wanted him to beg.

"Matti, please, please, don't hang up." Markus' voice was hoarse, like he'd been screaming for an hour. "I'm sorry you went through all of that. That you've been dealing with this on your own and that we didn't see it. You're right, we're a bunch of self-obsessed pricks and I am — god, I'm so sorry, little brother. Truly." He let out a muffled sob and must have handed the phone to Alina because she came on the line next.

"Matti?" she asked hesitantly.

"Yeah." I sighed, weary already of this.

"I'm so sorry too," she whispered.

"Why? None of this is your fault. You weren't there. Put Markus back on." I was possibly a tad more brusque than I should have been, but fuck all of their feelings right now. I'd tiptoed around them my entire life.

"I can't," she whispered. "He's not here anymore. He handed me the phone and walked away with his face in his hands. I heard the front door slam."

"Go find him," I demanded.

"Okay, okay. We'll call you right back."

I hung up.

While I waited for them to call me back, I grabbed one of the little Rebels practice balls and started dribbling around the apartment. I texted Abby to see what she was up to, but didn't get a response. My stress levels continued to rise and the cortisol sent a rush to my feet. I concentrated on the movement. Left-right-left-step-over-feint-right-go-left-right-left-right.
Flipped the ball up with my toe and bounced it four times on my left foot, then four on my right. Big flip up to my head, hold...

I Can Feel It Calling in the Air — Markus' obnoxious Phil Collins ringtone.

"Yeah?" I answered.

"Matti, sorry I ran out like that. I feel like such an ass for not noticing anything was wrong, for missing out on the fact that you needed my — our — help. I'm sorry that you went through all of that on your own, that we made you feel less than. We screwed up, royally," Markus said.

"It's fine, it's done now. All over. So stop treating me like an annoying little kid, okay?" The kinetic movement had slowed my heart rate. Helped me order my thoughts. I'd never had to learn how to impose order on my brain outside of sports. My therapist called it a "coping mechanism," and maybe it was, but things seemed much clearer with a ball at my feet.

"I won't, and I'll make sure Max and Ella don't either," he promised solemnly.

"Okay, then we're fine," I said as I deflated into our stiff leather couch.

"Fine, fine. I still feel like crap. But that's on me, not you." He sighed heavily. "You called to talk about Abby, though, right? Sorry I derailed everything, but you're together now? For real?"

"Er, no. Not together really, more like we've agreed to bang it out if we get pissed at each other. Or if we get horny, or whatever. She's hot, she thinks I'm hot, we're a good team. That's about it but, yeah, I do like her. She's a good person," I hedged and deliberately left out the fact that I couldn't sleep anymore unless she was tucked up next to me, wrapped in my arms. That she was the first and last thing I thought about every day. No one needed to know that.

"Huh. Sounds like you're together," he muttered dryly.

"Whatever. That's not the point," I said.

He laughed. "What *is* the point?"

"The point, big brother with all of the worldly knowledge about women, is that she's pulling away from me, blocking me out. Something is bothering her and she won't talk about it. When I push, she distracts me with sex, which is awesome, don't get me wrong —"

"Matti."

"I know, right? I don't like being distracted like that. I'm trying to help her, but she's skipping her workouts, not letting me come to appointments and completely overcommitting herself to stuff that's not helping her get back to playing shape."

"What other things is she committing to? Not that that makes any grammatical sense —"

"Markus."

He laughed. We were more similar than either of us wanted to admit. "Sorry, tangent."

"She's doing more and more with the youth camps and is now helping coach the Northwestern soccer teams—at first it was conditioning training and speaking to them about going pro. Now it seems like it's actual coaching, which is incredibly time-consuming."

"Aren't those good things?" he asked, sounding genuinely puzzled.

"I mean, yeah, but she's avoiding her workouts—how can she come back if she's not pushing herself anymore? Then there's all the stuff with her family. She won't talk about them, but we ran into someone from her home town and they were super nice. I feel like that separation is bothering her too."

Markus went on high alert. "What do you mean family separation?"

"She doesn't talk to them, like ever. Hasn't seen or spoken to them since she was maybe nineteen and won't go into details with me. It's probably something that could be worked out, but she's pretty stubborn. Maybe…" I paused. "Maybe that's what's bugging her. She's not feeling great and needs more support than me. Maybe she's missing her family."

"Matti, no, I don't think—"

"Yeah, that's got to be a big part of it. Whenever I get hurt, I want you guys around, like security duvets or whatever."

"Blankets?"

"Yeah, that too. Anyway, maybe that's what she needs, a reunion or something to help her refocus on her goals. What do you think?" I asked as I jumped up and began to pace excitedly. *This could be perfect.*

"Matti, did she tell you why she no longer speaks to or sees her family?" Markus asked gently.

146

"No, not really. Only that they never saw eye to eye on anything and weren't super supportive of her decision to play soccer. But that was a long time ago and I'm sure they see things differently now with all of her success. Maybe they're too embarrassed to make the first move."

Markus sighed and I was sure he was thinking about Alina, who was still estranged from her only living family member, her sister. "I don't know, Matti. Your intentions are good, but this might be something you want to keep your big foot out of. There might be more to the story. If you want to help her get back to playing, I don't think that this is the right approach."

"No, this is perfect. She won't talk to me about her recovery anymore, but maybe she'll talk to her mom. I've got to get their contact information." *Look at me go, all about the matchmaking and helping others.* This was going to be great and I couldn't help but start to picture all of the ways Abby would shower me with gratitude in the bedroom. "I gotta go, Markus. I bet Sylvie will know how to get in touch with them."

"Matti, wait! Think this through, okay? Don't do anything rash. Maybe talk to Sylvie about them." Markus' voice was rising with concern.

From the background, I could hear Alina's muffled words. "Oh god, he's not going to try to do a family reunion, is he?"

"Yeah, yeah, got it. Will do. Thanks for the talk — hey, when are you coming out to see us? Christmas? Can we do Christmas in Chicago?"

"Christmas? Matti, what the hell? I mean, sure? Or everyone could come here, I don't know how Alina is going to feel about traveling since she's already feeling like total ass and puking everywhere—ow! Don't hit me, woman!"

"Cool, cool. Christmas in California, see you in a few weeks! Gotta go," I said distractedly as I fumbled for my phone to end the call.

"Matti—"

Whoops, disconnected.

Unfortunately, Sylvie refused to give me the information for Abby's family. Accused me of being a very sweet but totally clueless lunk for trying to force a reunion. Markus' warning could be brushed aside, I figured. He didn't know Abby. But Sylvie did. And in no uncertain terms, she detailed exactly how badly a staged family reunion-slash-intervention would blow back in my face. Sylvie tried to coach me through better strategies for talking to Abby, but I doubted they'd help. Words could be cheap and I wasn't entirely sure how much she trusted mine yet.

There had to be something that I could do to help her, show her that she could trust me and that I really was someone who was on her side. Maybe even that I was someone who was worthy of being with her for real. But, then again, that was probably wishful thinking. While our physical trust was there, her emotional walls were up higher than they'd ever been and I didn't know how I could break through them to show her how important her recovery and happiness were to me.

Chapter Fourteen

Abby

As I limped through the door, I was greeted in the kitchen by the absolutely stunning sight of Matti fresh out of the shower and wearing nothing but a towel around his waist, his tattoos blazing and wet blond hair whipping around, little droplets flying off to spatter the cabinets. He was singing along with Duran Duran, which was absolutely blasting over the recessed speakers. The floorboards were shaking.

"Matti! What are you doing?" I shouted. We were late to dinner with his coach and literacy specialist and I had been ready to apologize for holding us up, until I'd observed the one-man dance party happening in our apartment.

Rather than respond, Matti grabbed me by the hand and pulled me up against him then spun me out to twirl away on my own. I had to admit, his awful singing voice had grown on me. He yanked me back to him and this time wrapped his other arm around me. The song came to a conclusion and he ducked his head to smooch my cheek as he whispered the last verse into my ear.

"Mmm, Stabby Abby, where've you been? You smell like sweaty gym socks." He sniffed my neck like a truffle pig rooting around in the Italian soil, making me snort-laugh.

I pulled back and smacked him on the chest and, against my best intentions, my palm curved over the warm planes of sculpted muscle, stroking the colorful tattoos inked across his sternum. He gasped sharply as I circled his flat nipples, which tightened when I tweaked them. He pressed a hand over mine, stopping me from continuing the playful torture.

"Not cool, Abby. We're late, hmm? And going to be beyond the bounds of politeness if you keep that up." He thrust his terrycloth-wrapped hips meaningfully against me and I could feel the effect I had on him.

I hummed and stood on my tiptoes to nip his earlobe. His arms tightened around me as I whispered, "Save it for after dinner, yeah?" He nodded and buried his head in my neck, his breath deep and harsh against my skin.

We stood there quietly for a moment, listening to *Hungry Like the Wolf*, which was blaring through the apartment. Finally he pulled back a minuscule amount and smoothed down the hair that had come loose from my ponytail. He kept my cheeks trapped between those big mitts as he scrutinized my face with an air of concern. "You okay, Abby? I feel like we haven't talked in ages."

I tore myself away from him and felt my jaw tighten. He had to be so sweet sometimes. "Yeah, I'm fine, but we're late for dinner with Sherman and Tiana. I need to change and you do too, if you don't want to get arrested."

Matti stared at me in confusion as I turned on my heel and headed for the bedroom, calling over my shoulder, "Come on, slow ass!"

He followed me a little uncertainly to the bedroom and we got changed to the soft tones of Duran Duran still playing over the stereo in the main living area. I put my makeup on in our bathroom while he dried his hair and pulled it back neatly, ducking away when I tried to ruffle the short hairs of his undercut. He made a mock-stern face and wagged a finger at me.

"Naughty girl." His dark gaze promised multiple hours of sweaty, sheet-twisting activity when we got home — little gold flecks in his light-blue eyes broadcast his filthy intentions. I drifted toward him and he stepped out of reach of my hands. "Finish getting ready, you minx. Now who's the slow ass?" He snorted.

I met him in the living room and he helped me into my coat, then grabbed his keys off the tray by the door and held out an arm. "Madam?"

"My good sir." I smiled at him.

My smiles were a front, though, and I sat quietly in my seat, twisting my fingers into knots in my lap. I'd had another rough PT session that day and it was slowly being beaten into my head with every failed agility test that I was very likely done.

"You okay over there?"

"*Mmh*? Yeah, sorry, it was a busy day and PT wasn't super great."

"That's kind of been a theme lately, hasn't it?" He was hesitant as he asked and wrapped a hand around my knee to reassure me.

I didn't want to reply, barely suppressing my cries that everything felt pointless, that I was never coming back. He glanced over and the worry in his baby blues steadied me. "It's fine, really." I sniffed a little and opened my eyes wide, hoping my gaze was broadcasting sincerity and not that I was trying to hold back tears. "I'm stressed out. I probably overcommitted a bit with the coaching and it's been a bunch of bad sessions lately, but I'm sure it will get better."

He seemed relieved that I was finally talking to him about where I was at emotionally. I hadn't realized that he'd even been aware, thought I was being so sneaky. Should have known he'd read me better than I ever expected. As we pulled up to the restaurant, where a valet waited, he unbuckled himself then me, pausing with a hand on my thigh.

"Listen," he said seriously. "I'm proud of how hard you're working. This coaching gig is a good thing to do while healing, but it's not you, right? Cut back a little, prioritize rehab. You're a player. Meant for bigger things. Don't lose sight of that."

My heart cracked a bit, I swore I could hear a rib creak from the pressure, and I frowned a little, my cheeks heating up. "I won't, Matti. Thanks."

He patted me on the thigh, gave me a squeeze and hopped out, tossing his keys at the valet before hurrying around to my side to help me down. I slapped a friendly smile over my resting bitch face and followed him more slowly. Matti took me by the hand and in we walked to a double date that I really wasn't looking forward to.

Coach Sherman still pissed me off after he'd treated Matti like a horny teenager who needed to be watched — maybe he was on some days, but he was *my* horny teenager—and Tiana was so gorgeous and mature that she made me feel like a frumpy kid trying on her mom's clothes and persona. It wasn't that she wasn't a genuinely kind and beautiful person, because she was. She simply carried herself like a woman in charge of her own destiny. And that was the complete opposite of where I found myself most days.

* * * *

We drove home from dinner in complete silence. As expected, it had been a lovely meal with one very nice person and one curmudgeon who was on his way to redemption in my book after I'd realized how much of his act was dictated by the ultra-conservative ownership group and his disappointment in himself over his failed marriage.

Over delicious steaks that had melted in our mouths like butter on warm rolls, caramelized Brussels sprouts and cauliflower rice pilaf, we'd talked a lot about intersections of sports and life. As a teacher who worked with young athletes, mostly on fixing the gaping holes left by the U.S. education system, Tiana's perspective was interesting. She and Coach Sherman cared, maybe too much, about making sure their athletes had the life skills necessary to conquer the world if sports failed, but they didn't understand the mentality that it took to go professional—the idea that there wasn't another option. Entertaining even the slightest doubt in yourself and your ability was basically admitting failure.

Tiana had pushed Matti hard to go public with his literacy struggles. Hard enough to make both of us bristle. She'd rattled on and on, saying that it could be a great addition to the youth camps if they also offered extra support in ESL. If he did it, he would be the face of the new program. Her sly suggestion that it would be a big boost for his reputation hadn't gone unnoticed and I'd seen Matti's eyebrows twitch. Sherman had been on her side, lovesick hearts spouting out of his eyes as his date blathered on about "*social responsibility*" and Matti's "*real chance to make a difference.*" To his credit, Matti had listened politely to her before shooting the idea down.

Finally I'd stepped in and spilled my glass of the smoky, spicy, full-bodied red wine we'd been drinking on the waiter's recommendation. I'd only had a bit left since zinfandels gave me a wicked hangover, but it had been enough to call over the waiter and a cadre of underpaid busboys that I'd immediately noted needed to be tipped separately and well.

Matti's grateful half-smile had told me he realized what I'd done, that it had been on purpose and for him. That smile had promised me time with his talented tongue between my legs, and my thighs had clenched with a flashbulb memory of the previous night, when he'd held my legs spread wide and flat against the bed as I'd thrashed and begged for his cock. I'd actually wept as he'd alternated cool breaths and hard sucks on my overheated clit before blacking out when he finally bit down gently as three fingers spread inside me to hit a very special spot that literally no man or toy had ever touched before.

My cheeks had warmed at the memory and he'd shot me a questioning glance that had turned predatory when he'd noticed the flush creeping up from my chest toward my ears. The curse of being a redhead with pale, freckled skin. He was fascinated by the way my blushes seemed to hide the freckles and had spent hours playing hide and seek with them, seeing which touches could elicit that response.

Sherman's eagle eye had caught the interplay and he'd grunted uncomfortably before asking if Matti had any birthday plans. Tiana's amused giggle muffled behind the napkin that she'd brought up to delicately blot the nonexistent stains on her lips had said she hadn't missed it either. I had rolled my eyes, missing the reference altogether, until Matti had replied that we didn't have any plans to celebrate his birthday — that the day after Christmas was a day that usually got overlooked in the boisterousness of family holidays and, besides, twenty-nine really wasn't anything to celebrate.

How did I not even know when his birthday is? Some fake fiancée I'm turning out to be. I was even more irritated to learn that the day tended to get lost in the turbulent rush of the Shellenberg family holiday celebrations. We were definitely celebrating. No way was I going to let this occasion slide.

Me glowering at the decadent slab of chocolate cake that the waiter had dropped in front of me had seemed to clue in Tiana that all was not hunky-dory in Abby Land. She'd tried to redirect by asking us if we'd been photographed lately, "*you two are so adorable together.*" Maybe at Christmas, Matti had said. The whole family would be getting together in L.A., which had been news to me and had made my mood sink further and infect the table. We'd finished up in relative silence and Sherman had taken care of the check after the requisite back-and-forth "*no, I'll pay for this*" between him and Matti.

I was royally pissed off when we left that dinner — not at Matti, at everyone else. It had been obvious to me for a while now that he struggled with who he was versus who other people expected him to be. More than anything, I wanted to fight everyone who tried to push him for more than he was ready — or able — to give. Smack anyone who ignored or discounted him when he tried to deviate from the image he'd maintained for too long. It was no wonder that he was barely able to open up to me. Every other time he'd tried, he'd been shut down.

It hurt, badly, and that pain only underscored what had been a hunch for a while. Much as it tore me up to admit it, I was in this now with him. We were more than a contractually bound fake couple who got to bang. There could be so much more if we could only be completely honest with each other. The problem was, I didn't know if he'd like me very much if I were totally open — if I wasn't who he thought I was, if I turned my back on playing.

Chapter Fifteen

Matti

I let Abby stew on the ride home before cautiously approaching her mood as we swung through the door to our apartment. She'd maintained a constant staccato drumming of her fingers on the armrest and her eyebrows had been deeply furrowed. They were still crinkled as she kicked off her shoes so hard one left a black scuff on the wall. Her gray eyes had gone icy on me again, too. I sighed. "Let me have it. Where did I screw up tonight?"

"You? You were perfect, although maybe you could have mentioned our holiday plans? Or that your birthday is the day after Christmas?"

I could tell it was more than that, although me forgetting to talk to her about the holidays probably didn't help. "Sorry, Stabby. My brother only invited us today since Alina can't travel because she's sick with this early pregnancy stuff, and I hate my birthday. I can't remember the last time I celebrated it. It always gets a little lost in the shuffle and I'll end up with cards a week later from my apologetic family members who only realize that they missed it—again—when they're all back home."

"That's terrible, Matti. Even if you hate your birthday, to not have them even mention it is pretty rotten." Her voice got choked up. "Even when you were a kid?"

I nodded. "But my friends at school always made a big deal out of it after the holidays."

"You were only home for one visit a year and they couldn't even—"

"Shh. It's fine. Didn't bother me then, still doesn't bother me now," I lied, and gently pushed her down the hall to our bedroom, nuzzling her neck from behind. Distracted, as I'd hoped, she leaned against me while I slowly unzipped her dress. It was pooled around her waist by the time we were at the door.

She hadn't worn a bra beneath it and my big hands spanned her ribcage, thumbs stroking the undersides of her breasts as we continued to walk unevenly toward the bed. One little nudge when we reached the bed and she toppled down, glancing back at me with laughter in her eyes as she tried to wriggle fully out of her dress. I helped her to inch it off and shucked off my pants too, then crawled into bed behind her.

"Sorry you've had such a stressful time of it lately." I started to massage her shoulders and her head dropped down to her chest as she groaned when I hit a tender spot. She scooted back until all of her weight hit my chest. I rested my chin on her head for a moment and wrapped my arms around her. "You want to talk about it?"

"No, I'm done talking for the day," she said after a short silence, then reached her hands back over my head and pulled out my hair tie so my gold and her auburn tangled together around her shoulders in a multicolored curtain.

I practically purred as she ran her fingers through my hair and teasingly scratched my scalp with her short nails. "Mmm, that feels good." I licked a path from her earlobe to her exposed collarbone.

If she could give me goosebumps, then I'd be giving them right back to her. Our relationship, sex and otherwise, was a competition, a constant game of one-upmanship. A push and pull of teasing touches and laughter, slowly escalating to a place where we trusted each other—with our secrets and bodies. I knew the places on her neck that would make her putty in my hands, and she'd learned that a pinch on my inner thigh when she went down on me was the exact amount of pleasure-pain to send me rocketing into another plane of existence.

She rose to her knees and turned, straddling me and staring with an unfathomable question in her eyes. The tension between us started to rachet up as I leaned back against the pillows and grabbed her ass. One fast smack on her right cheek jolted her forward and I pulled her the rest of the way to my face, angled her hips down toward me. She gripped my hair to keep from toppling backward and the slight pain made me groan as I dipped my head to slowly lick her sweet cunt, swirling my tongue around the tiny bud of nerves at the apex of her thighs. The sweet burn of her soft skin against my stubble made her moan and I leaned back to smile up at her, her inner thighs pink from the rough treatment, her eyes glowing like stars in her flushed face.

"Come here, I don't want all that pressure on your poor knee." I tugged her down to sit on my lap. The slickness of her pussy spread over my cock as she rocked back and forth over it.

She slowly lowered herself to her forearms. "Let me worry about my knee," she murmured as she kissed me with a gentleness that was at odds with the wicked gleam in her eye and the heat of her core pressing insistently against me.

I gasped as the tip of my cock slid inside her. "You're the boss."

"That's right, I am. And maybe you better not forget it tonight." She slid down an inch and squeezed me and the room seemed to combust as she held herself there, head tossed back and the ends of her hair tickling my thighs. My eyes rolled back and sweat broke out on my forehead.

"Abby, please, go deeper." I gasped again, reduced to begging for the nirvana I knew I'd find once I was fully inside her. She had a tight grip on my wrists, holding them above my head, and while I could have easily broken free, she was running the show tonight. "How long have you been imagining this?" I asked in a voice that was so low I almost didn't even recognize it as my own.

"Since I walked in earlier to you, a towel and *Rio*," she said breathlessly as she sank down farther, bringing her pebbled nipples into range as I arched up to rub against them. Felt the slow drag as she lifted herself off me.

"Christ, Abby, you wreck me." I groaned as she lowered herself onto me, this time bending forward and offering her breasts for me to suck. She let go of my wrists and I immediately wrapped my arms around her, pulling her tighter so I could kiss her, tongue her, from her collarbone to her pretty tits as she began to pick up the pace above me. "How do you want me?" I managed to grunt out as she started to circle her hips. The friction of her overheated skin against mine contrasted with the silkiness of the cool sheets and I was burning up, desperately trying not to come like a teenager with a hot girl for the first time.

"Lay all the way back," she commanded as she rose above me, letting me slip out, and I gasped at the loss of her heat. She kissed me then, a slow unhurried kiss as she crouched above me, letting me stroke her velvety skin everywhere. Her hands wound themselves in my hair and she pulled on it until I raised my head high enough that she could slide another pillow under it.

"Clever girl," I murmured against her lips. She smiled at me, all playfulness amidst that scorching, electrifying heat of the moment, and I felt my heart expand. I wanted that smile aimed at me twenty-four-seven, three hundred sixty-five days a year for the rest of my life, if she'd have me.

"Shut up," she said with that grin still on her face. It turned into a heated smirk a moment later. "I think it's time to put that talented mouth of yours toward something other than talking." She moved up my body so her knees rested beside my head and, grabbing onto the headboard, lowered herself down to me.

Before she could drop all the way, I grabbed her ass and nipped the inside of her thigh. "Not to break up the moment, but...maybe what's good for the goose?"

She rolled her eyes at me, but her smile never faded. "Say please."

I pinched her ass and she laughed. "Please, Abby."

"Please what?" She started to put more weight on my hands and my forearms trembled while my dick throbbed with the lack of attention. I was light-headed with my need to get my tongue inside her.

"Please suck my cock, Abby."

She pulled herself upright and smoothly turned around, hovering above me for one moment as she stared at me. "For you, anything."

I grabbed her and pulled her the rest of the way down to my face and the moan and voracious noise I made as I swiped my tongue through her wet folds seemed to electrify her. She tried to pull away, as if the sudden attention was almost too much, but I wasn't having any of it. She was coming on my face if it was the last thing I could possibly do. She moaned brokenly above me and my vision went dark as I lost myself in her hot, tight pussy.

A second later, the warmth of her mouth engulfed the head of my cock and my hips jerked uncontrollably, driving me deeper into her throat than she was ready for. She shuddered above me and wrapped one hand around the base, thumbing the thick vein that ran up the underside, and sucked hard. I tried to still my body, to concentrate on nothing but her pleasure, and she relaxed enough to accommodate the uncontrolled, shallow thrusts I couldn't hold back. She took everything I was giving her and the rhythm between us began to build, winding us both tighter and tighter.

A bolt of lightning seemed to gather at the base of my spine and I nipped at her clit and started to tease her back entrance with my thumb, hoping to get her off before I lost it completely. She pulled off my dick and groaned my name while groping in the bedside table drawer, which had a small bottle of edible lube that we'd been messing around with.

My tongue was buried in her pussy and she could barely form sentences aside from *more*, *please*, *fuck* and *Matti*. My dick lay throbbing on my stomach, forgotten, as she rocked above me, chasing her orgasm. She grabbed the hand that been teasing her ass and dripped lube on it and sent it back to where I'd been slowly circling her asshole. One fingertip tugged gently on the rim and she moaned into the light stretch as I slid in to my first knuckle. When I hit that point, the hard limit we'd established, I bit down hard on her clit and she convulsed above me.

On shaky legs, she turned back to face me and leaned forward for a spine-tingling kiss, not seeming to mind that I was covered with her fluids. I brought a hand to the back of her head while the other grabbed my dick tightly in hopes of staving off my own orgasm for one more moment and kissed her mercilessly, my tongue as busy in her mouth dancing with hers as it had been earlier between her legs. It didn't take long for her to recover and she swung off of me, then crawled between my legs and bent back to her task, holding her hair to the side so I could watch her slide a few drops of lube up and down her fingers.

I shuddered as I realized what she intended. We'd talked about going further with ass play and she maintained that she wasn't ready for more — unless I was too. The one-upmanship of our sex life was going to be the death of me. I nodded at her, my eyes wide as the anticipation built. She smirked again and I realized in that moment I'd let her do anything to me — anything to see her owning her power.

She dipped her head and gently started to work me over again. As her fingers slid to tiptoe around that tight ring of muscle, I yanked her hair to draw her gaze upward, needing her to see that I wanted this too, that we were good and she best carry on before I died a tiny little death. She cocked an eyebrow at me, hummed "this okay?" around my dick and waited for my fervent nod before sliding all the way back down my cock till it hit the back of her throat.

She held there and followed all the steps I'd done with her, circling the area, pressing a fingertip in slowly, slowly as I relaxed, then sinking a finger deep. With a little more lube, a second finger joined the first and caught up to the rhythm of her mouth. Never ever in my life had I felt so full, little white sparks exploding in my peripheral vision as she continued to work me in tandem.

"Abby, baby, please, fuck me like that. God, I wish you could fuck me like that at the same time as I fuck you. Harder, Abby, fucking harder." I was losing my mind and it was all from this beautiful, gorgeous woman owning my body, taking and giving pleasure. I wanted her, I wanted everything with her, and as I came, a montage of images that could be our future flashed before me. Abby in a white dress, crouching down to embrace a little redheaded boy and blonde-haired girl on a sandy beach. Her strong freckled arms wrapping around my waist from behind as we stood in a vineyard. Everything. I wanted everything with her.

As we collapsed back onto the covers, I pulled Abby right side up and tucked her into my armpit. We were silent as the air around us cooled, the sweat drying on our bodies. Then she squeaked and dove under the covers, leaving me lying on top of them in my naked postcoital bliss.

"I can't believe we did that. I can't believe *I* did that."

I lifted the quilt and grinned at my shy girl, crouched down with hands at her cheeks to hide that delicious blush. "We sure did, or rather, you did. And I'm proud of you. Pretty sure I'd let you do that to me anytime, anywhere." The emotional release of that moment still had me in its grip as I pulled her up to look me in the eye. "Seriously, you're incredible. I love watching you own me, when you take what you want from me."

She rolled her eyes, trying to play off the emotional intensity of what we'd done, and heaved herself out of bed, then stretched out a hand to me. "Let's get cleaned up, sexy. That lube might be edible, but it's sticky as hell when it dries." Her eyes were warm, full of new confidence and wonder—even through her practical focus on aftercare.

"*Mmhmm*, good call. Help me up?" I yawned and stuck my hand in hers. She gave a yank and my boneless legs almost collapsed completely as I tried to stand.

She snickered. "Seriously, you're welcome. Glad you discovered a new pleasure center."

I scooped her up and she let out a whoop of surprise as I hauled her cute ass into the bathroom.

We showered and I wanted to say more, how much I loved being with her. To ask if she realized what tonight had meant to me, if it meant something similar to her. I was falling hard, if not completely there already. But I held my tongue and helped her wash up, let her do the same for me, then wrapped her up in a fluffy white towel. She fell asleep before me that night and I stayed up watching her sleep for a while, too keyed-up from what we'd done to relax.

How could I ever give this up? Ever give *her* up? The answer was simple—I couldn't.

Chapter Sixteen

Matti

The sound of multiple generations shrieking and the acrid scent of burnt pine needles was apparent even from outside the modern glass and stucco mansion as we rang the bell. Our gazes clashed involuntarily as the sounds passed through the door, lots of questions in Abby's big gray eyes and raised eyebrows. I shrugged. My family was chaos. Pounding feet followed by an exasperated shout from my sister. "Girls, leave the door. I've got it!"

The massive frosted-glass door opened slowly and two pairs of eyes appeared roughly at my waist level. My six-year-old hellion nieces, Tess and Trudy. "Onkle Matti!" they shouted in German, and babbled on asking me if I'd brought a soccer ball, if I wanted to play because no one else did, and how they were sorry about the fire but it was a little one and everyone had overreacted.

"Girls, English? This is Abby, my fiancée, and she has no idea what you're saying. I'm sure she's very interested in hearing about the fire," I said and grinned at Abby.

Her eyebrows hovered near her hairline. "Fire?" her perfect lips mouthed at me.

"Matti? Is that you? I never thought I'd say this, but thank god you're here." My sister Ella appeared behind her daughters, pushing her flyaway blonde bangs back. She was wearing a fuzzy white sweater that seemed to be streaked in gray and brown ash and stank of skunky tree sap, like a resiny joint that had been lit and extinguished in a hurry because the cops were coming.

"Aw, Ella. You missed me and you know it."

"Absolutely. Girls, go find your father. Matti will play with you in a bit—you will, right, Matti?"

"Of course," I said and watched the girls take off back into the house my brother and his wife had recently bought on the beach south of L.A. I could see the rest of my family clustered around a singed evergreen through one of the big windows, my mother gesturing theatrically before flopping down on a chaise and covering her face. My father hovered over her in concern. "*Oomph*," I grunted as a sharp elbow dug into my ribs. "Oh, Ella, this is Abby, my fiancée."

"It's so nice to meet you—" Abby stepped forward and extended her hand to my sister, who looked at it, then looked down at her own dirty hand and sighed, waving us in.

"Nice to meet you too. Welcome to the Shellenberg family madness—burned Christmas trees and all," she said over her shoulder as she hurried back toward the living room.

Abby was nonplussed and gave me a "what is wrong with your family?" eyebrow wiggle. I shrugged again, helplessly. My sister wasn't always comfortable with social niceties or new people and often came off as cold and abrasive, but there were reasons for that no one ever talked about.

Ella had struggled for years trying to fit in and operate normally amidst a family that simply ignored differences. I hadn't told Abby about Ella since it didn't feel like my business to share, but now I could see how toxic our family had always been at dealing with things outside the mental norms. I was both complicit in it and a product of it.

The noise grew louder as we reached the group around the tree. Everywhere I could see was open space and glass, one room flowed into the next, and they all seemed to lead to an enormous outdoor deck and living space right on the beach. Markus and Alina were going to have an interesting time baby-proofing this house.

"Matthias! Come give your mother a hug!" my mother ordered from her dramatic fake faint on the chaise lounge.

I dutifully headed to her first with Abby attached to my hand like a limpet, following behind me. I nodded at Max, Martin and my dad, who were all standing around the still-smoking Christmas tree and shaking their heads. Neither Markus nor Alina were in sight.

"Mother," I said as I dipped down to give her a hug and kiss. "This is Abby, my fiancée."

"Abby, my dear! It's so lovely to meet you. We've heard such wonderful things from Matthias and I'm sorry that this is all pretend because we need more women in this family. Don't shake your head at me, Loren!"

My dad ducked his head and held out a hand to Abby. "Abby, nice to meet you. Anyone who can handle his nonsense is fine with me."

The rest of my family laughed and Martin murmured a hello from the base of the tree, where he and Ella were attempting to restack an enormous pile of gifts.

I bristled immediately. *Come on, really?* Within five minutes I'd been reduced to the baby of the family, a man-child who would never grow up. Abby squeezed my hand gently and I glanced down to see her worried face light with a slight smile.

"No, the pleasure is really mine. It's nice to meet you all and I'm not sure what planet everyone here lives on, but your son, brother, whatever, is a fairly delightful adult." She emphasized the word adult and my mother opened her mouth to say something before biting it back. Her jaw snapped shut with an audible click. Everyone else looked away.

Max snorted, ran a hand through his wavy dark brown hair and walked over and held out his hand. "Abby," he said in what I thought of as his billionaire businessman voice. "A pleasure." He winked at me.

"Where's your wife, Maxi-poo?" I asked idly as he proceeded to eye Abby in a way that made me extraordinarily territorial.

"Couldn't make it," he said without taking his eyes off Abby, who was slowly turning red.

Max and I were going to have to have a talk. I was the only one allowed to make her turn that color. "Right, we're going to go find our rooms and drop off our bags. Anyone know where our hosts are?" I asked as I tugged Abby's hand out from Max's.

"Upstairs, I assume," Ella said as she jumped up and brushed herself off. "Here, let me show you."

Martin stood too and muttered something about checking the garage for Markus and left. My mother's hands fluttered like irritated butterflies around her face, futzing with her earrings and necklace while my father rolled his eyes at all of us and headed for the bar cart where Max was already pouring himself a drink. He raised it to us ironically as we headed out. "Welcome to the family circus, Abby!"

Ella led the way up a set of floating stairs to a long hallway with enormous framed photographs of urban scenes interspersed with colorful abstract canvases that I recognized from Markus' apartment in Berlin, which he'd sold after locking things down with Alina. I'd tried to buy his swinging bed but it had had to stay with the apartment. *Pity*.

She stopped at the end of the hall and opened a door to a large guest suite that was all white with a few gray accents. "For you two. Also, Abby, I'm sorry about downstairs. I have a hard time meeting new people and this has been incredibly stressful. The girls set the tree on fire, which you saw, Markus is losing his mind about impending fatherhood, Alina is sick and cranky, Martin refuses to do anything but commiserate with Markus and Max is—well, you saw. Dark and broody."

Ella nervously pulled her hair tie out and whipped her hair back into a tighter ballerina bun on top of her head. I recognized that gesture immediately, as I'd been about to do the exact same thing.

"It's fine, Ella, don't worry about it. I'm nervous too," Abby said with a small smile. "Your family is kind of a lot to take in."

Ella's relieved sigh said a lot. "Yeah, they are." Then she surprised both of us by reaching out and pulling Abby into a clumsy hug. "Glad to have you here. Thank you for coming."

Abby dropped her bag onto the floor and flopped backward onto the bed. The fluffy white duvet poofed up around her and resettled with a soft *shh*. "Holy mother of god," she said with a hand over her eyes. "I'm already exhausted."

I nodded as I grabbed the lintel of the doorframe to the en suite bathroom and stretched. The groan as my back unkinked from the four-hour flight made Abby eye me with interest as I straightened up. "Want to take a shower?" I asked. "I hear California is in the middle of a drought, so showering together will save water. You know how I am about limiting our environmental footprint."

Abby laughed and extended a hand. I yanked her up and pulled her to me. She crashed into my chest, wrapped her arms around my neck and squeezed.

"Thank you for coming," I said softly into the top of her head as I buried my nose in her tropical-smelling hair.

She nodded against me and rubbed her nose against my chest. "Of course, any time."

* * * *

An hour later and we'd stalled as long as possible between our shower and some quality time testing out the sturdiness of the bed frame and the acoustics in the guest room. My nieces were banging on the door that I'd thankfully locked. Abby was dozing next to me, the sheet wound around her naked body, which was flushed with what we'd been doing only a few minutes ago. She sat bolt upright and stared at me in alarm as the banging changed over to scratching and muttered German.

"Locked it," I said smugly and stretched out an arm to roll her underneath me again.

Unfortunately, someone had taught my nieces to pick locks. We heard a series of clicks and a shrieked "Got it!" that barely gave us enough time to dive completely beneath the covers as two tiny blonde hellions came crashing through the door and leaped onto the bed, effectively killing any and all moods.

"Why are you in bed, Uncle Matti?" they chorused as they bounced around at the foot. "Come play with us, you've been up here forever!"

"We were, uh, sleeping?" I said. "It was a long flight."

They laughed and bounced higher.

Abby peeked her head out and her gray eyes were flashing. "Girls, I realize you don't know me, but if you don't get your adorable little butts out of this room and shut the door behind you by the time I count to three, something very bad is going to happen."

The girls stopped dead and stared at me in concern. I bit my lip, trying not to laugh. I don't think anyone had ever told them no before. I nodded at them seriously. "Very, very bad," I intoned.

Tess and Trudy glanced at each other and frowned, then turned back to us, then to each other again. "We're going," Tess said. "But you better come find us when you're done sleeping."

They bounced off the bed and out the door, slamming it behind them. Abby's gray eyes seemed to scream bloody murder. "Your family…" she muttered. "They are impossible." She slowly slid one tantalizingly bare leg out from under the covers and let the sheet pool at her waist, exposing the most gorgeous set of tits I'd ever had the pleasure of teasing.

I tackled her back into the pillows and held her wrists next to her head as I bent my head to swirl my tongue around first one, then the other nipple, feeling the vibrations of her moan echo through my body.

"Matti, no," she whined. "We have to get down there. Dammit, I hate it that you're so good at this."

"Stabby Abby, I need to repay you for dealing with my family and putting those two in their place. So shut up and let me," I ordered as I continued to kiss my way down her body to devour her pussy.

"*Mmhmm*, Jesus," she cried out as I slid two fingers inside her. Her fingers knotted in my hair as she ground against my face.

I raised my head. "It's Matti, thanks," I said with a shit-eating grin and ducked back to my work as she grumbled something about assholes before moaning and convulsing around my fingers and tongue.

* * * *

When we finally appeared downstairs, Abby was still a little flushed and both Max and Ella gave us a knowing smile. Max tipped an imaginary hat my way and turned back to pour himself another drink. I wondered how many he was at for the day. He didn't seem overly inebriated, but everything about him was darker than the last time I'd seen him. He was rumpled and the circles under his eyes could have rivaled mine after a week-long bender.

"Where's Markus and Alina?" I asked, still not having seen them.

Ella frowned. "Alina is probably up napping. She's been having a rough first trimester. Markus, I don't know. He keeps disappearing with Martin." Martin and Markus had been best friends growing up and remained close.

"Where are the girls?"

"Outside, hopefully staying on the sand and not going in the ocean," she said, sounding completely defeated. "Mother and Father are supposed to be keeping an eye on them."

"I'll go relieve them of their duties," I said and turned to Abby. "You want to come?"

She shrugged. "Sure, let's go mess around with some kiddos."

"Thank you." Ella sounded relieved.

Max strode over to the patio doors, glass in hand. "Maybe I'll come with you guys. Ella, you should go take a nap or something. You need your rest right now too."

They were twins and had always had a sixth sense about each other. I wondered if Ella's news was that she was pregnant again. Max had sounded a little protective. It would explain why Markus and Martin were off together — fatherhood bonding.

Max led the way outside, then excused himself to find food after pointing out my parents overseeing a massive sandcastle construction effort just down the beach.

Abby and I slumped into a lounger together and watched the chaos below us. The girls saw us and started waving madly. "Come on, let's go play with some kids." She heaved a sigh, stood and pulled me from my chair. "The sooner we play with them, the quicker the time will pass until you get to fuck me again."

"That is definitely a plan I can get behind. Or in front of, on top. However you want me."

She swatted me on the arm. "Behave yourself in front of your family, you animal."

"Never, baby. Bad boy, remember?" I winked.

* * * *

Markus and Martin had finally appeared right before we all sat down to dinner, reeking of cigarettes, cigars and whiskey. Markus was extraordinarily gallant and apologetic for not having been present, but also quite wobbly on his feet. Martin had collapsed in his chair and muttered a "nice to see you" while Ella had yanked on her ponytail in frustration. She and Alina were both fairly green at the stench wafting off of their beloveds and Alina couldn't stop hiccupping.

Max sat there giggling into his always-full wineglass. My parents did what they did best and pretended all was completely normal. Totally and perfectly fine. The twins were sleepy paragons of good behavior, having been exhausted by sand soccer and pacified with promises of a visit from Santa. Ella put them down as they started nodding their little heads during dessert and met us in the living room.

Ella had noticeably been avoiding wine and our mother immediately called her on it as we relaxed around the completely unnecessary fire on the warm L.A. night.

"Do you have something to tell us?" my mother asked eagerly, sloshing her own recently refilled glass all over the coffee table.

"Maria —"

"Hush, Loren, I want to know if we will have another grandchild soon!"

Finally, Ella nodded. Martin staggered over to her and held her tightly while she looked like she wanted to vomit. "We're pregnant!" he shouted.

"I'm pregnant," said Ella quietly.

"Yup, *she's* pregnant," Abby helpfully supplied. Always a lightweight, she'd had at least two glasses of wine and a cocktail. "Not *we*. God, I hate it when men try to claim a participation award in pregnancy. Procreation, sure, but pregnancy, fuck —"

Alina laughed and hiccupped loudly, cutting Abby off. "Too right," she agreed. "Fuck you, Markus." She hiccupped again.

"Of course, darling." He stared at her with besotted eyes. Terrified as he might be of fatherhood, he was absolutely, completely in love with his wife.

My mother gave everyone a dirty look. "This is wonderful news!"

Ella nodded grimly. "It is. We're very happy about it. Now, please excuse me, I'm exhausted and need to sleep." Martin trailed her up the stairs to their room.

Alina made a move to stand, as if she wanted to follow, but Markus had her on his lap and seemed to be holding her captive.

Max clinked his wine glass gently. "I have news too," he announced.

"Oh, more grandchildren!" my mother exclaimed.

"Not exactly. Nicole and I are divorcing. Amicably, but there's a small matter of disagreement about ownership of several of our biggest producing vineyards. But we should be fine. Absolutely fine."

"What?" My mother clapped a hand over her mouth.

Abby was highly amused by Max's nonchalance as he poured himself another drink and shoved her own glass out when he waved the bottle vaguely around the room.

"Good girl," he murmured as he poured, and I rolled my eyes.

"Our vineyard? You're losing our vineyards, Maximilian?" My mother was distraught. This had been her family's business for hundreds of years.

"No, no. It's fine, no worries, Mother."

"But—"

"Mother, stop talking," Markus finally chimed in and Max threw him a grateful look. "He's taking care of things, leave it."

Abby elbowed me and I cleared my throat to forestall my mother from unleashing another tirade. "So sorry, Max. Are you okay?"

"Been better, but everything will be fine. And you, Matti? Any news you'd like to share?" *Someone clearly wants the subject changed.*

"Not really," I answered.

"Oh, Matthias, I do hope you're not getting kicked off another team," my mother said, switching her attention to a new target.

Markus interjected, "Knock it off. Don't talk to him like he's a naughty teenager."

"Not helping, Markus," murmured Alina.

"No," he said stubbornly. "They should know. Everyone should know. We were not fair—"

"Fair?" my mother exploded. "Fair? What on earth do you mean? Matti has always had every opportunity. We've spoiled him, really, and he can't even be bothered to be grateful—"

"Moth—" started Markus.

"Now hold up for one fucking second." Abby lurched to her feet and, before I could grab her, staggered over to stand in front of my parents. She rarely lost her redhead temper, but when she did, it was totally and absolutely without any sense of remorse. "You people are the worst. Worst parents in history, completely terrible. How dare you even think about lecturing him? Do you honestly have no idea what he's gone through?"

"What on earth is she talking about?" My mother and father peered over their glasses at me.

I shrugged helplessly. "I—"

She steamrolled back into the conversation, words spitting out through a clenched jaw. "Talking down to your son like he's a child. Your *adult* son who you've ignored for most of his life." I glanced at Alina and she raised a fist in solidarity.

"Do you even realize you've forgotten his birthday every fucking year?" Abby shouted. "Every year, since he left at home at ten—which is way too fucking young, but I'll get back to that in a second—you've forgotten his birthday. And then there's the fact that he's struggled with school his entire life and you didn't fucking care. Do you not realize that ninety-nine percent of the crap he's pulled is mostly to hide the fact that he's practically illiterate? But none of you...none of you supported him. Cared enough to figure out what was going on. You shipped him off to Spain to be someone else's problem. You're horrible parents."

"Yes, horrible," Max or Markus — possibly both — interjected.

Alina hissed at me. "This is great, but maybe you should stop her before one of them starts physically attacking the other."

I got up from my chair and hurried over to Abby. Standing in front of her, I held out a hand. She automatically high-fived me, such an adorable little jock, and I scooped her up and over my shoulder. "G'night, everyone. We're going to bed."

"Fuck all of y'all, we're gonna go bang," Abby slurred upside down.

Max and Markus raised their glasses again and she flipped them off as I jogged toward the stairs. I heard Alina say, approvingly, "I like her. And, Maria, she's right. You really are dreadful sometimes. Now I'm going to bed too. Markus?"

I opened the door, stepped through and closed it behind us, then dropped Abby on the bed, where she slumped to the side. "You're the best, Stabby Abby. Thank you."

"Right backatchyou. You're my favorite person," she muttered.

"Aw, I'm flattered. Let's get you cleaned up and ready for bed."

"*Mmhmm*, then we can bang?" she asked hopefully as I picked her up again and carried her into the bathroom.

"We'll see, Stabby. Maybe I'll go down on you for a bit."

"You're the best, Shellenberg. Love you." Her eyes closed and I don't think she realized what she'd said because, in the next second, she was snoring in my arms.

I held her tightly and stroked her hair, then kissed her forehead. "I love you too, Stabby. Love you so much."

* * * *

By the time we got home from a lazy brunch with my brothers and sisters the next day, my mother was ready to apologize in her usual dramatic fashion. As per usual, she made it all about her and, while Abby looked like she might murder her with a wine bottle, I forgave her. Over dinner Alina asked if I wanted to do a big birthday thing the next day, but as I was about to say no, Abby interjected.

"We won't be here, actually, but thanks."

Everyone stared, but she didn't seem to notice as she chewed with her eyes on her plate.

"Uh, Stabby? What are you talking about?" I asked.

"He calls her Stabby!" Trudy whisper-shouted to her sister.

"Can we call her Tante Stabby when they get married?" Tess whispered back.

"Girls," reprimanded Ella. "That's enough."

"We're not going to be here," Abby repeated and wiped her mouth.

"Where are we going to—" I started to ask.

"Yeah, I booked us a trip to Mexico. Surprise? Happy Birthday?" She flushed, seemingly flustered by the sudden attention. "I mean, if you want to stay here and hang out, I can probably cancel."

"That's so romantic," Alina murmured to Markus.

"They're adorable," he whispered back.

Max snorted.

"No, no, we can go." I was touched, tickled pink. And she was turning my favorite color as everyone stared at her like they were seeing her for the first time. "In fact, maybe we need to go get packed."

Just like previous night, I scooped her up from her chair, pulled the fork from her hand and dropped it on her plate, where it landed with a clatter.

"Put me down, you big lunk. I wasn't finished!" she protested.

"'Night, everyone, what a great Christmas. See you all next year!" I shouted over my shoulder as I galloped away with Abby trying to wriggle loose.

"Fake engagement, my ass," said Ella and everyone gasped and the twins crowed about a swear jar.

I laughed under my breath and kissed Abby lightly on the lips. "The best, Stabby, the absolute best."

"You too, Matti. You too."

She never lost the smile on her face when she drifted off a half-hour later. I stroked her forehead as she lay across my chest. When we were in Mexico, I decided that I'd tell her how I felt, that I was done with contracts and that I wanted this to be real. Hopefully she wouldn't live up to her nickname when I did.

Chapter Seventeen

Matti

Abby dragged me by the hand through the heavy sand back to our little rental. We were around the bay from the main community beach, separated by a brief rocky stretch that no one seemed interested in navigating and reachable by a very dubious road through the jungle.

It was perfect. She was perfect. *Everything* was perfect.

"Last one in has to either do the cooking or decide where we're going for dinner tonight!" she shouted as she sprinted ahead of me.

I felt a twinge of worry for her still weakened knee, but she seemed to be almost fully healed and I followed more slowly—not minding the whole cooking responsibility or the view of her cute bubble butt bouncing away from me in peek-a-boo bikini.

"What's it gonna be, hotshot? You cooking for me, naked, or are we going out?" Sassy Abby was out and ready to play when I reached the door, leaning against the frame with one little hand propped on her hip. Screw dinner, I wanted to untie the strings holding that swimsuit together.

"Naked cooking, baby. Naked cooking." I shucked off my trunks right there on the porch and swaggered in, loving the way her eyes got big and glazed over as they followed my path. "You coming?" I asked over my shoulder as she stood frozen in the doorway.

"Oh, yes. I am definitely coming," she muttered as she tagged along after me. I could feel her hot gaze squarely on my ass as I whipped an apron over my front to protect it from splatters and started pulling produce and some chicken we'd bought earlier out of the fridge.

"You will be tonight, count on it." I smirked and she punched me lightly.

"I'm holding you to that promise, Shellenberg." She stepped around me and grabbed some lime juice and juggled it with an ice cube tray. My lady had learned to make a mean margarita over the past few days.

"Here, want one?" She handed me a drink while I finished slicing up vegetables and tossed them in a hot pan.

We brought the pitcher of margaritas she'd made out to the lanai with our food when it was ready. It was so peaceful out there. The stars and moon seemed to be close enough to touch.

"You're on clean-up duty and making more drinks," I informed her when we were done.

"Christ, you're bossy." She had a glow going, not quite buzzed but playful.

"Fine, I'll help you out."

"You're staying naked, though."

"Now who's the bossy one?" We smiled at each other and carried plates and food inside, along with the pitcher, to clean up companionably like an old married couple.

It was our last night in paradise and I don't think either of us wanted to be away from each other. The past few days had been magical—there was really no other word for it. We spent most of the day naked on our patio, sometimes venturing into our swimsuits and heading to the public beach, where we'd sit under umbrellas and drink margaritas and ice-cold Mexican beer. We ate our weight in ceviche and grilled shrimp in adobo spices with avocado and lime juice in thin little tortillas. Then we'd stumble home love-drunk and windswept and fuck all night. I had high hopes for that night too.

Abby hummed along with the scratchy music that warbled out of the little boombox in the kitchen as we washed dishes. Me washing and rinsing, her drying and setting them carefully back into the cupboards. I took over from her with the pots and pans while she made another pitcher of margaritas.

"Can you lighten those up a little?" I asked as I watched her dance around the tiny living room slinging booze and lime juice. "You're probably going to have a wicked sunburn after today."

She laughed. "Yeah, no problem—I'll cut the tequila in half. I don't want to be super hungover tomorrow either."

"Perfect." I swept her up in my arms and carried her and the pitcher back out to the lanai, where we snuggled onto a lounge chair to watch the stars move.

"Can I talk to you about something?" Her voice was tentative as she swirled her drink, making the ice cubes dance.

I reached over to smooth a flyaway hair off her forehead. "Of course, always."

"I feel like I haven't been completely honest with you…" She trailed off and my stomach sank a little.

"What do you mean?" I was more than a little hesitant as she reached for my hand.

"Most of this comes from seeing you with your family, and I know I've told you a little bit about my own growing up, but I didn't go into everything." Her eyes were glassy and this time it wasn't desire or the alcohol talking. She was screwing up her courage to open up. To tell me everything.

I heard about her childhood, the trauma of her family abandoning her, and finally realized how serious it was — how badly she'd been hurt by them and how it still made her wary and distrustful. She told me that she never wanted to see them again, never even think of them, and I believed her wholeheartedly.

My heart broke for the little girl she'd been who'd never fit into the space they wanted to force her into — no matter how hard she tried. Then she said that she wasn't sure how, or when, but somewhere along the line, things between us had turned real for her. Or at least she wanted them to be. When she stumbled to a halt and stared at me with pleading eyes, all of the ice completely melted, I could barely speak as I pulled her into my arms.

I finally gasped out, "God, Abby. It's been real for me almost since the beginning."

"You promise?" she asked hesitantly. "I'm scared of this. Of how I feel about you, like I never want to let you go."

"I'm here for you, always, if you'll let me be."

She blinked at me as she assessed my words, then sighed. "I think you're stuck with me, Ratty."

That trust settled on me like an uneasy but soft and comforting blanket. I could do this, be whatever she needed whenever she needed. Teammate, best friend, lover, anything. "Good, because you're super-duper stuck with me, Ms. Stabby."

Up to that point, I'd never made love to anyone in my life, but that night I made love to Abby McKinnon. She kissed me and rolled over, asleep within seconds. I watched her for a few minutes, counting the freckles that had come out to play, dotting across her cheekbones. The crooked smile that brought out a shy dimple in her cheek when I tucked a lock of hair behind her cheek broke me and I grabbed my phone, took a quick picture.

Setting the phone down, I curved around her, tucking her head under my chin and felt contentment settle over me like a weighted blanket. Nothing would ever be the same. We were done pretending.

* * * *

"Oh, snuggle bug, got your bag?" I asked as Abby came up to me with a rolling suitcase behind her. Two tiny paper cups with something steaming inside were clenched between her fingers. "One of those for me?"

She handed one over and we both took down those shots of espresso like we'd taken down racks of tequila shots in Mexico for the last five days. We both grimaced and I took her cup, stacked it with my own and dropped it in a nearby trash can. Despite our best intentions from the previous night, the emotions of it all had us in hangovers worse than any caused by alcohol.

"I feel like absolute shit." She groaned as her sunburn crinkled under her frown. The last day in Mexico, Abby had become bold under the guidance of Lady Tequila and foresworn sunscreen since it was slightly overcast. The woman looked like a gorgeous tomato.

"Oh come on," I teased as I snagged her roller bag handle. "Let's get home and I can rub you down with aloe. I called a car and they're here."

She grumbled unintelligible things about making me pay later, that she wouldn't be such a jerk if I were the one with a sunburn, that I needed to put on a hat or something because people were staring and she was in no mood for a photo op. The last one made me walk faster, tugging her along like a little caboose on my unstoppable train.

When we got into the apartment, Abby headed straight for our bedroom to take a shower and I followed her more slowly while I flipped through pictures of our trip on my phone. My heart expanded on the second-to-last one, which showed Abby tucked into bed last night, the sheet wrapped around her, auburn hair swirling around her freckled shoulders, fast asleep.

The final one on the roll was a selfie, me next to her, kissing her forehead while she slept. Everything was covered but my tattoos were showing, and it was pretty clear that the sheets were the only thing between us and the camera. Together we were such a beautiful mess, and I didn't think I'd ever been so happy, felt so complete, in my entire life.

As she came out of the shower and crawled into bed with me, she curled up into my chest, snuggling into my armpit. I kissed the top of her head and she tilted her head up to blink those big gray eyes at me. "'Night, baby. Thank you for such an incredible Christmas and birthday. I'll never forget it."

She poked me in the ribs. "Anytime, Ratty, anytime." She scooted up enough to give me a big smacking kiss on the lips. "Now let me sleep, you insatiable beast."

My little Ice Queen had melted completely, we were real and I hoped that she never stopped giving me crap, calling me "Ratty Matti" or rolling her eyes when I hollered for "my Stabby" in public. God, I loved her so much.

Chapter Eighteen

Abby

A few days after our return home, I went to a scheduled check-in with my med team. I'd been avoiding this appointment, rescheduling and rescheduling it, for too long. I knew my recovery had plateaued, but I hoped that they would be ready to present me with something new. Maybe a new PT technique, yoga, meditation, something. The tiny voice in my head was starting to get more persistent as it whispered that I better start thinking about what I was good at besides soccer. Or who I even was without playing the game.

"And as you can see here, the scans show that the ligament has tightened to the point where it's never going to be as flexible as it once was." My doctor stood in front of a light box, pointing at the joint pictured. My knee joint. He shook his head dolefully, like he was imparting a death sentence. To me, it was. "While you've healed, we're afraid there's very little chance of additional improvement."

"Can you say that again?" I asked slowly. Perhaps my vacation hangover plus latent sunstroke was making me hallucinate.

"You'll still be able to work out, play recreationally even, but I'm afraid that playing professionally would be incredibly ill-advised if you want to avoid permanent damage to the knee joint. We're talking major loss of mobility if you reinjure that leg," he said patiently.

"So, I'm done?" *This can't be it. It can't.*

"I'm afraid so, unless you want to risk permanent damage that will leave you reliant on a chair or cane. As it is, if you don't continue on with your PT, you'll probably have significant pain to manage as you age. I'm relatively sure you'll be able to avoid that if you stay active," he said with some sympathy. "Talk to Angela about this. She's worked with a lot of professionals who've stopped playing."

I nodded wordlessly and slipped from the table, heading for the door.

"Oh, and, Abby?"

I turned back.

"Take care, will you? Stay active and push yourself, but be careful of that knee."

"Thanks, doc," I said, my Midwestern politeness automatic in the face of a medical professional. I stumbled out of the office and headed to my car, where I slid into my seat without seeing anything.

The thing they never tell you growing up when you're good at something—like, really, really good—is that there may come a time when you won't be able to do that one thing that you're good at anymore. It may not be your fault or your choice — sometimes that agency is taken away from you by circumstance.

When that happens, you're going to crash and burn because you've never done anything else. Worse, you've never *been* anything else. It's a gross betrayal and there's no one to blame. The ground disappears beneath you and the vertigo is terrifying. Everything you give up to be a professional something-or-other that depends on very specific mental or physical abilities slams into you when your abilities fail. Everything.

I was twenty-eight years old and had never done anything but play soccer. That had been my whole life and my teammates had become my family when my blood relations abandoned me. I'd given up everything for this beautiful fucking game and now, when it was taken away, there was nothing left of me. I didn't know who I was anymore. Maybe the answer was that I was no one. No one important.

I couldn't go home. Matti would notice my withdrawal — I'd been plateaued in my therapy for weeks, but he was so damn positive that my comeback was inevitable. It made me feel terrible, like I was letting him down now that it was official. I was done. Maybe I needed a second opinion.

The gray slush on the January roads flew up to splatter my windows as I drove through pothole after pothole to get to the Northwestern athletic complex from the hospital. Steph, one of the assistant coaches I worked with, was finishing up a film review and I'd asked her and Angela, my PT, to meet me for coffee.

It was a short ride, but a slow one as I didn't want to bottom-out my Prius on the monster cracks and puddles in the road. I wished for a half-second that I'd let Matti buy me the car he'd wanted to get me in the first place, a customized hybrid BMW X5. My little baby wasn't doing so hot with the craptastic roads. *Fucking Chicago.*

A text from Matti was waiting for me on my phone when I pulled up to the main entrance of the complex and parked in the temporary loading zone to wait for Steph and Angela, asking how my appointment had gone and when I'd be home. My windshield washers *shhh-clunked* back and forth in a comforting metronomic rhythm as I considered what to even say. I glanced up and saw Steph and Angela beelining toward the car under a shared umbrella and quickly typed out a fast response.

Appointment was fine. Be home for dinner. X.

There, I'd even included a kiss.

"Abbbbby!" Angela was, as usual, ebullient. I'd never seen her in a bad mood, no matter how much surly crap of mine she put up with.

"Hey, lady," said Steph, the much more measured of the two.

"Hey, guys, coffee today, or should we go bigger?" I asked.

Angela craned her head around to question Steph in the backseat. "Ice cream?"

"Yes!" both Steph and I said in chorus.

"Uh-oh," said Angela softly. She probably knew exactly what I wanted to talk to them about — she was on my care team.

I managed to avoid their probing looks and leading questions until we were all seated at a little café table in the ice cream shop near campus. Finally Angela leveled me with a flinty stare and threatening jab with her dripping spoon. "Spill, Abby."

"Do I have to?" I whined.

Steph rolled her eyes at me and glanced at Angela. They both nodded. "You're the one who wanted to meet up with us. Spill," threatened Steph, echoing Angela.

"Fine. Dearly beloved, we are gathered here today to discuss the news I received this morning at my appointment. Doctor Mitchell says I'm done playing professionally. I'm thinking about seeking a second opinion. What say you?" I gestured grandly with a spoonful of butter pecan that was coated in a caramel swirl.

Again Steph and Angela stared at each other, having an entire conversation with eyebrow twitches and blinks while shoveling more ice cream into their gaping pie holes.

"You wanna take this?" Steph mumbled to Angela through a mouthful of strawberry and chocolate swirl.

Angela nodded. "Fine, yeah. I got this. Abby, as your PT, I've got to say that you need to listen to Doctor Mitchell. You know you've been stuck for the last month. No improvement. Even with more therapy, I don't see the joint ever bouncing back to performance-ready. Stronger, sure, but not more flexible or tight enough to handle the flexion needed for playing midfield."

Steph took over with a furious spoon gesture that spattered the table with decadent abstract art. "And don't give us any nonsense about changing positions and everything being a-okay. Because that ain't gonna happen on my watch, or hers." She elbowed Angela, who shrieked when a flick of chocolate appeared on her high cheekbone.

"Steph is right. Your joint simply cannot and will not handle the stress of playing at the professional level. In any position." Angela reached over and grabbed a napkin, swiped off the ice cream and tossed the crumpled paper in my face.

The faint scent of dark chocolate made my stomach growl as I contemplated whether or not the butter pecan with mouth-wateringly salted caramel sauce may have been a premature decision. "Guys, come on. It's been a couple of months stuck on a plateau. That's nothing. There are other surgical options, I'm sure. I can still come back—"

Steph cut me off. "No, baby girl, you can't," she said gently. "You're done. Ang told me about the latest scans. I know it sucks, but you have to listen to the doctors and the rest of your care team. Do you know why I stopped playing?"

I twirled my spoon across my fingers and shook my head. She'd gone to Northwestern a few years before me and we'd never overlapped. After she graduated, she'd played a brief stint in Portland but had dropped out and turned to coaching soon after. I'd snobbishly assumed she hadn't made the cut, hadn't been as good as me, hadn't worked as hard. The "those who can't play, coach" mantra was a real one to any professional athlete.

"I stopped because I ended up with my fifth reported concussion—in all reality, it was probably more like my ninth, but five was what my records said, and the coaches cut me."

"Ninth? How are you still functional?" Angela practically shouted.

Steph shrugged and continued. "I was bitter and pissed off, trying to find my way, working retail, when the blinding headaches and forgetfulness started. Eventually I saw a neurologist, who told me that I better not ever let anything even tap me roughly on the head again or I was in serious danger of brain damage. As it is, CTE is likely as I get older."

Angela shook her head so hard I was sure I heard her brain slosh around. "Nine concussions," she muttered.

Steph shushed her. "Yeah, nine. Till that day, I was still trying out for teams. When the doc gave me that news, I quit cold turkey. Called Williams crying and begged for a job. I was bitter as hell that my playing career was cut short, but you know what?" She paused and pointed her spoon at each of us in turn, and we sat raptly awaiting her response. My ice cream was melting into a slurry of sweet goodness and I didn't even care. The knot in my gut was going to make it impossible to finish.

"It was all for the best. This—coaching—is what I was meant to do. I'm way better at teaching and mentoring players than I was an actual player." She sighed and dug back in.

"Steph, I'm sorry. I had no idea." I reached out to tap the back of her hand. "Seriously. You're amazing."

She waved me off. "Prove it by thinking about this. Just because you've always been an athlete, it's not the only thing that defines you, nor is it the only thing that can bring you joy."

Angela chimed in, "Yeah, I think you need to do a joy inventory, Abby. Sit down and take a minute, write it all down in your journal with a glitter pen while you sip tea and wallow in the atmosphere created by a warm down comforter and scented candle. What brings you fucking joy. Write it all down."

Her spoon scraped bottom and she gave it a decidedly sexual lick to clean it. She wiped her hands, balled up her napkin into the empty cup and tossed the whole thing into a nearby trash can, where it made a wet plopping sound as it landed on the other discards. "Then talk to us about making a comeback."

"Fine," I said. "I'll inventory my fucking joy and get back to you."

We cleaned up the rest of our mess and headed back to the car. No one brought up my injury or recovery status again and I managed to let it go too. Their threats had had their intended effect and I got a hug and sloppy peck on the cheek from each of them when we got back to the athletic center. They stood outside and shouted at me.

"Love you, girl. Take care of yourself — and your sexy-ass fiancé!"

"Ooh, we didn't even talk about him! Abby, let us back in the car. We need to go to a bar."

I flipped them off and honked the horn, then drove off, hoping that I'd painted both of those two busybodies with some serious slush. They were well-intentioned, but I still desperately wanted to believe that a second opinion could cure everything. While I'd enjoyed coaching the kids at the camps, working with Williams' team, and wouldn't mind continuing to help out while I healed, coaching had always been a stop-gap measure to keep me near the field as I prepared for my comeback.

There was no other option, right? Or maybe I needed to stop listening to Matti and my own stubbornness and start actually using my brain. Because even if it wasn't at that exact moment, the time would eventually come that I would have to hang up my cleats and find something new. Maybe it was time to open myself up to new possibilities.

Chapter Nineteen

Abby

Sometimes I hated being such an early riser. I especially hated it on the occasional morning where I had to yank a very reluctant Matti out of our bed. Case in point, the day when we were already running late to filming an early morning local news show. Naturally, I was already showered, made up and dressed, whereas he was still a tantalizing shrouded lump of tatted-up muscles and messy blond hair curled up under the covers. He'd fallen asleep with the elastic still in his hair and the little sumo knot that peeked out from the duvet made me smile. Christ, I was so in love with this big doofus.

I grabbed the baby top knot between my thumb and index finger and gave it a yank. "Dude! We're going to be late, move your ass!"

He groaned. "Stabby, there's no way." A colorful forearm snaked its way out from the quilt and he grabbed my thigh in a death grip. His hands were so big that they almost wrapped around my leg, and I sadly remembered how less than a year ago my quads had been so tight that he wouldn't have even made half the circumference. I mourned the loss of my soccer player thighs.

"And did you call me 'dude'?" he muttered as he gave a yank and I tumbled back into the bed to land on top of him. "*Oomph.*" All the breath left him in a whoosh, but he recovered in lightning speed to flip me over on my back so I was now the one tied down in stifling blankets that smelled like us while he hovered above me, planking on his forearms, completely bare.

I managed to sneak a hand down and pinch his muscled backside and he rolled off with a squeak and a hurt look as he rubbed his ass.

"Not the nicest wake-up, Abby. It started out with such promise, but ended with a whimper."

"Sorry, big guy, but we've got ten minutes before the car arrives to take us down to the station." I kicked my way out of the nest of bedding with possibly more force than necessary. Some days it seemed like he took nothing seriously at all. Since we'd signed our updated "we're totally together, but hoo boy does engagement seem awful serious" agreement, every day had been marked by an unexpected level of tension.

He was so tender and open with me, but still steadfastly refused to come out with his backstory publicly. Which I understood and supported, to some extent. What was worse, in my mind, was that he continued to maintain the fairly immature persona that people loved, and it frustrated me to no end. We'd spent so much time together working on his reading and writing that—while he might be a little slower than average—he could function in a textual world without much difficulty. He was a serious person too, but couldn't be bothered to correct the narrative because he was afraid of exposing his perceived weakness.

I was so proud of him and I cared about him, truly, but sometimes I'd think I'd liked him better as a fake fiancée than a real boyfriend. It was like he'd killed off my patience for his habitual nonsense with all of his expertly given orgasms and refusal to go public with the real him.

"Aye aye, captain." He jumped up and headed for the shower, completely naked, and shot me a sassy wink over his shoulder. "Join me?"

I couldn't help my reluctant smile, nor could I stop the rising blush on my cheeks. He somehow went from drooling, passed-out lump to full-on siren with "come back to bed so I can devour your sweet body" eyes in seconds. *Boo*.

"Hurry up, hotshot, or Sylvie will kill both of us."

* * * *

"Oh, you're so lucky you've got such a natural glow!" the makeup artist cooed as he shot me a wink that turned into a smirk as he subtly angled his head toward Matti, who was gesturing wildly as he made his own makeup artist throw her head back and laugh uncontrollably.

I watched as she wiped some leaky mascara from the corner of her eye. "Oh, honey, you've got to tone it down, save some for Rachel and Dean." Rachel and Dean were the popular hosts of the morning show that we were supposed to be visiting to hype the work of the Rebels with Chicago Public Schools and the youth camps.

"Oh, don't you worry about Rachel and Dean. I'm saving the best for them." He smirked right back at her and glanced over at me. "Stabby! Looking good!"

I rolled my eyes, my ire continuing to rise. Maybe it was his early morning "I take nothing seriously" antics still bothering me. Maybe it was the fact that when I'd tried to raise the idea of taking on more coaching responsibilities because I was worried about my plateauing recovery, he'd brushed me off.

Every time I'd tried to talk to him about my recovery — or lack thereof — since I'd gotten the word from my care team, he'd redirected to talk about working out together and seeing if Sylvie had set up any tryouts yet. Very much the positive thinker, he had tunnel vision when it came to doing anything but playing soccer.

Fifteen minutes later we were both made up, my hair all teased out and Matti's smoother than glass. He looked me up and down, his brow furrowing when he saw my hands crossed in front of my chest, my toes tapping in a pair of stiff new cleats. "I think you forgot something," he said as he whipped one of his ever-present hair ties off his wrist and tossed it to me. "You hate having your hair like that. Here — use this."

Dammit. That was all it took. With one casual observation acknowledging my discomfort and a toss of a frayed red elastic, I completely lost whatever minuscule grip I'd still had on my heart. The walls I kept frantically reconstructing to keep him from completely barreling in like he owned the place — like he owned *me* — crumbled. I could see how easy it would be to lose myself completely in him, even as he seemed hellbent on showing me that I owned him right back.

"Thanks," I choked out as I bent over and whipped my hair into a ballerina bun on top of my head. "Slightly better than the sloppy ponytail."

He grinned at me. "I do love that ponytail. Nice to have something to hang onto—"

Mortified, I tried to shush him with zero success and his arm descended heavily on my shoulder as he tucked me up against him. "Ah, c'mon, Abby. We're engaged, remember?"

Before I could answer, a small horde of runners called our names and whipped mics and mic packs onto us, then pushed us out onto the field of the Rebels' indoor training facility, where we would be taping a segment in support of our work with the youth camps. A few of the kids who participated were already out on the field passing balls back and forth and jumping up and down. Their excitement and nerves were palpable, and echoed by the way their parents stood on the sideline whispering to each other while clutching coffee cups from the craft services setup.

"Places, everyone," a disembodied voice hollered from behind me, and a runner pushed Matti and me over to the heavily made-up and locally famous figures of Dean Shannon and Rachel Midas. They were both shorter than I'd imagined, a few inches above me but a good eight below Matti. He theatrically crouched down to offer his hand. Dean harrumphed and turned bright red, while Rachel bit back a laugh.

"Welcome, welcome, you two, to our humble show," she said in that bright, cheery morning voice that was the alarm clock for so many sleepy Chicagoans.

"Thanks, guys, for having us. You ready to play with some balls?"

I let Matti speak for both of us. He had all the words while I contented myself with surly glares and rolled eyes.

Dean and Rachel giggled politely. "That's what the plan is," Dean hopped in. "Hope that works for you two hotshots."

"Oh sure, Abby and I feel really strongly about this program and we're excited to be involved with it."

Dean smirked. "Then this should be a walk in the park for both of you. Just follow our lead, make some jokes and, honey, stop scowling. Smile a little, show us that pretty face."

Matti frowned at him. "She's always pretty."

"Of course she is," Rachel smoothly stepped in. "She's beautiful! After our intro, we'll cut to a quick commercial break, and when we come back it will be time for you to run some drills with these adorable kids. Are there any questions?"

We both shook our heads and I raised and lowered my shoulders a few times and wiggled my jaw. I hated being on camera. And I *really* hated being told to smile.

"Don't be nervous, Abby! You've really taken the town by storm and this is meant to be light-hearted fun — so, don't be afraid to ham it up for the cameras." She winked at us and Matti, like it was an uncontrollable response, winked back. I huffed out a breath and rolled my eyes again.

"Places, everyone, final marks. We're going live in five — four — three — two — one!"

"Good morning, Chicago! I'm Rachel Midas with Dean Shannon and we're here today with two superstar athletes who are excited to share the work that they've done with the Rebels' Little Flames camps!" She gave Dean a playful smile as she handed over the narration.

"That's right, Rachel. Looking forward to seeing what these kids can do shortly, but first. Matthias and Abby, welcome to the show."

"Thanks, Dean, Rachel. We're happy to be here — we're both big fans of the show, right, Abby?" He nudged me.

"Right, Matti. Huge fans. The biggest." I grinned and felt a cool breeze on my teeth as my mouth stretched wide. "We also get to talk about something near and dear to my heart, so I'm pumped." I'd never felt less pumped in my life. Nor had I ever used that word un-ironically.

"So, Matthias, let's start with you. Tough loss last week against Dallas."

"It was, Rachel, it really was. But we did our best and that's what counts."

"You had a nice run there, too, didn't you? Tell us what that's like."

"I mean, I'm a defender, right? A protector. I happened to be in the right spot when Dallas' striker came down the field."

"A clean tackle though, that was well-done."

"Thanks, Rachel."

The awkwardness was choking me as Dean cleared his throat. "Abby, tell us what you've been up to here in our great city. We love the social media of you two out and about exploring the town."

"Yeah, we're really getting into the Chicago vibe. I'm helping Matti and the Rebels out with their youth camps and also recently started assistant coaching the midfielders at Northwestern, which is where I went to school for sports management." That was good, right? I definitely sounded a little stiff, but nothing too terrible. I frantically combed through my brain to come up with some sort of funny anecdote.

"That's not all she's doing," Matti chimed in. "It's great that she's helping out with the coaching and camps and stuff, but she's really here to rehab after a knee injury and prep for her comeback, right, Abby?"

"Oh, is that right? When do you think you'll be back?" asked Rachel, leaning forward and tapping my hand.

"I mean, sure, I'm training, but I'm not sure when —"

"She'll be ready by the summer." Matti shouldered in again and my cheeks started to burn.

"This is fantastic. Can't wait to hear more about the comeback, but we need to take a quick break and then talk some more about these camps!"

Matti and I flashed uncomfortable smiles as Dean deftly took the attention off of us.

"And…we're out."

"Phew, you two are adorable with the way you finish each other's sentences and support each other!" Rachel grinned at us and went over to join Dean by the camera crew.

"Stabby, I'm sorry. I shouldn't have interrupted you," Matti said quietly once we were alone.

"You shouldn't have, but that is so you — you act, don't think!"

"Hey, that's not completely fair," he protested.

"Feels that way to me sometimes. Why can't you support me when I talk about the camps and coaching? I love it, it's not all about playing." I crossed my arms across my chest and could feel my heart rate rocket against my forearm.

"Because you're a player, not a coach! You're only twenty-eight, not ready to retire. Come on, Abby." He shot me a disappointed grimace, the corners of his mouth turned down and that damn little crease that only formed when he was exceptionally frustrated or stressed making an appearance.

I was fuming quietly. He was so earnest and I knew his intentions were good, but this bullheaded stubbornness was annoying.

"Trouble in paradise?" Dean interrupted us with a leer and, when we shook our heads, he laughed. "Sure, kids, sure. I know a lovers' spat when I see one."

"Back off, dude. We're fine," Matti snapped at him as he wrapped an arm around me protectively.

"And we're back in five, four, three, two, one!" shouted the producer as Rachel hustled over to us, arriving at her spot in time for "one."

"Hey, sports fans, I hope you're ready for this. I think it's time to see what our pro athletes are up to aside from scoring on the field," Rachel enthused, seemingly unaware of how dirty that sounded.

Matti picked up on it and I elbowed him in the ribs as I saw his mouth open to make a smart-ass remark. His jaw shut with a snap and he gave me a wide-eyed "who me?" innocent look.

We walked over to where the kids were playing and Matti started running them through a few drills while I continued the conversation about the camps with Rachel and Dean, talking about the scholarship programs the Rebels were supporting along with the ESL and basic literacy work that we'd started this year. I knew Matti didn't want to go public with his own issues, but we really wouldn't have gone in this direction if it weren't for him. We cut to a break and I handed over the mic pack so I could help with the final drill—a scrimmage, where Matti and I would "captain" each of the teams.

I joined Matti by the kids and held up a hand. "Who's ready for a scrimmage?"

"We are!" they screamed in chorus. "And we're gonna kick your butts."

Matti counted them off, then he and I each took a side to play against each other. The trash talking between the two of us began immediately and I could only thank whatever providential messenger had nudged me to get rid of our mic packs before we started. The kids caught every other insult and were rolling on the ground as it devolved into the two of us playing off each other. It ended with a dirty tackle on my end as I shoved grass and dirt down his shirt. The kids dogpiled on top of us.

"Matthias? Abby? We really should get back to—" Rachel tried to capture our attention, but Matti held up a hand like a boss to cut her off. He'd risen up on his forearms to hold the weight of all the squirming, giggling children off of me.

"Kids? Time to get off!" one of the parents shouted from the sideline and, with a chorus of "*awws,*" the weight above us started to release.

"You okay there?" he asked, and his voice was husky with concern as he swiped at a clod of grass hanging from his ear. "This would be a lousy place to reinjure yourself."

"Oh, I'm fine, sweet pea." I grinned up at him, both of us now pink-cheeked, covered in dirt and grass stains. "Come here. You've got a little something right—"

Matti obliged and drew closer and I could see the lighter striations of gold and gray in his baby-blue eyes warm up as our bodies came into contact.

"—here!" I shouted as I rubbed another clod of turf directly in his face. He shot off me and started pawing at his face disgustedly.

I rolled over onto my back, laughing uncontrollably. Tears leaking out of my eyes messed up the carefully applied makeup.

"Hmm, that was quite the experience, Rachel, wouldn't you say?" Dean's dry observation cut through.

Matti crawled back over and collapsed next to me. He pulled me over to his lap for a kiss. "Think Sylvie will be pissed or love this?"

I frowned as I drew back, wiping my mouth with my hand. All of a sudden this wasn't funny anymore. The kisses weren't going to make up for it and I'd gotten sucked into his bright supernova personality again. Everything was fun as hell in that place, but here we were on a field, covered in dirt, when all we were supposed to have done was act cute and talk up the camps. The kids and parents on the sidelines were whooping it up and cheering us on—at least a few people were enjoying themselves.

Rachel and Dean appeared in front of us, a camera guy with a shoulder cam right behind him to catch the closing shot. "You two about done?" Dean asked.

Our eyes met and I could tell he was struggling not to laugh. I started to apologize, but Matti laughed and held out a hand for Dean to haul him up, then he returned the favor for me.

"Whew, you two." Rachel mock fanned herself. "Is everything this fun with you?"

"Oh, we're a barrel of laughs all the time." I was sweetly sarcastic. "You should see us battle over the remote." Matti eyed me with a heated stare, remembering the last time we'd tried — and gotten distracted from — watching a movie. "Thanks so much for having us."

Matti held out a filthy paw and waved at the camera genially. "Yeah, thanks. We should really do this again sometime."

"And that's a wrap!" came the disembodied voice of the show runner.

"Oh my god." I turned on a heel and stalked off the field with as much dignity as I could. Behind me I could hear Matti continuing to chitchat with Rachel and Dean for a few minutes, smoothing everything over and saying how much the kids and the two of us had enjoyed ourselves.

"Abby, wait!" He caught up to me in the green room, where I'd pulled off my cleats and pitched them into the corner.

"I don't want to hear it," I grumbled. "Give me my jacket and let's get out of here."

"Stabby, wait. Are you...mad? At me?" He tossed my jacket and it landed directly on my head.

"Yes!" My shout was muffled by the million layers of down. I pulled it off and thrust my arms into it then held them up to Matti. "I hate looking like an immature brat and this was supposed to be about the kids."

"The kids had fun today. I heard you talking up the camps and you did a great job. I wanted to make things a little more fun," he said as he swooped me up like a bride. "Sorry if I took it too far. You can bitch at me all you want on the way home, but both of us know that

that was way more fun than it would have been otherwise."

He smirked like the smug bastard he pretended to be all the time and, once more, the line between my Matti and everyone else's was blurred. I sighed and nestled my head in the crook of his jaw.

"Fine, take me home and get me cleaned up. But you've got to stop interrupting me. Take this kind of stuff seriously, too. I mean it. I was really pissed off there."

"Yeah, yeah, I know and I'm sorry. I shouldn't have interrupted you like that." He ground his chin into the top of my head until I shrieked and punched him. "Seriously, sorry." His strides matched the steady thump of his heart as he easily took the steps out to the parking garage by twos. "C'mon. Let's get you fixed up."

I went along with him, but the disquieting feelings of frustration from this morning kept getting bigger. How could he not listen to me, interrupt and correct me publicly like that and think that a fast "sorry" would fix everything?

He was refusing to see what I was trying to shove in front of his face. I was done playing and scared about that fact. I needed him to support the version of me that I was slowly becoming—no longer a player but someone else. And I needed him to find his way to making his public persona the one that I saw—we couldn't work if only one of us was willing to grow up.

We weren't the same people who'd entered this agreement back in July, and we weren't even the same people who'd said that we wanted this to be a real relationship for the first time not even a month ago.

Things had changed, and I needed him to acknowledge that.

Chapter Twenty

Matti

Even though we'd been home for more than a week, we were still moving on vacation time and were late, late, late for a fundraiser for our youth camps. All Rebels team members and their families were required to be in attendance, all dressed to the nines. Even those who rarely bothered to show up at the camps would be there under orders of management to "*support the cause, look nice and not raise hell.*"

Abby kept me waiting, impatiently, while she finalized her makeup for the evening. I sat at the island texting my brothers on our new group chat that Abby had initiated for me back in Mexico after a few too many shots of tequila had rendered me incapable of saying no when she'd demanded my phone and texted my brothers saying we were family, dammit, and needed to start communicating like one.

On the chat, Markus was moaning about Alina's morning sickness and Max was screwing with him by sending GIFs of people puking. It may have taken me ten times as long as it would have anyone else, but I managed to answer Markus' frantic attempts to change the subject by telling them about the crap weather here, how bad I wanted to be on the beach still and how little I liked being stuffed into a tux for fundraisers. My few sentences stopped the ribbing dead and both immediately congratulated me for *"using my words,"* then it was back to giving Markus more crap.

A faint scent of the tropics and the clipped sound of stilettos on our polished hardwood floors pulled me out of the perfect GIF search and my jaw dropped as Abby strode into the room, her long athlete legs eating up the space between us. She was wearing a floor-length, clingy gold dress with little cap sleeves. The narrow column accentuated the smooth curves of her compact body, draped just so over her ass so that I couldn't stop myself from smacking it as she pushed past me. The sound echoed as my hand popped off those tight muscles. She pulled a coat off the hook by the door, swirled it around her shoulders and spun to face me. "You like?" she asked with a crooked grin and motioned to me to push my mouth closed.

I nodded and managed to croak out, "Very nice, Stabby. The kids will love it."

She rolled her eyes at me. "You look very handsome too. Come here and let me tie your tie."

I adjusted myself as subtly as I could, but she still caught me and pinked up delightfully as I moved into her space. She quickly whipped the tie into shape and paused with her hands on the lapels of my tuxedo coat then, quick as a bird, she rose up on her tiptoes and gave me a peck on the lips. "Very handsome."

She settled on her heels and stepped away slowly. I caught her by the hand and pulled her back toward me. We stood there for a moment and I could hear the hum of the heating vents kick on, the smell of her hair and my aftershave mingling together as I inhaled deeply. It was a sensory memory that would be locked away in my heart.

"Time to go," she said softly as she took a half step back.

"Mmhmm, maybe we could be late," I offered as I tried ineffectively to reclaim her in an embrace.

She smacked me in the chest and winked at me. "Nope, let's go. I promise I'll make it worthwhile later."

I grinned. Abby always kept her promises.

* * * *

"You shouldn't have done that!" Abby's frazzled laugh cut through the crowd as she wound her way through all of the rich fucks we were hoping would empty their wallets for the cause.

I moved away from the group of advertising bros who'd cornered me with an apologetic shrug and turned to her. There were two bright red spots high on her cheekbones, maybe from the champagne, maybe from embarrassment. "Shouldn't have done what, Stabby?"

She hissed at me. "Don't call me that in public, weirdo! Shouldn't have—"

"Told everyone the truth? That the camps and I would be a mess if it weren't for you and all of the work you do that no one pays you for or recognizes?" I asked with the half-smirk I knew drove her wild.

She punched me and I dodged her fist. "That! Exactly that," she mumbled as I caught her around the waist and hugged her tightly. "It's embarrassing."

"Like I give a fuck. Not to mention all of this talk about doing stuff in public is getting to me."

"But I care," she tried to claim as she switched from batting at me with her little hands to biting me since I wasn't letting go.

"Mmm, Abby. We're sort of in the middle of people right now." People had their phones out and I grinned down at her. She scowled, so ferocious, before finally laughing. I tapped her nose. "Let's get out of here."

Abby made a show of trying to bite my finger again and wriggled out of my arms and started for the door, her usual long strides hampered by the tightness of her dress. I could see her hands flexing at her sides like she was itching to hitch it up so she could run. The sultry, "come get me, asshole" look she shot over her shoulder went straight to my dick and I took off after her.

"Thank you for being there for me tonight. I needed you." She wrapped herself around me like a python as we descended the elevator to the parking garage.

"You're grateful for me?"

"Mmhmm, I need you. And I'm gonna show how bad you as soon as we're out of camera sight," she whispered in a sultry voice with a nod up to the little lens in the corner.

We barely made it to the backseat of our SUV before her dress was torn off and thrown to the floor. My pants dropped to join it and she was on my lap, grinding her wet pussy up and down my hard cock, which was pressed up against my stomach as I lay back across the long bench seat. Every few swipes she'd teasingly drop a half inch onto my cock, and I begged her to fuck me. Luckily our car was in a dark corner spot in the parking garage of the fundraiser's hotel.

"Mmm-mmm, no, how do you ask, Matti?" she murmured with a smirk as she slowed the grind, grabbed my wrists and held them over my head.

"Fucking hell, Abby, let me inside you." I begged and thrashed, but she had a tight hold of my wrists and was applying the perfect amount of pressure to the ulna nerve to keep me still as she teased me.

"If I let go of one of your hands, will you keep it there?" she asked, and at my frantic nod, she let go and held my cock away from my body so she could slowly slide down it. We both moaned as I bottomed out inside her and I shuddered as I watched a drop of sweat bead up on her upper lip.

"So big, you're so big and it gets better every time." Her eyes rolled back in her head and her inner muscles clenched around me like an iron fist in a tight velvet glove. "Grab the door handle," she ordered as she started to raise herself up on her knees above me.

"Yes, ma'am," I said, and my voice was hoarse as I tried to encourage her to move faster. "You like this, huh, Abby? Being in charge."

She nodded and canted her hips forward a little, dropping her hands to press against my thighs. They slid and caught on the fine hairs, the sheen of sweat we'd started to work up changing the friction between us.

I managed to grunt out another line of dirty talk that I knew would tip her over the edge of control. "Take over, baby, use me to get off. I need to see you come."

Her eyes went from lit up to sparking furnaces as she beamed at me. "Ask and you shall receive. Anything I say, you'll do?"

"Anything," I murmured and bucked up slightly in counterpoint to the slow rhythm she set above me. The anticipation was killing me and I felt like I could barely breathe.

"Excellent, keep holding on. I want you as still as possible."

Fuck.

She rose up and spun around until she was facing the other way and grabbed that side of the car's "oh shit" handle to steady herself as she began to speed her movements up and down. Every downstroke her pussy clenched around me, and it felt like I was going deeper into her than I'd ever been before. I still wasn't used to being bare in a woman and the feel of our supersensitized skin gliding together was an unbearable friction.

"You can let go now. Fuck me harder."

Faster than lightning striking a weathervane I had my hands gripping her hips, raising and lowering her over me. "So close, Abby, so close. Come for me." I'd barely finished speaking when she began to wail my name as she came harder than I'd ever seen her come before. Somehow she managed to reach down to my balls and pull them tightly as I ground into her on the last stroke and it was my turn, her pleasure giving me my pleasure.

We untangled ourselves and slouched our sweaty bodies on the cool leather of the seat. She rubbed a damp strand of her hair off of her face and peered up at me. Her cheeks were bright red and her eyes glowed like hot coals, the fire between us barely banked. "I love that we're so good at that."

"Me too. Let's get home and do it again, yeah? I think I still owe you one for embarrassing you earlier."

"Mmmhmm, clothes first." She smiled wickedly as she tossed me my pants and rolled her dress on. Proper motivation, I was finding, was the key to success.

Chapter Twenty-One

Matti

Like clockwork, Abby rolled out of bed the day after the fundraiser and silenced her alarm. No snoozing for my girl, and she bounced from the bed straight into the shower. I'd never lived with a morning person before and it was absolutely atrocious. But she was changing me, and I struggled out of our warm cocoon to stumble into the kitchen and get coffee brewing for her to take to the office.

Divvying up the morning jobs had happened effortlessly and I marveled again at myself — half-asleep and hungover, but so tweaked about a girl that I was up at six in the morning after going to bed at two to make her coffee before work.

My cup burned my hands as I cradled it while inhaling the bittersweet smell that steamed from the white cafeteria-style mug. A text flashed across my screen and I set down my coffee to reach for my phone, but Abby's whirlwind arrival distracted me as she sprinted down the hall. "Late again, I'm so damned late!" she muttered, clearly furious with herself.

I'd learned months ago to let her rage in the morning. Early bird she might be, but she was also a royal bitch before her first caffeine hit of the day. I nudged her full travel mug over to her as she slammed open cupboards looking for it. "It's full," I said as I tossed a granola bar at her back, where it smacked right between her shoulder blades.

"Bless you," she murmured as she tore open the packaging with her teeth. She shoved half the bar in her face and gulped coffee to rinse it down.

"How are you usually so refined, yet manage to eat like a feral animal in the morning?"

The middle finger she jabbed into the air in my general direction was answer enough as she took another sip of coffee, wincing at the burn.

"Sleep well? I certainly did. Very well and very satisfied."

She blushed bright red. "You are such a turd sometimes, Shellenberg. Stop winding me up."

"Mmhmm, think of me when you're working like a busy beaver all day. Sitting here all alone, dreaming of ways to wind you up." I took a sip of my own coffee and considered exactly how pissed off it would make her if I could convince her to be really, really late today.

Her blush intensified somehow. "You are a very bad influence."

"So you've said." I took another sip and smiled at her. "But you love it."

She shook her head at me, full lips pressed together in a firm line, and I couldn't tell if she wanted to smack me or kiss me. I wondered if *she* even knew.

We leaned against our respective counter spaces and continued to sip our coffee. "I'll be home around four," she offered.

"Good, I'll be here. Cook dinner tonight?"

"Definitely, you pick the recipe and text me the ingredients. I'll pick up anything we don't have on the way home." Her phone buzzed with an event reminder. "Crap! I really have to go."

I watched affectionately as she dithered. She either wanted to kiss me or hug me, but she was wary that I was going to keep messing with her. "*Winding her up*," as she liked to say. Putting her out of her misery, I reached over to squeeze her in a fast embrace and kissed the top of her head. I managed to swipe my phone from the counter as I tore myself away from her and headed back to the bedroom.

"See you tonight." Her regretful sigh lingered behind me as she left.

Back in the bedroom, I set my mug on the nightstand and flopped back onto the messy bed. The linen sheets were still all soft and warm, a faint scent of us hovering above them and wrapping around me. Home, security, Abby, love. It was all there, all falling into place. I had dreamed about her for a long-ass time, far longer than I'd ever waited before making a move in the past. She scared the fuck out of me, but she'd said she was in this for me, for real, and I was going to hold her to it.

I buried my nose in her pillow and inhaled, groaning slightly as I flashed back to the way she'd owned me last night. That look in her eyes, both playful and proud of the control she'd held over me, the reactions she could coax from me. My pleasure in her very capable hands and the trust that had blazed from her eyes as she'd nodded to turn control over to me, the switch happening in a blink of an eye as I'd flipped her on her back and plowed into her.

My phone buzzed again, reminding me of the message that I'd ignored while fixing my lady's coffee. I scanned through the short message, nothing but a command from Sylvie to call her when I got my sorry ass out of bed. For that she could wait, and I settled back into the pillows for a quick, one-handed trip down memory lane.

* * * *

I called Sylvie back about an hour later as I finished scrambling eggs and pulled bacon out of the oven. Sometimes I took the command to treat myself a little too far and I knew my workout later that morning was going to be rough.

"Matthias." Her voice grated on my still slightly hungover brain.

"Sylvie, what's happening?" I slid the food onto a plate and headed over to the island where the jar of Mexican hot sauce, a glass of orange juice and another mug of coffee awaited.

"A Premier League team wants you back in the U.K., playing for them next week. What do you think?"

I choked and the hot sauce I'd liberally poured over my eggs went straight up my nose, searing my sinuses.

"Matthias?" she asked, sounding vaguely impatient.

"Yep," I croaked. "Hang on." I blew my nose inelegantly into a napkin. "Okay, say that again?"

"A Premier League team — Tottenham — wants to pick you up for an absolutely obscene amount of money. They want you ready to start for them next week. Apparently there was an injury and Dierckson is out." Lars Dierckson was a Swedish defender who'd made a name for himself over the last few years, following in my footsteps. We both played the same position, but he had taken on my party boy mantle and lowered the bar on whatever was considered socially acceptable. I despised him.

"They want me to replace Dierckson?"

"Yes. A defender for a defender." She sighed. "And there's more. Somehow they think that this whole 'good guy in a serious relationship' cover you and Abby have very convincingly put together is fake. In their words, they want the 'real you' back."

I could imagine the air quotes and my hackles started to rise.

"It's a huge contract, Matti, absolutely huge — enough to retire on even if you only play one more season — "

"Sylvie, it isn't fake," I cut in.

"What's not fake?"

"Us, me and Abby. I mean, we're not, like, really engaged or anything, but we're definitely a couple."

Sylvie snorted in derision. "Dating with your grandmother's ring on her finger? You kids are fucking adorable."

"Hey — "

"I get it, Matti. But the thing with Tottenham is, they don't give a shit about your personal life. They want you back in the Premier League and they will actually pay you extra to go out and make a scene. They've lost more than a defender with Dierckson injured, they've lost their main headline generator and a fan favorite."

"Sylvie, I'm not that guy anymore," I tried to tell her.

"I know, you're very mature now, Matthias." She snorted again.

"Come on, Sylvie. That's bullshit."

"I know, sorry. I'm not used to you being so amenable, I guess. So, what do you think?"

"What about Abby?"

"What about Abby? I don't understand."

"What will she do over there? Assuming she wants to go, that is."

"Um, you're not kidding, are you? The two of you are really together?" Sylvie asked slowly, as if I were three and had miraculously delivered a Shakespearean soliloquy.

"You know we are, and I know she's told you that too." My irritated tone left no room for argument and she hummed in response.

"Yes, yes, she did and you're right, having her over there would be great for exposure. If — I mean, *when* — she comes back, it will be good to have her right there for a tryout. I do still have a few lines out for her and there's been some interest that hasn't gone beyond initial conversations," Sylvie said thoughtfully. "But does she want to leave? I mean, she's building a life in Chicago too. Every time I've chatted with her lately, she's been a bit hesitant. I'd assumed you two would be long distance."

"She will, if I'm going." We were a team. We supported each other. "Maybe not right away, I know she's really wrapped up in coaching and the camps. Plus her med team is here."

"Okay, how about I push the teams I've been chatting with about her? Let them know she's on her way back and looking for a home?"

"That would be great, but you should probably talk to her first. Make sure she's even interested in playing for those particular teams when she's ready for her comeback."

"Of course, of course. You're in, then?" she asked, seeking that final confirmation.

I took a massive breath and felt my T-shirt tighten across my chest. "Yeah, we're in."

"To be clear, kiddo" — her voice was affectionate finally — "you're single, as far as they know. They're expecting your previous antics to give them an attention boost. Ironic, no?"

"Sylvie, there's no way I'm going back to that bullshit image. Abby would kill me and I don't know if it's even something I can — "

"No buts, it's part of the package. Sorry, but if you can fake being engaged, I'm pretty sure you can fake being single for a bit. Don't worry about it."

At that moment, I felt much more than a small bit of foreboding about what Abby would think if we had to fake a break-up and me being single.

"Sylvie, really, promise me you'll try — "

"All right, Matthias, I've got to run. I'm about to hop on a plane to Chicago. Will get in touch with a few teams for Ms. Abigail Jane and a contract from Tottenham for us to review. I'll try to get the party boy clause cut out. Toodles."

Click!

She'd hung up on me.

I pulled up my group text with my brothers and sent out an SOS of sorts. An animated GIF of a guy lurching for a phone with blood running down his face, a shadowy stabby figure behind him.

Seconds later a FaceTime call lit up from Markus. Alina hovered behind him in the background and I could hear her saying, "Is he okay? He's not, like, really dead, is he?"

His eyebrows were at his hairline and he was a little out of breath, no shirt on as he sat on a lounge chair on his deck. "Matti? Are you all right?" He frowned as he took in the video image of me, sitting at my kitchen island, calmly sipping coffee. "You're fine. What's the deal with the SOS? Oh, wait — "

A chime and Max's dark hair and eyes filled the screen. He was also shirtless, and I could see someone behind him shrugging into a robe. My eyebrows took the opportunity to meet my hairline and Markus was actually turning into a tomato as we contemplated the fact that our very reclusive, uptight brother...had...sex.

"What?" Max's grin was positively demonic. Some rustling from his end and the video blurred as he moved around. When it cleared, he was sitting up against the wrought-iron spindles of a bed with a few pillows behind him. "You're not dead, I see."

Markus shook his head in shock.

After so many years, it was thrilling to see my oldest brother at such a total loss. Even better, having my super uptight, next oldest brother actually doing something...naughty, apparently. "Nope. Not dead. Although you... What is it the French call post-sex, Markus?"

"Le petite mort?" Markus mumbled, now trying to hide a shit-eating grin even though his cheeks were still a bit pink.

"Yeah, that. Maxi-pad, you look like you got some."

Max's grin went feral. "I don't kiss and tell."

Alina popped her head into the frame with Markus'. "Max!" she reproved him. "Oh! Sorry, I really didn't think that... Never mind." She disappeared.

"Max? I need to get going. Next week Tuesday?" an unfamiliar feminine voice with an American accent called out.

He winked at us and Markus groaned. "Same time, Char — " He clearly tapped the mute button as he kept talking. Finally he came back to us and tapped his phone again. "So, what's the big emergency?" he asked, suddenly all business.

"You sure we can't talk about this 'Char' anymore?" I asked innocently.

"No, the matter is closed," he clipped out.

"Great, fine. Next Tuesday maybe?"

Max's eyes threatened to shoot sparks and Markus snorted. "Give him a break, Matti. Tell us what's going on."

"Fine, fine. You guys aren't any fun. The thing is, a team in London called Sylvie and they want me. Quite soon, actually. Like, next week. They have an injury and are willing to buy out my contract here, then pay me an obscene amount of money to move back."

"Wow, Matti, that's great!" Markus was definitely more excited, Max's brow furrowed in thought.

"What's the catch?" asked my middle brother, the genius businessman.

"They want the *'real me'*, not this fake guy in a fake engagement," I said with a sigh.

Markus reared back like someone had slapped him. "But this is the real you, the real you *now*. Right?"

Max nodded to himself and frowned. "Of course it is, but they want the Matthias Shellenberg spectacle. The circus."

"Yeah, that. They want the circus."

"What about Abby?" both my brothers said at the same time, and I started laughing.

"What about her? I mean, she'll back me, it's a great opportunity — even if they're not going to get the circus they expect."

"Idiot. Will she go with you?" Markus sounded concerned.

I could hear Alina in the background again. "He's not breaking up with her, is he? I loved her and I still need to get her number!"

Markus shooed her away and rolled her eyes at us. He dropped his voice. "Text me her number after this, will you? I keep forgetting to ask."

Max started laughing and made a whip cracking sound.

"Sure, sure. Seriously, what do you guys think?" I started to gnaw on my thumbnail and jog my knee up and down.

"You take it," said Max immediately. "Take it, amend the contract to get rid of that spectacle bullshit and get the money."

"Talk to Abby," sad Markus, almost at the same time. "Figure it out together."

"She knows how big of a deal this would be for me. She'll back me. She gets me."

"Then it sounds like you made your decision, didn't you?" Markus still seemed a little disturbed. "But I don't think you should automatically assume that she's going to be happy about this."

"She'll be fine, Matti can handle her," said Max with his slow, dismissive drawl. "I need to go, guys. Have a dinner to get to." He clicked off as Markus and I said goodbye. Then it was the two of us staring at each other.

"Did you ever think you'd see Max immediately post-coitus?" asked Markus. He shuddered.

"Nope, I honestly thought he was asexual." I was highly amused. "Did you notice the rope on the bed frame?"

"What? No! What are you talking about?"

"Rope," I said patiently. "Actually, it looked more like a ribbon, maybe a scarf. Looks like our brother is into a little bondage. I didn't notice any red marks on his wrists, so I'm guessing he likes to be in charge—"

"Matti, that's the last thing I need to think about," Markus cut me off and his face turned a pale green.

"Same."

We were silent for a moment, contemplating our brother's heretofore unknown sex life.

I shook myself out of a very disturbing reverie. "Thanks for the time and advice, Markus."

"Don't forget to talk to Abby. Leave it open, okay? It's a discussion, not an automatic yes," he reminded me.

"Yup, totally." I winked and clicked out. I felt lighter after talking to them and started thumbing through my recipe app, humming as I clicked on a new vegetarian entree and sent the ingredients over to Abby with a tap. I had to get running for practice, but I made a note in my calendar to pick up something special for dessert to celebrate the new contract and our move.

Chapter Twenty-Two

Abby

The day after the fundraiser, I'd barely settled into my workspace at the office for the Rebels' philanthropy organization when a message pinged my inbox from Coach Williams. He'd been harassing me for weeks about making a more significant commitment to the Northwestern teams, but this email laid it out in stark terms. A salary, benefits, full-time, well-paid work — more than I'd made at Chelsea. To be a coach, though, not a player. It was too much and not enough at the same time. I didn't know if anything would ever be able to compensate me for giving up the one dream that had been wholly mine.

I stood up from my desk after shutting out of my inbox with a hard poke to the trackpad and went to the window where I could see the lovely blank façade of the cinder block and brick building next to the office. My phone buzzed back on my desk and I wanted to scream that everyone needed to leave me alone, but I knew that it was probably Sylvie with instructions for another event or something.

More singing and dancing from the oh-so-entertaining Abby and Matti show—only everyone called it the Matti and Abby show. Fuck that. Or maybe she wanted to float another team by me for my inevitable comeback. She and Matti both had selective listening every time I said, *"No, I'm not interested in meeting with a new team right now."*

"Sylvie, we're not doing another event for at least a week and, yes, Matti's schedule is now fixed for the next ten days. No, I'm not interested in talking to a new team right now. Back off."

"Abby McKinnon?" an unfamiliar voice asked hesitantly.

"Oops, I'm so sorry! Yes, this is Abby."

"Please hold for Doctor Warner."

"Um, okay? How long will I be—" Tinkly piano music came from the speakers as the woman took me literally at my word. I quickly paired my headphones, jammed them in my ears and set my phone aside while I turned back to my laptop to review a proposal that Matti's teacher, Tiana, had sent over to add a new tutoring component to our camps.

Had to hand it to her, she did *not* want to give up. Matti was going to hit the roof. I got his fears about people finding out, but it seemed like he'd come so far. It would be a great thing to take this one additional step and I didn't totally understand how he wouldn't want to support this for the kids. Tiana wanted to use his name, face, everything, to further her cause, and I didn't know which horse I backed more in this race. But, maybe it wasn't my race and I should bow out.

"Abby?" a man's voice cracked in as the piano abruptly cut off.

"Yes? Doctor Warner, I presume?"

"Yes, that's right. Great to finally connect with you, Abby. I know I'm not part of your regular care team, but Doctor Mitchell has been filling me in on your progress."

"I didn't realize he could do that."

"Teaching hospital and we're on the same rounds. Listen, I'll keep this brief unless you're interested. My office is, like Mitchell's, focused on sports medicine and rehabilitation. I'm a surgeon and have been working on a new procedure for knee reconstruction. It's still considered experimental, but it has the potential to considerably improve your chances to return to playing professionally."

"I'm sorry, what?" I swear I was usually more on the ball than this.

"New procedure that could fix your knee. If you're interested and willing to participate in a clinical trial," Doctor Warner said patiently. "While results are still early, I can promise at least a sixty percent chance of bringing you back to full strength. That's sixty percent better than you're at right now, right?"

I nodded, quickly realized that he couldn't see me and muttered, "Yes, I've been told that my playing days are done."

"Well, if you're willing to join our trial, we have a sixty percent chance of changing that. The recovery will still be extensive, but you'll be no worse off than you are right now if things don't go perfectly."

I swallowed hard. A sixty percent chance of regaining everything. "I need to think about it," I said slowly.

"Can you let us know by the end of the week?" Doctor Warner sounded a little surprised.

"Sure, sure. I'll call you back." I took down the numbers he rattled off and set my phone aside.

Sixty percent chance. After an experimental procedure and what promised to be months of agonizing recovery and rehabilitation. Months on top of what I'd already invested. *Sixty percent chance.*

The numbers bounced around in my head for the remainder of the day as I wound up my office tasks, headed over to the field house to drop off some new conditioning workouts and manned the weight room for the midfielders. It was snowing when I finally left and my windshield wipers swish chunked *sixty-percent, sixty-percent* as I drove carefully to the grocery store, then to our apartment.

"Matti? I'm home," I yelled as I lurched through the door with a dozen plastic grocery bags dangling from my hands and cutting off circulation in my fingers. Balancing on my good leg, I used my right to reach back, hook around the door and, with a flick, slam it shut.

"Be right there." His faint voice came from our room. A trail of muddy gear led from our entryway down the hall.

I sighed at the mess. Maybe even yesterday I would have dropped the bags and dashed back there to tackle him onto the bed. But things had changed with one email and one phone call and I didn't even know who I was anymore, much less who I was with him. Instead, I unpacked the bags and started to put things into the pantry and refrigerator.

First the cat then the bounding footsteps of Matti flew down the short hallway until he slid the final, short distance to sweep me off my feet and dance me over to the floor-to-ceiling windows overlooking the balcony. "Stabby," he murmured as he kissed me soundly. "I missed you today."

I squirmed against him as I tried to detach myself, but every move tightened his hold on me until I gave up and kissed him back. Getting lost in our mouths moving against each other, hands starting to roam, until an unhappy chirp from my cat separated us and he set me down gently.

"Save it for later, eh?" He grinned and walked over to fill the clearly starving cat's food bowl.

"Yeah, later," I responded and tried to resettle my clothes. The bastard had somehow unhooked my bra without me noticing and I slid it through my sleeves before chucking it at him.

He stuck his tongue out and panted like a comic book dog as he kissed the cups reverently. "I've been daydreaming about this moment all day. The moment that you'd gift me with your bra after a long day at work. Thanks, baby."

"You're so ridiculous." I sighed. "Come on, let's start cooking."

"Sure," he said as he bent down to pull a cutting board from a low cupboard and I ogled his ass momentarily. "Like what you see, hmm?" He grinned up at me as he busted me and I could feel my cheeks heat up. That telltale blush that he seemed to eat up whenever he caught me.

"Again, ridiculous. You." I swatted him with a towel and leaned around him to grab a few pots off the hanging rack.

He set the iPad with the recipe between us and the two of us moved into our respective duties, him chopping everything, me measuring and assembling. "How come I never get to chop?" I complained, as I always did.

"Because your name is Stabby and I'm not giving you the opportunity to live up to it," he answered, as he always did.

I smiled, glad that some things remained the same.

"How was your day, dear?" I asked after a moment of silent chopping and measuring.

"Oh, fine. Good workout, talked to Daniel—you want to go to dinner with him and Mer this weekend, maybe?"

I hummed noncommittally.

"That's what I thought. I said I'd let him know later on in the week."

"Great, I'd like to, but I'm usually shattered by the weekend."

"I know. I love the shattering process."

I elbowed him and he shot me my favorite smirk, which faded away quickly as his forehead wrinkled.

"Something else happened today."

"Yeah?" I poured the chickpeas I'd rinsed from the colander into the pot on the stove.

"Yeah, Sylvie called."

"Oh, what does she want from us now? Tandem skydiving? Judging a dog show?"

"Ooh, I'd love all of those. But no. That's not why she called."

"Ugh, don't keep me in suspense. What happened?"

Matti took a deep breath and I glanced at him in concern. "Is it your contract?" I asked.

"Not this current one, I guess? Tottenham called her. They want me and they want me now. They'll buy out my contract from the Rebels and pay an exorbitant amount of money to get me back to the U.K. for a game next week."

My eyes bugged out. "Next week?"

"Yeah," he said quietly as he set aside his knife and came over to encircle my waist. "Next week. There's an injury and I'm needed. They also don't want anything to do with a morality clause."

"What does this mean for us?"

"If you didn't want to be with me, we could go our separate ways right now. But if we're really in this for real, which I am and I'm pretty sure you are too, we figure out how to get you over as quickly as possible. Sylvie is already in talks with a few teams for you."

"What?" I didn't know if words could express the degree of flabbergasted he made me with those two convoluted sentences.

"I mean, we're a package deal, right?" He pulled back and his eyes searched my own. "If they want me, they need to be cool with my Stabby girlfriend. You are my Stabby girlfriend, right?" His lips tightened with anxiety.

I reached over and smoothed out the little crease between his eyebrows.

"Yeah, of course, that. But I don't know about this—"

"London, Abby! Can you believe it? We get to go back!" He picked me up again and twirled me around till I was dizzy and I couldn't help laughing at his excitement. For a second. Until it really sank in. The "we" that we'd been using so regularly that it was second nature meant *me*, too.

"Hold up. I can't go anywhere right now."

"What do you mean? There are great physical therapists over there and, like I said, Sylvie says she's gonna put a few lines out to clubs who were interested in snagging you after Chelsea let you go. It's a perfect opportunity."

"If I'm *playing*, it's a perfect opportunity," I corrected him gently. "But I'm not playing."

"Right now, you're not playing, no. But you will be soon enough. Come on, Abby, come with me. Please? I need you. We're a package deal, right?"

I didn't think I'd ever seen him that vulnerable before. All of the words that we never said, punctuated in little red hearts, seemed to flood his gaze, but I could see fear starting to grow and snuff out the light. And I was going to kill that light completely. Be yet another person who pushed him away with a cheerful goodbye. "I can't come with you."

"What do you mean you can't?" His voice was dull and dangerously soft as he pushed me back a few steps, giving me space that I didn't want. I tried to step back into his proximity and he halted me with a tiny head shake.

"I can't because I can't play anymore and I want to keep building on the foundation I've laid here. Coach Williams wants me to come on full-time as an assistant coach, the camps need me, all of this is important to me."

"Am I not important to you?" His voice cracked on the "I" and I could see him starting to withdraw from me.

"No, no! Of course you're important to me, Matti! But I can't drop this new life I've been trying to build."

"I don't understand you, Abby. I seriously don't." He thrust a hand into his hair to yank out the messy bun and, with choppy motions, tied it back again. I could see his hands trembling slightly. "You're giving up? What the hell is wrong with you? You're a player, not a coach." The disdain in his voice when he said the word "coach" was sharp enough that it sliced through my chest. A direct shot to my heart.

"I mean it, Matti. I can't play anymore. My med team told me right after we got home from vacation—"

"Over a month ago? And you never said a single fucking word about that to me? How could you not tell me?"

"I've been trying to tell you for weeks, but you haven't been listening to me! This isn't about you — it's not me trying to hurt your feelings." I watched as he pushed off the counter and started to pace back and forth.

"It's a little bit about me. I mean, I've been paying for your treatment and everything, so, yeah, it's a little about me."

"Don't be a jerk. They told me I was done and I didn't want to admit it. Then, when that doctor called today and told me about the experimental surgery, I thought, maybe, and then — You know what?" I was getting angry now, throwing down the rhetorical questions. "I thought about it, and I thought about you, and I realized that playing is not my everything. Not if I don't allow it to be. And I'm not going to allow it to define me anymore. I am more than a player, just like you are more than a player."

Matti was still pacing and I joined him, both of us too kinetically wired to be still. We were two planets orbiting each other in increasingly tighter and angrier circles. "Being here with you, doing all of these new things, has helped me unlock parts of me that I never wanted to admit existed. I care about other people. I love teaching people to do new things, to accomplish things they only dreamed about. Watching you tackle your fears and insecurities has inspired me. I'm *not* just a player."

"Okay, okay. Fine, you're not only a player. I understand. A little. Can you think about it? Please? I don't want to lose you."

I could tell that while he meant it when he said that he didn't want to lose me, he didn't really understand my decision. He was ready to dismiss me again, but at least this time he could see that I was serious. That determined glint in his eye said that this was only a temporary withdrawal until he could think up an alternate argument to sway me.

"I'll think about it, Matti, but I need you to think about this too. I'm not the same person you met back in London. I've changed from the woman who made that dumb fake engagement pact—and, no, I don't regret it, because it's you and it's me and I never would have given you the chance otherwise. But you need to see that people grow and change and, in a relationship, they grow and change together or the relationship fails. Are you ready to accept my growth?"

He shrugged and nodded, dismissive gestures negating any words he could say. "Sure, fine. Promise me you'll think about this. Really. It could be a great opportunity for both of us."

I nodded and he seemed relieved, then he wrapped me up in one of his spectacular Matti hugs. "I'm sorry I yelled. I was really excited and thought you would be too."

My voice was muffled by his shirt. "I am excited for you, but I want you to consider whether this is what you actually want, or if it's what you *think* you want. Maybe it's what you wanted before we moved here and started to settle in. Maybe you've changed too."

He hummed something he probably intended to be soothing and affirming, but was obviously an avoidance tactic. I wanted to call him on it until I felt his hands still trembling as they held me, his heart rate pounding away beneath my ear. Matti was terrified and there would be no getting through to him or talking him around tonight.

"Come on." He set me down and pulled me toward the kitchen. "Let's eat and watch a movie or something." He shot me a shaky version of his usual smirk. "Don't forget the deal, Stabby. We've got to bang this out—no going to bed angry."

"Yeah, yeah," I said and tried to muster a smile as he ushered me to the table and headed to the kitchen to serve us.

It felt like I was watching him leave me behind and it was a weird premonition. This was the start of the end, I knew it. It was all so clear. He'd never accept my changing until he accepted his own evolution and owned the reasons behind the changes he'd recently made. This wasn't going to go away and I didn't think it was something we could bang out of our systems. He didn't want me to be anything other than the simplest, easiest version of me to complement his exhausting life. And I wasn't that person any longer.

Chapter Twenty-Three

Abby

The next morning I woke before my alarm and struggled out of the nest of Matti's suffocating snuggles. I showered, made my own coffee for once and slipped out the door before he woke up. Space was what I needed — from his puppy-dog eyes and the raw physicality that drew me in and tied me up in knots. The ability he had to persuade me to do things his way, forgetting what was my own path.

It was a Northwestern day, which meant that I got to travel north instead of south. A far easier morning commute on Lake Shore Drive — all those suckers going downtown could kiss my ass. I parked in the parking garage nearest the field house and navigated the crowds of very tall kids in purple, their lanyards jingling from their monogrammed backpacks and equipment duffels.

The swimming and basketball teams were currently feuding and things were taking a turn for the weird as the swim team broke into an a cappella song and dance number while the men's basketball team catcalled them. The tall forest of dudes seemed to vibrate with the need to sweep in and take over. *How sweet.* The crowd around them held up phones and I ducked to avoid everyone.

The utilitarian office I shared with Steph was quiet, her little row of succulents that formed a barrier between her and any visitors at the front of her spartan desk the only bit of color in the grayish-beige interior. The fluorescent lights above flickered and I made a note that we needed replacements, if we could get on the facilities schedule—I hadn't figured out yet why that was such an impossible mission. Academic bureaucracy was a real pain in the ass.

Steph arrived a few minutes after me and I pretty much attacked her. Told her about the experimental treatment option and Coach Williams' offer.

"So you didn't turn either of them down, then?" she asked, her mouth puckering like she'd bitten a sour grape.

I shrugged. "Nope, I didn't want to rule anything out."

"But you didn't accept either. I would have thought that you'd jump all over that surgeon and tell Williams to shove it."

"Me from a month ago would have agreed with you. Things are different now."

"Ooh, is this because of that beautiful man back at your house?" she teased and it stung, really stung.

"No! Why does everything have to be about him?"

"Whoa, I'm sorry. Point taken. It's not about him." She reached out and grabbed my hand. "Seriously, I'm sorry."

I sighed. "I mean, it's not him, completely. It's *us*. Before we were a thing, all I wanted was soccer — to play, to be the best, to win. Maybe it's the injury, this move here, working with everyone to coach and teach, what being in this relationship has taught me, but I'm not the same person. Not as single-minded. I want more in my life than perpetual grass stains, aching joints, athlete's foot and the taste of blood in my mouth."

"I get it," Steph said softly. "I do. I started down this road because I had to, but now I'm so grateful that I did and wish that I could have made the decision on my own without feeling like there were no other options. This is what I was meant to do."

"You've inspired me, you know?"

She did an exaggerated, shocked, finger to her chest move with an unnecessary campy flourish.

"Yeah, you." I rolled my eyes and laughed. "I'm not the most open-minded person in the world. I have tunnel vision and never considered not playing. It was like there were life or death stakes on it and, between you and Matti, I've realized that it's just a game. A beautiful game, yeah, but not the only one — and there are millions of ways to have it in my life besides playing it."

Steph's eyes were watering suspiciously and she quickly wiped a hand across her brow. "Fucking allergies in here," she muttered and launched herself at me. "You're going to be great, Abby. The greatest, whatever you end up doing."

I peeled myself away from her overexuberant hug and sighed. "I hope so, but I'm worried."

"I know. It's nerve-wracking making such a big change, but you've got this." She rubbed my shoulders briskly.

"No, no, I'm fine with the decision itself, but I'm worried because Matti was offered a contract to move back to England and play for Tottenham. They want him next week." I plopped back into my desk chair and put my head in my hands.

She sat down heavily too. "Wow. Does he want to go without you?"

I fiddled with a pen and muttered, "Um, no. Not exactly. He expects me to pick up and move with him because we're together, and I don't feel ready to. I'm building something here."

"Eek. For real?" Her face was skeptical.

"Yeah, he was so damn excited yesterday when he told me, and when I didn't immediately jump on it, he got pissed. Like I never support him or something." I was starting to recover my anger and rant.

"Yuck. What are you going to do?"

I sighed. What was I *ever* going to do with Matti Shellenberg? That was the operative question that had been nagging me for months. "I don't know. It's a good question."

"Keep me posted." She threw a wadded-up tissue at me and it dropped softly to the floor between us, unable to make its expected trajectory.

We both went heads down for the next few hours until lunch when I had to go over to the hospital to meet with my medical team. I'd requested a meeting to discuss the surgery option with as many people as could make it. While I was already pretty sure what my answer would be, I still wanted to get their input.

Doctor Mitchell, Angie and the other members of the team who I'd worked with sat around a table in a small conference room that smelled like burned coffee and burritos. My eyes watered.

"Sorry about the smell, Taco Tuesday meets office coffee disaster."

"Oh, it's fine," I managed to choke out.

Doctor Mitchell grinned and held out a hand for me to shake. "Abby, good to see you. You wanted to talk about Doctor Warner's surgery?"

I nodded and pulled my collar up over my nose, I didn't care how juvenile I appeared. This was foul.

"As he probably explained, it's a new technique that he's pioneered. Interesting, but with mixed results." He pulled up a PowerPoint presentation and indecipherable charts and graphs swam across the screen. My eyes glazed over. "There've been twenty-eight individuals who've gone through the surgery and post-surgery recovery period. Most of the candidates are younger, high school and college-aged. That said, they were in your exact position with regards to where their progress plateaued. Sixty percent of them have recovered fully and gone on to continue to play at previous levels—you can see here playing time, their stats, mobility results, etc."

I nodded, still not completely sure what he was pointing to. "But what about the forty percent who were not helped?"

"Those individuals were no worse off, but they still had to invest the same amount of time to recover and rehab to get back to the exact same place they were at before the surgery."

"So they lost time?"

"Yes, exactly. They lost time, to the tune of six to eight months."

Angie jumped in. "Lost time and additionally went through extensive mental and physical counseling. You can imagine the rollercoaster of hope these individuals were on."

"That's what I'm most worried about," I confessed as my fingers knotted into a cat's cradle pattern in my lap.

"It's definitely something you should consider," Doctor Mitchell allowed. "I'm not going to advise you either way. All I can do is present the data from the trial where it currently stands."

I glanced at Angie. "What would you advise?"

Angie glanced over at Doctor Mitchell, who nodded encouragingly at her. "It's up to you, Abby. For me personally, I don't know that sixty percent is compelling enough. I would wait and see how the trial plays out for a little longer. If the ages were more widely distributed and we could break the data down by that demographic, I'd be more encouraging. A twenty-eight-year-old knee joint is different than a sixteen-year-old, or even twenty-two-year-old, joint, when it's been as heavily used as yours."

My fingers were knotted in the fringe of my scarf that still hung like an itchy snake around my neck. If Matti had been there, he would have grabbed my hand, massaged my fingers, told me to take the surgery. It was a chance and any amount of pain would be worth me being able to do what I was meant to do. I shook my head, dismissing the imaginary Matti. I couldn't live for him or his idea of me.

I felt like I was suffocating from the stench that I still hadn't acclimated to and the attention of all these medical professionals. I took a deep breath and almost choked. "I'm going to pass for now. Can you please thank Doctor Warner for me and let him know to keep me in the loop as the trial progresses?"

"Sure thing, Abby," Doctor Mitchell said as he stood and extended his hand again for me to shake. "It's been a real pleasure and I hope that you find a path that works for you and your recovery, whichever you choose."

Everyone but Angie filed out after him. She drew me in for a fast hug. "You made the right call. I know it was a hard choice for you, but I don't think it's a good option at this point. We can revisit as the trial continues."

I grunted at the strength of her arms wrapped around me like steel coils and wiggled loose. "Christ, how much have you been juicing? Your hugs are more like a bear trap than Matti's."

"Ooh, how's that hugging going?" She poked me in the shoulder and I had to flinch away.

"Stop it. It's fine, he's fine, we're fine. Thanks for your advice on this, I'm glad you agree." I zipped my jacket and wrapped my scarf around my neck, the itchy wool a comforting tickle.

Her eyes narrowed. "So we're not going to talk about him?"

I waved a hand in front of my nose. "No, not in a room that reeks of Taco Bell and Starbucks. Ugh, how can you even stand this?"

Her nose wrinkled too. "Fine, fine. Girls' night soon?"

"Sure, maybe this weekend or something. It's a rough week for me, I can fill you in later." I turned for the door, but Angie reached out and grabbed a hold of my sleeve.

She shook me by the shoulders and I tried ineffectually to loosen her grip. "What's going on? Are you okay?"

"Yeah, yeah. I'm fine. Just tired. Lots of decisions to make and, sorry, but I'm really not ready to talk about it right now."

She stepped back and stared at me, like she was trying to read my poker face. My cheeks flushed under her affectionate scrutiny. "Okay, I'll let you off the hook this time. But this weekend, you're telling me everything."

"Roger that. I gotta go now. Williams wants to talk to me." I slid away from her hands after I gave them a squeeze, and headed for the door.

"Stay strong, Abby!" She called as the door swung closed behind me.

I drove back over to the Fieldhouse, a little late for my meeting with Williams, wondering if we were talking about workouts or the job offer he'd emailed me.

"Come in," his deep voice called out curtly when I knocked at his office.

I took a deep breath and eased the door open. "Hey, it's me."

He waved me in and motioned to a chair. I struggled out of my outerwear and laid the layers on the back before flopping into the seat. "What's up?"

"Abby, we need to talk about my email from yesterday. We've talked informally about this, but I've been quite serious the entire time and I've got to know where you stand. I need a conditioning coach and an assistant for the midfielders on the men's team. The spot is yours if you want it, but you've got to give me a straight answer."

My fingers knotted into the convenient tassels of my scarf again. "I do, Coach. I do. I'm nervous about it, but I want it. It's time for me to move on from playing."

Williams' shocked face brought up Matti's when I'd said "no" to him yesterday. "You will?"

"Yes, print the contract. I'll sign right now. I'm ready."

"Alrighty then. Do you want to negotiate for anything?"

I shrugged. "I probably should, but I trust you."

Williams stared me down and I met his eyes without blinking. "Give me a minute. I need to print you a new copy." His rare grin broke through the stern coach face. "I lowballed you."

"Thanks, Coach."

"No, thank you, Coach." We smiled and he extended a hand. I shook it then stood up and jittered around his office while he messed around on his computer before excusing himself to go grab the contract off the printer. He handed it to me. "Hot off the press," he joked.

I scanned it quickly and noticed that the salary had gone up quite a bit. I raised an eyebrow at him. "You dick, you *totally* lowballed me."

He laughed. "HR has a starting point and encouraged me to start there — I'd already planned on moving it up whether you tried to negotiate or not. I'll tell them you played hardball."

"Give me a pen, you dastardly sneak." He handed one over and I signed with a flourish. "There you go, you've got yourself a new coach."

He took the papers and stood, then shocked the hell out of me when he rounded his desk and gave me that kind of clumsy quick hug that dads give their kids when they're proud of them. "Welcome aboard, kiddo."

It had been a day for hugging Abby, apparently. Hopefully Matti would feel the same way when I got home and broke the news.

* * * *

My stomach roiled as I took the elevator up to our apartment, a jazzy instrumental version of Taylor Swift's *Shake It Off* taunting me through the speakers in the ceiling. "Matti?" I called out as I opened the door and toed off my shoes at the rack so I didn't track slush all over the floors that had been cleaned by our housekeeper.

"Right here," Matti called back, and as I walked into the living room, I saw him and Sylvie with their heads down looking back and forth between their two tablets.

"What's this? When did you get into town?" I asked as I unwound my scarf and tossed my jacket and hat on the back of one of the bar stools by the island that separated the kitchen and dining space from the living room. The last person I wanted to see right now was my agent.

Matti had started a fire and the gas flames flickered hypnotically as I sat down as close to it as possible. Chicago winter had me chilled to the bone from the ins and outs at work.

"Abigail Elizabeth," intoned Sylvie, ignoring my questions. "Glad you're here. We're house hunting and contract finalizing for this guy. Now we need to talk about you. Your comeback is going to be incredibly exciting and there are a few teams already interested. I've let them know — "

I interrupted. "No need. I'm not going. Matti and I will have to be long distance. I signed a few hours ago with Coach Williams. You're looking at the new conditioning and midfielders coach for the Northwestern men's soccer team." My wide grin slowly slid off my face as I saw the gross light of betrayal flash through Matti's eyes.

* * * *

Matti

Sylvie glanced between the two of us hunkering down in our respective corners, getting ready for a fight, and attempted to mediate. "Abby, are you sure about this? There are medical facilities we could check out in London that might have a second or third opinion, a different treatment option. It's a lot to give up and if it's the playboy image thing for Matti that's troubling you, I'm trying to get the team to loosen up that requirement."

"What playboy image thing for Matti?" Abby shook her head. "Never mind. Look, I mean this. I'm starting something new. My playing days are done. This is my choice and I need you both to respect that."

"Well then." Sylvie stood and started stuffing things into her enormous tote. "I see you two have a lot to talk about. Call me when you've made some decisions, Matti."

She reached over and gave Abby a squeeze. "Congratulations, kiddo, you're going to be a great coach. I'm proud of you," she whispered. Abby nodded, but her eyes never left me as she moved over to take Sylvie's place on the long couch. It crackled as she sat. Like us, it was still too new to bear any weight without complaining. The door shutting seemed to echo as Sylvie exited the apartment.

"Matti—"

"Don't 'Matti' me in that reasonable Mom tone. How could you have made this decision without even talking to me?"

She sighed. "I'm sorry."

I yanked my hair elastic out and shook my head, dropping my face into my hands. "Are you?" My voice was muffled. "From here it doesn't seem like it."

"That's because you're hiding in your hands," she tried to joke.

I raised my head slowly and she could only meet my eyes for a moment before dropping her gaze to her lap, where her fingers started to twist and twine together.

"You're really doing this. You're giving up on everything. Your career, me, this thing we've been building together. That's it?"

"No! That's not what I'm doing at all! My path is changing a little. I can't play anymore, and you know what? I don't know if I'd want to if I could. I have to think about a career after soccer and I feel lucky that I figured it out before I would have been forced to retire—I mean, I was pretty much forced to retire, but this is my decision."

"But, us?" My hands were starting to shake and I could hear a low buzz, like a tattoo gun. My skin was crawling and demanded the emotional release valve of a needle digging into it at hundreds of strikes per second.

"We're not over, unless you want us to be." Her voice was quiet, pleading with me. "We can stay together—I want to stay together. It will have to be long distance for a little bit."

I exploded. "Abby, I'm not doing that. I'm not doing long distance, and I'm not doing it with someone who would so easily give up on herself, on her career, someone who would watch me leave without trying to fight for me."

"What do you mean, watch you leave without trying to fight for you?"

"Exactly what it sounds like! You couldn't even talk to me about this, ask me to compromise. Jesus, Abby, I thought we were a team. Teammates don't do this to each other. You're abandoning me, sending me off with a kiss and a wave to get me out of your hair."

"What the hell are you talking about?" Good, she was getting angry now. "I'm not leaving you, I told you I wanted to be with you. We'll need to be long distance for a while, but I'm sure we'll figure out — "

"There's nothing to figure out! I don't want to be with someone who turns their back on themselves. Someone who gives up without really putting in the work. Christ, it's like I don't even know you anymore."

"Matti." Her voice pleaded with me as I jumped to my feet and started stalking around the ugly modern furniture. "Come on, it's not like that. This can work. I'm not giving up on myself or my career. My path has changed, but that doesn't mean that our relationship has to end."

"If you're not trying to be a player anymore, you *have* given up on yourself. And you know what, maybe that's okay. I don't want to be with a quitter or a liar. Besides, the club wants me to be single, so maybe this is for the best." I immediately wanted to take that back.

She was off the couch like a shot, pacing after me. Both of us were too kinetic to be contained. Her hand had a death grip on her ponytail and she yanked it with every word out of her mouth. "Are you kidding? Fuck you, Matti Shellenberg. Fuck you, and fuck this entire situation. I'm not reasoning with you. You want an excuse to be single and go back to the bullshit life you were living before me? How dare you try to police me, my career and my decision-making for your benefit. Just because you're afraid that an injury and choice like this might happen to you, fucking stop projecting onto me."

I reeled back. "That's not it at all. You're not listening to me. This is my dream, everything I've ever worked for. Last chance, Abby, are you with me or not?"

She was breathing hard and I could see her eyes were glassy as she struggled not to cry. My brave, stabby girl was going to bawl and it was my fault because I couldn't stop talking... But she was leaving me, was seemingly totally fine sending me off. Every rushed goodbye from parents, siblings, teammates and friends seemed to echo in my head as I watched her. *Bye, Matti, it's been fun.*

"Not, I guess. Not if this is how you're going to treat me and my decisions. Not if this is how easily you'll revert back to the fake person you were before me." She gulped back a sob and made tracks to the guest room, scooping Spock up on the way. The tiny cat *mirped* reproachfully at me and his eyes seemed to scold me over her shoulder as the door shut behind her.

Even the cat could see that we were over. I'd miss him too.

I rammed a hand into my hair and kicked one of the little Rebels practice balls as hard as I could at the obnoxious couch. As it thudded harmlessly to the ground, I grabbed my phone and sent out a text to my team letting them know I'd be leaving and seeing if people wanted to meet me out for a celebratory drink.

Chapter Twenty-Four

Matti

A buzzing beneath my pillow and prickly kneading woke me up way too early the next day. It seemed to happen in waves, the way my nauseous stomach seemed to be sloshing around, and matched the painful, sunburned feeling on the back of my hand. Why did my hand hurt? I could feel every thread on the comforter rubbing against it. *Oh*. The tattoo studio... The club...

My eyes slitted open and I crawled my left hand out from under the covers to hover in front of my face. When I saw the colorful, swollen appendage dangling there, I went from hungover half-asleep zombie to full-on wired. I'd gotten a new tattoo and, now that I thought about it, my other hand prickled too. I pulled my right arm out and glanced back and forth. At least they matched. On my right hand, a swallow. My left, a bird cage with a heart-shaped key slotted into the lock on the open door. How symbolic.

I slid my slightly less painful right hand beneath my pillow to pull out my phone and see what was causing the buzzing. A raft of notifications from social media and a new text from the owners' group of my shiny new team. I read that first—always better to rip the bandage on the bad news off first.

Great to see you in top form, Matti! Can't wait till you bring that energy back to London next week.

Another social media notification flashed. I'd been busy the night before and it slowly started to come back to me. Meeting the guys at the tattoo studio after leaving the apartment, a three-hour sitting, then the club, the—wince—body shot girls and champagne waterfalls as a goodbye tribute for me. The cigars, strip club. All of it chronicled in great detail by other people.

Instagram was particularly unkind, as I was tagged in all sorts of semi-compromising positions. I dropped my phone on the duvet and scrubbed a hand over my face and through my hair, where it immediately got caught in a nest of tangles. A rapid-fire knock on the door left me with a pit of dread in my stomach and I pulled myself to a sitting position, ready to face the music. "I'm up."

Abby barged through the door waving her phone in front of her like a red flag in front of a bull. "What have you done?" Her voice was a hiss that cut off as she approached the bed and stopped dead with a wrinkled nose. "It smells like something died in here."

"Probably me." I waved my freshly inked hands in front of her face. "See?"

"Oh my god, Matti. What were you thinking? Anything at all?"

I sighed. "I'm sorry. Things got out of hand last night. I left here angry with you and the entire situation."

"You know better, I know you do. You knew this would happen. You had to know." Her voice was choked up and I could see her eyes glisten as she tried to hold back tears. "How did you think this would make me feel?"

"I don't know, I wasn't thinking," I repeated and I couldn't even meet her eyes as she scrolled through the social media posts. Champagne bottles recorked themselves and body shots were done in reverse as she scrolled up and down, making a flip book of my entire debauched night — which, to be fair, was actually pretty tame compared to some of my evenings.

"This isn't you. I know it isn't."

"Maybe it is," I muttered.

"Do you really think that?" she asked quietly and sat down at the very edge of the bed, where she immediately started pleating the twisted sheets between her fingers.

We were so close now, my foot right next to the knee she'd pulled up on the bed, but the distance between us had never felt larger or deeper. My stomach churned as I thought back to our conversation the night before. We hadn't settled anything the previous evening at all, she'd left the choice in my court. Whether or not I was willing to change with her or not.

"I don't know," I finally copped. "Everyone else seems to think I'm like this. Maybe the me you've come to know is only temporary."

Her cheeks flushed and she swiped at her eyes with the back of her hand. "You know, when you told me about the offer from Tottenham, I was excited for you.

So excited. I knew that it would be hard for me, because we'd need to be apart for a while, but my happiness for you exceeded my own concerns and I knew we'd be fine because of all the work you've done, the way you've grown in the past six months."

"And now?"

"I don't know what to think. The Matti Shellenberg I fell for isn't this guy." She waved her phone at me where a picture of me licking a line of salt off of a woman's bare abdomen shone out at me. "This is the guy I hated, the guy who dumped spiders on my plate at a fundraiser in London and made everyone laugh at my expense. This is the guy who turned himself into someone he wasn't because he was ashamed of himself."

Each word that came flying out of her mouth was a precise dagger thrust to my kidneys and heart. So smooth I didn't even feel them till they sank all the way in and the blood started pooling internally. She was slicing me to ribbons with her words, making me bleed with the tears she was clearly trying so valiantly to hold back.

"I don't like this guy very much and don't think I can stay with him," she finally ground out quietly.

"Fine," I said, and felt like such a tough guy when my voice didn't shake. "This is me, and if you're not into it, it's probably better we go our separate ways now. Other people can accept me at face value. I tried to be someone else for you, but it clearly didn't work out."

"So that's it? *This* is it?" Her eyes were huge in her chalky-white face, dark circles like bruises beneath them. She started to breathe in short gasps as she waited for me to put the final nail in our coffin.

"Guess so. See you around, Stabby." I lay back down and covered my aching head with my pillow, blocking out the sight of her stricken, tear-streaked face. The smoke starting to pour out of her ears. Good, she was pissed. I needed that. She needed that or this was going to hurt worse than any motherfucking injury I'd ever had in my life. *Clean break, Abby. Stay pissed and get the fuck out.*

She stood up and moved to the door. "You know, I can tell you're lying to yourself to make this okay. You messed up, you know it, but you aren't going to admit it. I feel sorry for you because one day you're going to look back on this moment and regret everything from even listening to that offer to now. I'll be long gone by then, but I promise I'll think of this moment every now and then and be proud of myself for seeing you so clearly."

The door opened and closed with a slam and she was gone, leaving me behind in a cloud of censure and disappointment so heavy it nearly suffocated me. I kept my eyes closed. Fuck this nonsense and the hangover from hell. I was sorry she'd gotten hurt, but this wasn't really my fault—she'd known exactly what she was getting into with me. But that reassurance didn't stop a few drops of moisture from leaking out of the corners of my eyes to stain the linen sheets beneath my cheek.

* * * *

Abby

The door shut behind me and I leaned back against it, listening hard for any sounds. I don't know what I expected, him to call me back and beg for forgiveness?

Maybe Spock to scratch at the door and meow, wanting to rejoin his mother after his father promised to abandon him? Neither of those things happened and I finally gave up the last shred of hope. It was over, this fake engagement experiment. Done.

Moving slowly as an arthritic hippo, I lumbered to the balcony door and stepped outside. The freezing late February wind whipped my face and froze my tears. I didn't even feel it.

Sylvie must have come over at some point because her knock on the glass startled me out of my halfway hypothermic state. She slid the door open, grabbed me by the elbow and pulled me back into the warmth of the apartment. My teeth started chattering immediately.

"You lovely little idiot. You're turning blue," she fussed as she slid a throw around my shoulders and guided me to our couch. "What on earth were you thinking going out there?"

"Did you bring the paperwork?" I asked to avoid her question.

"The dissolution of your relationship agreement? Yes, I brought it."

"Give it to me."

"You're sure, then?"

I nodded and she handed it over without another word, extending a pen for my signature. It was a standard no-contact, nondisclosure agreement regarding everything having to do with our relationship over the past eight months. I read through carefully and signed with a shaking hand, in disbelief that everything that had happened, all of those feelings could be cut off with nothing more than a pen stroke. I slid it back to her and she stacked the pages neatly and tucked them away into her tote.

"Abby, I don't like this at all," she said quietly. "This isn't good for either of you."

I got up to grab a bottle of water from the fridge and slammed it shut when I saw that we were out. "It's not your business anymore."

"I know, but being together changed both of you for the better – you have to see that." Her eyes were big with concern and every day of her sixty-some years of life experience came hurtling down on me. At that moment she was more motherly than my own mom had ever been.

"Oh, I do. But he doesn't. I'm not going to be with someone who's afraid of sharing who he really is with people, someone who makes up a front that's the opposite of himself. Someone who is so afraid of change that they're willing to sabotage a relationship because they resent the other person's growth. I'm done." I grabbed blindly for a glass to fill with tap water to drown the throat-prickling tears that threatened. "Besides, why'd you do all of this for him? How could you not think of me?"

Sylvie threw her hands up, palms turned out to me. "I understand, really, I do, and you're absolutely doing the right thing for you. I'm sorry that I didn't realize that you were serious about doing anything besides playing. I've known you for a long time and in all that time, you never seemed to consider any other options. I took that for granted and didn't see how you've changed."

She wrapped me in a careful hug. "I'm proud of you, Abby, so very proud. I hope you'll still keep me involved in your career as a coach. May I keep an ear out for possible opportunities? I imagine that coaches are also in need of sponsorships and whatnot."

I hugged her back, wringing out those lingering feelings of betrayal. "Please, I'd like that. For now though, I need to pack a bag. I'm getting out of here. Tell him I'll be back for my stuff and my cat later when he's at practice."

"Sure, Abby Jean, of course." Sylvie wrapped me back up in another hug that smelled like oranges and spicy tea and I felt a wave of longing for the family that had let me go so easily.

"Thanks for everything," I said as I gave her a final squeeze.

My overnight bag took no time to pack since I was only grabbing stuff from the laundry—no way was I going back into our room. As I zipped it up, slowly put on my jacket and dragged my feet into boots, I kept one eye on the master bedroom door. It never opened and no noise came from inside.

"Bye, Sylvie, I'll be at Steph's. You know, in case he asks or if you need me," I finally said after hovering by the door for altogether too long.

"Be good, Abby. We'll talk soon." She waved a knitting needle at me and promptly dropped the half-made misshapen bundle of loose knots onto the floor.

And that was that. Eight months of my life. My heart, which had been held together by hastily applied bandages, shattered all over again as I collapsed behind the wheel of my car in the parking garage. I sobbed, letting everything come out—a lifetime of disappointing and being disappointed in people who should have been my support system.

Chapter Twenty-Five

Matti

"Matthias Shellenberg!" A very loud, very authoritative feminine voice was shouting right into my eardrum.

"Mmm. Lay off, Stabby, I'm getting up."

"She's long gone, Matthias. Long gone. Now get that tight ass out of bed."

The owner of the voice smacked my ass and I flinched — she packed a wallop. The door slammed shut and I finally pulled my head out from under my pillow.

"*Merow*," chirped the cat, who looked at me reproachfully.

"What are you doing in here, anyways, silly cat? Didn't your mom feed you this morning? Your mom —"

Holy shit, Abby. She was gone. We were through, but the cat was still here. Was he mine now? A minor thrill of fear shot through me at the idea of keeping another being alive. A major bolt of regret and self-disgust followed as the foggy details of our fight crystallized in the cold, watery light of the February afternoon. I threw on a pair of joggers and a T-shirt from the floor that passed the sniff test, scooped up the cat and headed tentatively for the door to see who had dared disturb me.

"Sylvie?" I called out and my voice echoed throughout the big apartment that we'd never gotten around to filling with furniture and knick-knacks.

"In here, Matthias."

With Spock purring in my ear, I crept closer and saw that she'd turned on the gas fire and was knitting something with a truly ugly chartreuse stripe.

"Where's Abby?"

"Gone."

"Gone where? What about the cat?" I thrust Spock out to her and she recoiled with a pinched mouth, like she'd tasted a lemon. "What about the rest of her stuff?"

"She said she'll back for it when you're gone for practice – it will depend on how long it takes her to find an apartment, I think."

"Oh." Now I was sad that I wouldn't get to keep the little guy.

"Sit down, Matthias." Sylvie's voice returned to grandma gangster mode as she fired out the order. I could imagine her with a sawed-off shotgun demanding that people stand and deliver.

I sat.

"You're lucky that your antics last night are something that Tottenham seems to appreciate," she spat out.

I nodded.

"Despite the bonus they would like to bestow upon you for making your exit from Chicago so memorable with the new tattoos, drunken shenanigans and sexual innuendo, I would like to say — as your manager — that I think it was an exceptionally ill-timed and disrespectful move on your part." She snorted and I knew she was remembering older stories about me that were far, far more extreme.

Sylvie continued. "Aside from the way you treated Abby — someone you assured me that you cared about, your girlfriend even — there is going to be massive PR fallout from all of the sweetheart couple press events that we had the two of you doing."

I tightened my hold on the cat and dropped my head in shame.

"You're going to be dragged quite a bit and I'd say that you've very effectively burned any and all bridges here in Chicago. The camps are disaffiliating themselves with you immediately and Coach Sherman has issued a statement regarding your behavior. It's abhorrent, in case you wanted the short version." She pulled up her phone to a video of a press conference and gestured for me to take it, dared me to press play. I ignored it.

"I'm sorry," I muttered into Spock's fur.

She tucked the phone away. "Don't apologize to me. You need to apologize to Abby, to the team and to all of the kids who looked up to you. You truly fucked up, you selfish twat."

At that, my head shot up and I stared at her in disbelief. She'd called me a *twat*?

"You better start packing. I'll head off the worst of the press, but you need to let me know if there's a specific apology statement you'd like me to make to any of those groups in particular. Perhaps you could write them down and send them to me when you're ready." She shook her head slowly at me. "I was trying to get Tottenham to drop that playboy requirement and now they're not going to back down. I'm disappointed in you."

"It wasn't only me," I said through clenched teeth.

"Excuse me? I'm pretty sure you were the one who made the decisions you did last night, the one who seems to have ended things for good with Abby when they didn't go your way."

"Oh, fuck off."

"No, no, I will not. You listen to me and you listen good, Matthias. You pull a stunt like this one more time and I am through with you. Done. Finito. And good luck finding an agent after me who will put up with your childishness. This is your final chance. I really thought you'd grown up. Clearly I was wrong." She thrust her half-assed knitting back in her tote with a level of aggression I'd never seen before.

I grabbed a kiddie soccer ball and punted it into the wall, where it dented the drywall.

"Get it all out, kiddo," she called as I flipped her off.

I picked up the ball and did it again, this time sending it through the wall. *Crappy pre-fab buildings.* As I went to pick it up again, I realized that my vision was blurred. Tears were sliding down my face.

"Oh, Matti," said Sylvie as she snuck up behind me.

"I fucked up," I whispered.

"You sure did." She wrapped me in a hug. "What are you going to do?"

"I don't know, I really don't. Move to London and try to do better? Apologize to Abby profusely? I don't know." I leaned into the comfort she offered and she reached up to gingerly pat my shoulder.

"Leave it, Matti. You'll figure it out, but if it's Abby you want, I think you're going to have to wait for a long time before she's willing to speak with you. You're both royally stubborn and the bullshit you pulled last night plus ignoring her wishes about choosing a new career is going to make her freeze you out. The girl can hold a grudge."

The door slammed behind Sylvie and I was left with my own bad decisions. A thousand memories of Abby ran through my head. The first time I'd realized I liked her more than two years ago, her anger when I pranked her, the soft confusion on her face the first time we'd kissed, seeing her so still and small wrapped in bandages in the hospital and dozens more of the last few months of utter happiness. It was over, though, and it was my own fault.

I texted Daniel and asked him to pick up the few personal items I had in my locker at the team's facility.

* * * *

When Abby texted me a few hours later, I felt a wild, fleeting hope that she would be open to listening to me. Instead it was a demand that I be out of the house when she came back for her stuff. So sue me—once again I chose to ignore her request and stayed. I was desperate.

"Have you found a new place?" I leaned against the doorframe as Abby knelt on the ground sorting T-shirts—one of hers, one of mine—and studiously ignored me. Spock had jumped into her suitcase and she was trying to simultaneously keep him out while stuffing her finished pile into the overflowing case.

She shook her head, at least silently acknowledging me.

"When do you start the new job?"

She shrugged and stood, shaking out her legs like they'd fallen asleep.

"Has anyone said anything to you about our break-up?"

The laser glare she shot my way would have leveled me if she'd been making eye contact. It punched me in the chest and I bowed forward a little to compensate for the piece of my heart she'd carved out.

"Fine. You don't want to talk, we don't need to talk." I left her to finish the job and went to the laundry room to pull out Spock's carrier. I grabbed a few hand towels from the powder room to make a cozy spot for him.

A half-hour went by while I messed around with my phone and she finally emerged from our room with two suitcases, a duffel and her backpack slung over one shoulder. Spock pranced out after her and sniffed the carrier before ducking in like a good little mama's boy. Ugh, I was going to miss him. I rushed toward the carrier and crouched down to give his purring little butt a quick scratch and gently shut the door.

"I guess this is it?" I asked unnecessarily from the ground.

She sighed and finally made eye contact. "This is it."

I peered into the carrier, the little green eyes of the cat staring sadly back at me. "Bye, Spock, take good care of your mama, okay, little man? I'm going to miss you."

Abby recoiled as I stood abruptly, backing away from me, and stumbled over her suitcases. I caught her, barely, and pulled her close. The familiar tropical smell of her shampoo overwhelmed me and I buried my face in her hair. She let me hold her for a moment, then placed her hands on my chest and shoved me away.

"Bye, Matti. I hope you get everything you ever dreamed of."

"Stabby—"

"No! You don't get to call me that anymore! You don't get to hug me, smirk at me, nothing. You've lost those privileges. Why are you even here anyways? You're supposed to be cleaning out your locker." The look in her eyes was so hurt and accusatory it set me back further.

"Daniel is taking care of it for me. I had to see you one last time." My tongue felt thick and inadequate at forming the words I wanted to say. "I'm sorry for how we're leaving things."

"But not for what's happened, huh?"

"Yes—no? I don't know."

"Very mature," she said in a low voice as she suddenly started rummaging around in her pockets before pulling out something small and square. "Here, this is yours. I don't want it anymore."

It was my grandmother's ring box. She forced it into my hand, wrapping my fingers around it. "This means nothing anymore to me. You'll want it for your real fiancée."

"But you said—"

"We both said a lot of things, didn't we?" She bent and picked up her suitcases, shouldered her duffel and headed toward the door while I remained glued to my spot by her sharp words. "Bye, Matti," she said again as she opened the door and walked out, closing it gently behind her.

My too-slow tongue was stuck to the roof of my mouth. All the words I hadn't said, the words I *should* have said, were stuck somewhere between my brain and mouth. Half-formed pleas to stay, to love me the way I loved her. The realization that she didn't deserve what I'd done, that she deserved far more than I'd ever be able to give—me, a guy who was too scared that no one would love the real him. I wanted to run after her, I wanted to drop to the ground and cry, but mostly I wanted her to open the door and say, "Matti, you fucking idiot. I forgive you. I'll never leave."

But that didn't happen because I'd blown things so spectacularly and all I could do was wait for the moving company to show up to pack everything for my transatlantic move. I glanced down at the faded blue velvet box that had been rubbed bare on the corners. With one finger, I flipped it open and balanced it on my palm.

She might have been right about me, but she was wrong about who the ring truly belonged to—it was hers. I shut the case with a snap, stuffed it into a pocket of my jeans. Grabbing my phone, I took a last photo of Chicago's skyline from our balcony. It went to Instagram with the caption, "Leaving my heart behind."

Chapter Twenty-Six

Abby

Staying with Steph was a mistake. I should have called Angie first, but something about living with someone who provided medical care for you felt like a breach of ethics. Or I overthought everything that didn't matter in my life while avoiding the big bads. One or the other.

Spock and Steph got off to a terrible start when she had a sneezing fit the minute I walked in the door with the cat carrier and the rest of my stuff from the apartment.

"Oh no, are you allergic?"

Her eyes watered furiously and her nose was already turning red as she swiped ineffectually at it. "No, not at all. Er, maybe a little bit."

"Crap, should I go stay with Ang?"

"No, no. We'll be fine. I love cats. Bring the little bugger in—I need to get used to him. Helllooo, Spocky!"

Spock meowed a cautiously chipper hello from the carrier and blinked his big green eyes at us. "You're not my daddy," he seemed to say as his gaze flicked back and forth between the two of us.

"Thanks for letting us crash. I promise it won't be for too long. I need to find a place of my own, stat."

"It's fine, really. I love apartment hunting and maybe I can help." She grabbed a tissue to blot her eyes, then blew her nose for good measure.

"That would be great, I'd like to stick around here in Evanston. I have no desire to go back into Chicago." That was the understatement of the year.

"Fair enough. There are some great old Victorians that have been subdivided up recently. I've been dying to get inside them." She took one of my bags and gestured for me to follow her to her guest room, giving the cat carrier a wide berth.

"Perfect, show them to me online and I'll make some appointments." I said the last as I headed down the hallway to the already cramped guest room with its full-size bed, big desk and tiny freestanding wardrobe.

When I came back out, Spock was cautiously exploring and Steph was valiantly trying to avoid scratching her reddened eyes. "I'm fine," she hastened to reassure me as she popped up and headed to her kitchen, where she started to rummage around in the cupboards. "Sit, sit. Do you want some tea? How did it go back at the apartment?"

"Crap, give me a second." I scooped up Spock and hauled him back to the guest room and dropped him off with a "sorry, buddy, we'll get out of here soon."

Cat properly disposed of, I plopped down on her poofy couch. "Sure, I'll take some tea. Thanks." I watched as she sneezed again, this time trying to hide it. "And maybe we accelerate the timeline on me moving. I'll keep Spock in the bedroom till then." She nodded as she filled the kettle with water from the tap. "But, yeah, the apartment. It went. He was there."

"What? Didn't he have practice today?"

I twisted around. "He did. But he threw a tantrum and decided to skip it. No surprise."

"Was it weird to see him, or did the closure help?" She started up one of the burners beneath her tea kettle.

"Yeah, a little. He kept trying to talk to me and apologize for the wrong things. I know he didn't cheat on me, that wasn't the point. He disrespected me and our relationship when he didn't get his way by running out and acting like the party boy who's finally been let off the leash." I nodded my thanks when she passed me a mug. "Oh, and his new tattoos are healing nicely."

"The bird and the cage?" she asked as she sat down.

"Yeah. Fucking symbolic."

"Totally. Ugh, fuck that guy. You need a good cleansing cry?"

I made a face at her.

"Fine. No crying sesh. Got it. Any more trauma you want to work through?"

I hesitated, still not sure if I was ready, but being with — and then so abruptly losing — Matti had made me realize that we only get one chance at life. That it was better to love and lose than never love at all. And that sometimes, letting go of a grudge or your past was important. "I don't know if it's trauma, but I think it's time I got back in touch with my family. My life is my own now and I get to choose who is in it and who isn't.

Even though he shattered my heart, I'm glad I tried with Matti. Maybe I need to give them another chance too."

Steph frowned at me. "That's a pretty big realization."

"I know, I know. But I've changed, I'm not as single-minded as I once was and maybe they're ready to reconnect and don't know how. I can be the bigger person here."

"You're sure?" She wiped her nose with a tissue again.

"I am. Not now, but soon."

"All right, Abby. Trust your instincts." She pulled out her phone and flicked through the calendar. "Well, we've got a free day. Why don't you get your computer out and we can start combing the rental lists? I'm apparently more allergic than I thought I was."

With Steph's help, I booked three apartment tours for the afternoon and we headed out to brunch, then furniture shopping. Matti's parting gift was burning a hole in my bank account. It was a truly astronomical sum from my impoverished perspective and while I didn't want to take his money, I also wasn't going to turn it down. Renting an apartment and getting furniture in Evanston was more expensive than I'd anticipated and I literally had nothing of my own since making the move from London.

We were in a very cute vintage furniture shop looking at painstakingly refurbished mid-century modern pieces when Mer Lopez, Matti's ex-teammate's wife, called me.

"Mer?"

"Hey, Abby." Her warm, lightly accented voice was sympathetic enough that I wanted to crawl into her arms for the biggest mom hug I'd never received. "You doing okay?"

"Sort of, but it'll get better. Just a little raw right now, with him leaving this morning and the amount of press calls that Sylvie and I have waved off, writing bullshit statements requesting privacy and everything else."

"Oh, girl. That sounds terrible. Can we get a drink or coffee sometime soon? I already miss you!"

"Of course, I'd like that. Once I'm settled in my own place, I'll invite you over for a girls' night. I want to hear all the WAG gossip."

"Sure, Abby. Oh, before I let you go — Daniel talked to Matti yesterday when he picked up his stuff. He looked terrible and all he wanted to talk about was how he could never make it up to you."

I immediately wanted to rescind my invitation, in no known or unknown universe did I want to be subjected to some sort of "stand by your man, he feels terrible and why are you making him feel worse" talk. *Diplomacy*, my mind silently whispered at me. *Be nice.* "I know, Mer, but I really don't want to talk about this." A brainwave hit. "In fact, I can't — we both signed NDAs."

She sighed heavily and I couldn't tell if it was because she wanted the gossip — cynical devil on my left shoulder — or if she genuinely felt bad and wanted us to make nice — naïve angel on my right shoulder. "Okay, okay. I'll remove my nose from your business."

"Thanks, Mer. Listen, I've got to go. We're on a tight schedule viewing new places. I'll let you know when I'm settled in."

"Sounds good, Abby. Talk soon."

That afternoon, Steph and I found the perfect place. It was a refurbished two-bedroom carriage house behind a beautiful Victorian mansion that was rented out to Northwestern's Provost. Safe, secure and lovely. Better yet, I could move in at the end of the week. And, thanks to Matti, it was also within my price range. I called the furniture stores where we'd been browsing and requested deliveries for Friday. I'd be moved in on Saturday. Sunday would be a girls' night with Steph and Ang. I was already exhausted and desperately missing the only man I shouldn't care about anymore. Matti.

Chapter Twenty-Seven

Abby

A few weeks after I'd moved into the carriage house, I'd left work early to oversee the delivery of the last piece of new furniture — the most fabulous chaise lounge ever to exist — when a phone call blared through the car's speakers. The car jerked to the left as I jumped and I fumbled to overcorrect. My heart pounding, I slid to a stop and answered the call.

"What?" I asked while willing my heart rate to return to normal. Who wanted to die on an only slightly icy road in Evanston, Illinois? *Not this gal*.

"Abigail Samantha!"

"Sylvie."

"'Tis I, indeed." Her voice was too spirited for the morning, and that particular tone always portended favors upon favors. The last time I'd heard it, I'd found myself agreeing to babysit my nemesis at a party. Resulting in...my current situation.

"How are you, my dear?"

I drummed my fingers on the steering wheel. "I'm fine, you know I'm fine. What's going on?"

"It's Matti."

I sighed and she echoed me.

"How is that my problem?" I asked and my voice cracked on the last syllable, bursting through the whole hard-ass, gives-zero-fucks façade I'd carefully constructed.

"It's not, dear, but I thought you might have some insight into what he's thinking?"

"What do you mean?"

"Do you still follow him on social media or anything? Has he reached out to you?"

No, none of that. I hadn't heard from him since he moved. Not that I cared. Or missed him. I'd unfollowed him on every platform and rewarded myself with chocolate every time I was able to stop myself from looking. It had been successful—I'd gained five pounds.

"No." I kept it simple.

"The thing is, I really don't know what to do about him."

I rolled my eyes so hard I was sure she could hear them rattle around in my skull. I wasn't there to be her Matti whisperer. "I'm not sure why you think I can help you, but I need to get going. My final furniture delivery is happening today and I need to be there before they arrive."

"Abby, wait! Can you check out his accounts? Help me figure out how to help him?"

"Gotta go, Sylvie." I hung up. No way in hell was I making anything having to do with Matti Shellenberg my business anymore.

* * * *

The delivery went smoothly and I'd slumped down on my lovely new chaise to make a list of other odds and ends I needed for my apartment, namely some kitchen gadgets and an extra set of bed linens, when Sylvie texted me again.

Please, Abby. Go check out his social media. What am I supposed to do with him?

Fine, fine.

I hit myself in the head a few times with my phone to prepare myself and searched out his profile. His feed was mostly promotional shots from games or team events, clearly not taken by him, with some minimal "Go Team" comments.

The personal ones, though — and maybe even the team ones now that I looked more closely — were a mess. His hair seemed a little greasy and straggly, the undercut growing out to an awkward length. Dark circles had been carved beneath his eyes and new lines that bisected his brow made him appear at least ten years older — a tired ten years older at that.

Where there used to be a mischievous grin or smirk, now there was a scowl or a jaw firmly set, lips pressed tightly and bloodlessly together. Most of the personal ones showed a messy apartment in the background, underscoring the fact that this professional athlete lived and breathed his sport with very little time outside for doing anything else. But the small percentage that weren't at games, team events or his apartment... *Holy crap, Matti. What is he thinking?*

I searched his name as a hashtag and more damning evidence rolled across my screen. Photo and video after photo and video of him out at bars and clubs, getting in fights. Before his rep had been of a genial good-time guy who liked a drink or two and was a mischievous rabble rouser. These photos made him out to be some sort of hooligan. The ones where he wasn't fighting all involved multiple women in barely-there club gear.

Tears started to fracture my vision. I zoomed in more closely, couldn't make myself click away, and saw that his eyes were equally disgusted, shuttered and distant. The drinks were always full, never a sip taken from them. He wasn't smiling, the light of desire wasn't glowing in his blue eyes. He looked like the wax figure of him on display at Madame Tussauds — a close approximation of the real man.

This was the face of a man playing a game that he wasn't into in the slightest, and he seemed absolutely miserable. Worse, he was driving himself straight into the mud. The headlines showed that he was playing without most of his usual sparkle and that he held the distinction as the most carded member of the team. It seemed like he'd taken the Dierckson role and run with it.

I should have felt vindicated, or maybe like I'd dodged a bullet getting away from this guy, but I couldn't. This wasn't the Matti I knew. This was an even worse version of the Matti I'd first met in London, the one that I now knew had been a front. My insides curdled like spoiled milk.

Part of me wanted to feel proud of myself for getting out of something toxic, but the rest of me knew that taking that track would be as willfully obstinate as he was being at that moment. He was still stubbornly playing a game that no one could win anymore. I wanted to shout at him, tell him off for disappointing me and everyone else, but then I wanted to hug him, cradle him against my chest and never, ever let him go. My eyes started to water and I considered whether or not a HEPA filter would get rid of these damn allergies. Against my better judgment, I tapped Sylvie's contact.

"Abby. Thanks for calling me back. I take it you checked out his social media?"

"Yeah, he looks like total shit."

"He's acting like a piece of one too," she muttered.

I snorted. "Sorry, not sure what to tell you, you know?"

"I know he hurt you, Abby, but he's hurting right now, really badly, and I blame myself. I didn't think it through when I brought the deal to him. I'd hoped that we'd be able to work around this goon part of the contract. But then he said he'd go with it regardless."

Something wasn't ringing true to me. "Wait, you *were* trying to get him out of that aspect of the contract? And then you stopped?"

Sylvie backpedaled. "Um, yes. I thought that he'd push back because of you and we'd finally see him publicly embrace some of those positive changes he'd made behind the scenes."

"Why would that matter to you? Aren't you watching out for his career? Surely this is a great opportunity for him and losing that clause may have tanked the deal. And why would you care about the two of us together so much?"

Now it was Sylvie's turn to snort. "*Psh*, Abby. Please. You've been around this game for long enough that you know how it goes. Sometimes money isn't everything, especially when your soulmate is on the line."

"Sylvie? Soulmate? Are you trying to say —"

"Yes! Yes, fine. I'll admit it. I've literally been waiting for years for the two of you to realize how perfect you are for each other and — just when I thought you were right there too — he goes and pulls this crap."

"The whole morality clause thing?" I asked slowly, feeling like I'd been hit over the head with a hammer.

"Oh, it was real all right. Chicago insisted on it, but when you two pulled that smooch and then the accident happened with him saying you were engaged, my heart nearly exploded! I was so happy!"

"Happy that I could have died?" I nearly shrieked.

"Obviously not, my dear, but finally my two favorite clients could pull their thumbs out of their asses and be forced to deal with the fact that they're perfect for each other."

"You've got to be kidding me," I muttered. "You set this up."

"No, not completely. I mean, you two did the whole smooch thing yourselves, and then the accident...that was all the universe pushing you two together."

"Sylvie, I'm glad you're invested in your clients, but this is a lot to take in. I can't believe you didn't push him harder to get out of that aspect of the contract if you felt so strongly about us together. He let me down when he made that decision."

"I messed up there, you're right, and I'm sorry for my part in your break-up. But, Abby, please. Think about this. He loves you so much. He's a wreck without you. I know you're a tough cookie and you'll ultimately be fine, but you're not you, not whole without him. And you know it."

"You're honestly trying to pull the fairy godmother thing right now?"

"I don't know what else to do. His family has been trying to talk to him, but no one is getting through to his stubborn ass. Is there anything you can do to reach out to him?"

"You've got to be joking. I'm not reaching out to him, he ruined everything. We're done. Over. The Abby and Matti show has been canceled."

"Abby, I'm sorry. I meddled and I know it was wrong but, please, think about this. I need your help to reach him. I know there are feelings still between the two of you. Please."

"Fuck you, Sylvie. I can't even comprehend how fucked up this is. I've got to go, we can talk some other time. Like maybe in a few years."

I hung up, furious, and smashed my fist into the back of the chaise over and over again. Matchmaking wasn't her fucking job, it was to be our agent — not our love life manager. *How dare she mess around with that.*

Jumping up and down, I rolled my shoulders and finally racked out twenty-five fast push-ups to get rid of the pent-up anger before deciding that I needed to get on with my plan for the day. A plan that would certainly suit my terrible mood. A trip to the most deadly place on earth on a Saturday — IKEA.

The drive took a half-hour and I parked closest to the warehouse exit. I slid my headphones in my ears and felt a pang of remorse — the UEFA podcast I'd been listening to had broken down Matti's team's last game. They'd won, but he'd been red carded and would be sitting out the next two games. I wanted to call him, but there was no way that would happen after Sylvie's disclosure. Instead I turned on a new podcast to cancel out the horrible IKEA on a weekend crowd and started loading my cart. My ongoing heartbreak could wait — my stubborn had a tight hold on me and I couldn't afford to wallow in my heartbreak at a discount furniture warehouse of all places.

The trick with IKEA is to know exactly what you're getting and go straight to the warehouse to pluck it off the shelves, working in reverse wherever possible. I followed my tried-and-true methods and was back in the car a shocking two hours later — I'd stopped for meatballs. *Mmm…delicious balls of fatty, MSG goodness.* My phone was connected to Bluetooth and blaring a Grrls of Pop playlist that never failed to make me ready to dismantle the patriarchy and keep my energy up for the hell of unpacking and assembling IKEA doohickeys.

A text notification pinged and I immediately grabbed my phone, hoping without reason that it was a response to a very carefully constructed message I'd sent to my mother's phone a few days ago. It was a flashback to every other time that my phone would ring and I'd irrationally hope it was her, calling to apologize. To tell me she loved me.

Instead it was a robo-text from a local pizza place thanking me for being such a great customer and offering me a discount on my next order. As the Grrls rioted around me, I stuffed my frustration back down. "Fine, one more chance?" I asked my reflection in the rearview mirror as I backed out of my spot. "Okay. Siri, call Mom."

"Calling Mom," my phone responded, then the ringing started. My heart was in my throat as I navigated through the parking structure and back to the highway. I'd almost given up hope when it clicked.

"Hello?"

"M-Mom?" I managed to stutter out.

"Abby?" Her voice sounded a little different than it had ten years ago when she'd cut me off so deeply and permanently. It was softer, more hesitant now. Almost penitent in that one word that somehow managed to convey ten years of regret and fault.

"Yeah, Mom. It's me, Abby. Hi. I know it's been a while, but I've been hoping we could connect. Did you get my text message?"

She was silent for a moment and I heard a muffled sob. Then, "Yes, I did. I'm so sorry I didn't reply. I almost didn't know what to say. I've wanted to reach out for so long. How have you been?"

As if ten years were nothing, as if the last time she'd talked to me I hadn't still been a teenager. A lifetime had passed. "Why? Why didn't you reply? How can you just ask how things are going?"

She choked as she laughed awkwardly. "I don't even know what to say. I've dreamed about this for years. How I'd apologize and the words that I'd say to try to mend fences. And what comes out of my mouth when I finally have the chance? 'How you doin'?'"

Her attempt at an Italian accent was atrocious and I laughed. The ice broken. "Should we start over?"

"If you don't mind. I'd like to do this right. I'm just so nervous."

I grinned and realized that my cheeks were damp, tears of relief snaking their way down as I drove. "I am too."

"Oh, Abby." She took a deep breath. "I'm so sorry. I wasn't a good mother to you, didn't encourage you enough, tried to force you into a role you weren't meant for. I pushed you away when I should have been proud of you. I can't take back those years or the words that I said. All I can say is that I'll try to do better."

I was silent, shocked into complete stillness like a rabbit who smells a predator but has no idea if they're hungry and ready to attack or decently full and keeping an eye out.

"When we saw that you were home—after you ran into Cynthia, she told us about running into you and that darling boy. That you seemed happy with where you were, it made me see the error of my ways and how much I needed you back in my life—"

"You talked to Cynthia?" I asked.

"Yes, she came over almost as soon as she got back from Chicago. Had so many great things to say about you, how well you looked, and that you were in love with a lovely boy. I've wasted too much time and want to know you, your fiancé. I want to be part of your life again. When you texted me, it was right as I was trying to figure out the right way to reach out to you."

"And you still didn't respond?"

She sighed. "I chickened out. Wasn't sure you'd be interested in talking to me or whether or not you'd let your small-town family into your new big-city life. I know that sounds bad, or like I'm trying to guilt you or something, but I'm not. You've lived so many places, seen so many things. How could you want to reconnect with a past that was too constrained and unkind for you?"

"Ma, I just wanted you back. This whole time. Yeah, I've seen a lot of the world now, but I missed you."

"I understand that now. Would it be all right if your dad and I came down to Chicago to spend time with you and meet your fiancé?"

My fiancé. Is that all I'm good for? Getting married and popping out kids? "Unfortunately, you're a bit late for meeting him. He's moved to England. Still want to hang out with your daughter if she's not being a good girl and getting married?"

"Of course I do. It's you I miss. I want you to be happy. Did you end up breaking up with him?"

"It's a long story, Mom, and not one I feel like talking about with someone who's only tiptoeing her way back into my life."

"Oh, sure, sorry. Am I, though? Tiptoeing back into your life? I'd like nothing more than to get to know you and to have some sort of relationship. I know it will take a while for you to trust me, maybe even longer for you to forgive me, but I want to try. If you'll allow it."

I bashed myself over the head with my phone before bringing it gently to my ear. "Mom... I don't know what to say. I've missed you for years, wanted you with me each time I celebrated a win. Every time the phone would ring—for years—I'd hope it was you."

She gasped on the other end of the phone and I heard a muffled sniffle.

"Maybe. I don't know. Can we start small? Monthly or weekly phone calls? Video calls? And promises that each one is a no-judgment zone. I can't handle any more of that in my life. If I catch even a hint that you're doing this because I finally found my way to being a wife and mother, I will end things myself."

"Yes, yes, absolutely, Abby. We can do this. Oh, thank you. Thank you, thank you for this opportunity."

We hung up after agreeing to a video chat date the next weekend and I drove the rest of the way home with a tiny sun glowing in my heart. Even though the loss of Matti and my worries about him were shadows on the otherwise bright aspects of my new life, I could feel the beginnings of a peaceful bedrock being laid down. I wished, with all of my heart, that he was still part of it, still reachable and still mine.

Chapter Twenty-Eight

Matti

London was a mistake. A horrible, horrible mistake. I cursed Sylvie every day for bringing me that contract, and my idiot self for agreeing to it. For not listening to Abby, for losing her. Nothing was right without her and I could feel myself sinking deeper and deeper into depression.

I should have done so many things differently, but Tottenham wasn't letting me go and it was hard to walk away from the money and prestige of a Premier League team when my behavior had basically made me persona non grata to anyone else. There was only one thing I'd been able to do since I moved — one good thing — and management had the nerve to haul me in for it since it didn't *"fit my brand."*

"Matthias, what's this about?" Ronan's hand struck the newspaper with an irritated slap that threatened to rip through the flimsy paper.

"It's a story about the charity I've started working with, similar to one that I was involved with in Chicago — setting up and outfitting soccer programs for children of new immigrant families." I picked at the cuticle of my left thumb, frowning that it seemed all jagged and puffy. How long had I been gnawing on it?

"You do realize that this is the opposite of your brand, do you not?" His patronizing, lightly accented voice was growing more strident with every smack of his hand to the newsprint.

"Sir, it's something that means a lot to me and I've kept it low-key to fit with what you've asked of me, but it's important. I'm not going to stop doing it."

"Matthias, we've invested a great deal in you and the rest of this team. We have consultants on hand to deal with branding and messaging and This. Does. Not. Fit. You need to drop it." The chair that he'd been leaning back on thudded back down to the floor of his posh office and I felt the vibration run up the metal legs of the uncomfortable visitor chair across from him.

"I don't see why it matters. I'll talk to them and have my name taken off of it. You know that this image isn't me — not really. I'm doing everything you wanted me to, but it's not me."

"Sure, sure, it's not. Listen, your level of play on the field has been high lately, but if you want to keep your playing time, you'll drop this. Immediately. Now get out of here, you've got practice and I have another meeting in three minutes and need to take a shit." Ronan waved me out.

The one good thing I'd been trying to do was being taken from me and I didn't know if I could handle the loss. I was constantly ill from staying out late — never mind that I didn't drink when I went out — and the pressure to constantly be in the spotlight acting like an asshole was killing me. They'd tied my pay and my playing time to headlines and social media stories. Clicks for cash—and I'd signed that contract like an idiot.

Almost daily, Sylvie's and Abby's voices rang through my head. "*This isn't you. Why do you feel like you need to hide who you really are?*" And, maybe most importantly, "*What have you done?*" My teammates were a bunch of hooligans with no respect for me, for the game, for anything but their images. We were a talented-as-hell group of egocentric assholes who barely played as a team. It was a miracle that we were winning at all with our selfish and boorish play. I was fucking ashamed every time I suited up, and even more so whenever I went out in public with them.

I felt lost. The charity group that I worked with now was the only thing keeping me sane and I was about to lose that too. If, that is, I wanted to keep playing the club's game. Frustrated beyond all reason, I called Sylvie.

"Matthias," she said, and sighed as if I were the bane of her existence. Maybe I was. Who knew anymore?

"Hey, Sylvie. Listen, I had a meeting with Ronan and he wants me to quit the charity work I've been doing."

"I'm aware."

"Okay, then you probably know that I don't want to do that. Can you set up a scholarship fund for kids? I'm talking equipment, tutoring, whatever those kids need, I'll fund it. Maybe my name won't be on the board anymore, but I'll still be doing something."

She was silent for a moment. "Is this really what you want? Seriously, Matti. I'm very concerned." I could tell — she rarely called me "Matti." It was almost always "Matthias," keeping me at arm's distance, professionally meddling.

"Yeah, I need to do something since I'm not allowed to do the work in person anymore."

"No, Matthias. Is dropping the charity really what you want? Is playing for this club really what you want?"

Now it was my turn to be silent.

"I ask this because I'd have thought you'd have come to your senses by now. I haven't wanted to say anything because I know how much playing in Europe means to you, but that contract is killing you and I'd be remiss in my duties as your agent if I didn't encourage you to really think about what you want right now. You ran from the start of something great in Chicago. Why, given your general level of misery, are you willing to stay?"

I groaned. "Chicago" was code for Abby. "Sylvie, you know it wasn't like that —"

"That's bullshit, Matthias."

"I don't want to talk about Chicago right now. Can you do the scholarship thing or not?"

"I can. Should I also convey your regrets that you'll no longer be able to volunteer in person?"

"Yeah," I said, and my heart sank at the loss. "Since we're on the subject, how is Chicago?" I drummed my fingers on the bench in the locker room. My teammates were starting to filter in for morning practice.

"Fine. Everything's perfectly fine, actually."

"Great, that's great. Glad to hear —"

"Abby's team is likely going to qualify for the national title, she's got an adorable little apartment, her family is starting to become a part of her life again and I think she's dating someone seriously."

"What? Are you kidding me?" I shouted.

"Yes. A little. Why are you mad? You're the one who cut her loose."

"I did, but I thought she'd respect me enough—"

"Oh, horseshit, Matthias. You're jealous and you know you messed up big-time there. It's not about you—I repeat, everything is not always about you. She's not dating anyone at all, but she seems to be at peace with everything in her life right now. We had dinner together a few weeks ago and I've never seen her so optimistic and focused. My little grump is turning into a regular sunshine. It's almost alarming."

"Alarming," I said, and my voice was faint as I watched the guys start to change. No one was talking and it certainly wasn't because we were focused. More because we all despised one another. "Sylvie, I've got to go or I'll be late for practice. I'm glad Abby's okay and thanks for dealing with the charity for me."

"Stop being stubborn, Matti. You should call her—"

I stabbed the red end call icon and continued to flip through my phone, ignoring everyone as they changed and headed out to the field. My camera roll had largely been purged of anything Abby-related, except that one picture from Mexico, her asleep on my chest, both of us naked and exhausted, but happy—she was grinning in her sleep and I had the cat that ate the canary smirk spreading large. I'd never been able to delete it.

A little thread of guilt and shame spiraled into the gaping hole she'd left in my heart and I hastily clicked back out. "Damn allergies, they need to dust in here," I muttered as I swiped at my eyes and opened my messaging app to the Brothers S group text that Abby had started for me.

SOS drinks tonight. FaceTime at 20:00 GMT. Figure out what that means for your time zones yourselves.

Markus and Max sent back GIFs from *The Hangover* and *Beerfest*. After a terrible practice, I dropped into a carry-out and grabbed two six-packs indiscriminately, then headed home. For the rest of the afternoon, I methodically stalked Abby's social media presence, sparse as it was, and immediately understood what Sylvie had meant. There she was, a smile that wasn't forced, eyes that didn't glitter with pain. The Ice Queen had melted and now she was this whole, real, beautiful person. Her focus may have shifted from the single-minded tunnel vision required for a player, but widening it seemed to have been the best for her.

Only one picture hinted at something slightly amiss and I devoured it, hoping against hope that it was evidence that she was as messed up as me. It was a candid profile shot of her on the field during some sort of Northwestern–Rebels exhibition scrimmage. She had her arms crossed tightly across her chest and Daniel Lopez was talking to her, him standing with his hands wide and palms facing up. Her mouth was turned down, her brow was furrowed and there was something a little lost and broken in her eyes. To anyone else, maybe, she would have come off as tough and in charge. But I knew her and had seen her broken looks before. She was not as fine as she pretended to be and my heart shattered again. This was my fault.

Bbbbb-t, bbbb-t... Who had determined that FaceTime calls had that kind of farting, blurt-y ringtone? It was a disgusting sound and I was already a beer deep on a gross Chinese takeout.

My propped-up tablet's screen split into two image panes. Markus, the urbane, effortlessly handsome film star that he was, had a highball glass of brown liquid cradled in his hands. Max appeared uncharacteristically disheveled. His tie was loosened, collar opened a few buttons more than was typical for him, dark hair sticking out every which way and even the arms of his shirt looked a little wrinkled. He was mid-drink directly from the wine bottle when the call connected and held up a finger for us to pause. Markus smirked and ran a hand through his own artfully mussed hair that was so much more like my own. Except shorter, and a little dirtier blond. He winked at me.

"Max. How disappointing that you didn't wait for our toast," Markus said in that stern daddy voice that I knew he'd been practicing. Max flipped him off as he set the bottle down with a gasp and wiped his mouth with the back of his hand.

"It's been a day, brothers. An absolute fucking day." He stared longingly at the bottle again. "So, what's the deal, Matti? You called this meeting of the minds."

"Hold up. First we need to toast, then Matti can unload upon us properly," Markus interjected.

"Fine, fine. Here's to brothers, drinking and minimizing driving," Max rattled off in a bored tone and Markus and I glanced at each other, then at him.

"It's truly uncanny how you manage to nail a situation in like seven words," Markus muttered.

"Anyways..." Max ignored him. "We're waiting?" He took another gulp straight from the bottle.

"So, I think I fucked up."

Max choked and sprayed wine all over the camera and Markus started to laugh uncontrollably.

"What? I'm being serious. I need help." I fiddled with the bottle caps that littered the counter and started sliding them into little frowny faces.

Markus recovered first and his eyebrows lowered. His frown could have threatened a teenager trying to get away with stealing their parents' booze. "Tell us how you think you fucked up." Damn, he was going to be a great dad.

I took a deep breath and tried to tamp down my irritation. Wasn't it obvious how I'd fucked up? Why'd they need me to spell it out— *Oh.* "I fucked it up with Abby when I took the Tottenham gig without talking to her. She's right, I didn't really treat her like an equal in our relationship."

"And?" Max said and coughed.

"And, and...I'm in love with her, but didn't bother to tell her, and instead of dealing with it head-on, I decided to run from my feelings."

"And?" Markus asked patiently, then slammed his Scotch and filled the glass again.

"Hold up, just a second," I said indignantly, then slammed my own beer, burped and flipped the cap off the next. "There we go. Quit trying to outdrink me. I'm the one in severe emotional pain here."

"We see that," Max deadpanned.

"And...?" Markus threatened.

"And, fine. I was incapable of being myself because I was scared to admit to who I really was—a dumb jock. When she got through to me, I wanted to keep her in the little box I'd assigned her to and couldn't handle it when she outgrew it. Because she did outgrow it and, in the end, she outgrew me because I refused to grow with her."

"Wow. I would have expected the agricultural references about growth from Max but you've really nailed it." Markus clapped at me, then held up his glass to the screen. Max and I dutifully raised our own, clinked our glasses and finished our drinks. Then found others. As one does.

"Proud of your personal growth, Matti," muttered Max, who'd yanked the cork out of a new bottle with his teeth like a total badass.

"Samesies," Markus muttered as he overflowed his glass.

"Samesies?" Max and I chorused and burst out laughing.

"Oh, shut up, children. Listen, Matti, what are you going to do with this new knowledge? Because you can't sit there being miserable with what you've realized."

"I don't know. Can you help me? That's why I called, really. I can't do this alone. I'm the moron who's never been in a relationship before." I flipped the cap into the recycling can like a champ and gave myself a silent high-five.

Max smiled indulgently, like I was a precocious toddler. "Sure, Matti. We've got you."

The next hour flew by with Max and Markus coaching me on strategies for groveling, the timing of the apology and the most effective methods of grand gesturing. My petty-ass ears perked up big-time when Max started detailing nefarious plans for screwing over Tottenham on my way out the door.

"Markus, are you done yet? You promised you'd go down — oh. Hey, Matti, Max."

"Ooh, is Markus late for an oral appointment?" I struggled with a straight face and Max snorted, little rivulets of wine leaking out of his mouth.

"Yes, yes, he is." Alina was stern but her cheeks were bright red and Markus was staring at her like a besotted fool.

"Okay, thanks, guys—"

"Hey, wait!" Max interrupted and suddenly his words were ultra-clear and precise. "Real quick, wanted to let you guys know that I've met someone and it's serious. Keep an eye out for an invitation soon." He clicked off.

"What the actual fuck?!" Markus and I chorused.

From the background, I could hear Alina muttering, "I knew that one was dangerous."

"Oh my god, Mother is going to kill him, right?" I laughed hysterically at my peacemaking, flying-beneath-the-radar brother getting busted by our mother.

"Oh she totally is," gasped Markus. "All right, Alina, all right. Listen, Matti, I gotta go. Talk soon, yeah? This was fun. Keep me updated on how the planning goes."

"I will. Love you, Markus."

"You too, baby brother."

We hung up and I started to dance around my apartment, cranking music loudly and air guitar and drumming as I raced through the rooms. When the song changed to something more contemplative, I decided to call Sylvie. *No time like the present.*

"Hello?" Sylvie's voice was a little croaky, like she'd taken up smoking again.

"Sylvie! My favorite agent in the whole agenting world. Hi!"

"Matthias, to what do I owe this honor? Two calls in one day?"

"Yeah, bear with me. I'm a little buzzed and just got off the phone with my brothers."

"Oh, shit sticks," she muttered.

"No, none of that. Here's the deal and I think you can agree with us. This Tottenham thing has been a huge mistake. The biggest of my career. Because of it I lost Abby and whatever bright future I'd been building." I continued to strum my imaginary guitar.

"True, very true."

"Okay, so maybe you know what I'm going to say here?"

"Honestly, no, the way I see it, things could go a few different directions—"

"First, I need you to call the club. Tell them if they don't remove the asshole clause in my contract and the whole clickbait incentive structure, I'm out."

"You know they're not going to remove it."

"Then I'm out."

"As you say," she murmured. "Anything else?"

"Yeah, I need to apologize to Abby. So, after you lay down that ultimatum and they say no, you quit for me and then I'm going to go get my girl. If she'll have me."

"Matti, I don't think it's going to be that simple," she said.

"Sure, that's what I pay you for. Make it that simple. You're an ace and I know you wouldn't have locked me into that horrible contract if you hadn't created a loophole for us to exit without punitive damages once I got my head out of my ass."

"How well you know me, Matthias."

"Abby does, and she told me you were the best."

"I'm flattered." Her voice was choked.

"So you'll get me out and I'm going to get moving on a serious grand gesture. Then I'm going to Chicago, and I'm going to need you to find us a few job options somewhere together. None of this long-distance bullshit. I need her, she needs me, and that's how it's going to be."

Faint applause from Sylvie's corner lit me up. This was going to work. Things were going to be fine. I just had to get the girl.

Chapter Twenty-Nine

Abby

Muddy water splashed up over the curb, soaking my trainers. Yet another gross, cold and rainy April afternoon in Chicago. Luckily, I had another pair in my locker at work. We were in the finals of the Big Ten Conference Championship and had been largely on cruise control, but this weather was going to throw a wrench in the works since our goalkeeper was a sophomore transfer from Florida and decidedly whiny about what counted as spring in the Midwest. One more practice, then the big game.

I was scarfing down takeout in my office, reviewing film and analyzing set plays from the semifinals, when my phone began to vibrate across my desk. The international number wasn't one I recognized, but the country code was +44 and I figured it was Teresa, who owed me a call back.

"Teresa, it's late for you. What's going on?"

The line was quiet except for an insistent buzz like a horde of bees were trapped in the mobile ether. Then a very familiar gravelly voice, "It's not Teresa. It's me. Matti."

My phone fell out of my suddenly nerveless fingers and landed directly on my sandwich, sliding off to clatter on the desk. I swore and picked it back up, wiping off the mayo with my sleeve. "Um, yeah. Matti. Hey."

The buzzing turned up louder and he raised his voice, but somehow made it softer too, like the sense of relief that I hadn't hung up on him was too much. "Abby, I'm so glad you answered."

My cheeks started to burn. His voice had always been one of my favorite things about him and I could picture him pulling out his hair tie and aggressively tightening it again. I cleared my throat. "Sure, Matti. What's going on? Are you enjoying being back in the League?" *Do you miss me as much as I miss you? Are you as sad as you look in social media?*

"I'm okay. It's not really been the deal that I hoped for, you know?" He groaned suddenly.

A voice from the background announced, "Almost done, bud. Doing okay?"

Matti answered, "Fine, finish it up. Don't need a break." The buzzing started up again.

"Sorry," he said into the phone. "I'm kind of in the middle of something."

"Um, it's okay. What are you doing?"

Matti grunted. "New tattoo, ribs, hurts like a bitch and I wanted someone to talk to me through it."

Oh. Not talk to me specifically.

Then, like he read my mind, "And I've been thinking a lot about you. I hope it's okay that I called."

I shook my head. "It's fine. What are you getting?"

"It's a surprise. I'll send you a pic when it's done. How are things with you? Sylvie says your team is kicking ass."

Sylvie was a vile traitor. I held my phone out and made a face at it. "Yeah, I'm fine. We're in the conference finals on Friday, then hopefully on to the national tournament next week. After that, we'll see."

"Cool," he said and moaned a little. "How's Spock?"

"He's fine. I'll tell him you say hello."

"Great, thanks. Listen, this is awkward and I'm sorry. For so many things, but I'm hurting and wanted to talk to you. Tell you about everything that's going on—Markus is about to be a dad and is finally excited about it, Max is apparently dating someone seriously and I'm—well, you know. Me."

"Sure, Matti."

"Ugh, this isn't coming out right at all. Not how I planned it. Usually tattoos get me in order—the pain focuses things for me. It's not working tonight. I think the stakes are too high."

"It's okay, Matti."

"It's not." He unintentionally echoed my thoughts. "It's really not and I'm sorry about that too. Fuck, I'm really screwing this up. The point is that you were right about everything. This move was a huge mistake. The club wants me to be someone I'm not and I'm finally not scared to be who I really am. And that's all because of you."

Tears started to tickle the corners of my eyes. Dammit, I'd sworn I'd never cry over Matti Shellenberg again.

"My brothers and my sister are all sitting in places that I want to be—not exactly like them, but close. They know themselves, intimately, and aren't afraid of anything anymore. Their partners helped them find themselves and supported them along the way. And that's what I want. It's also what I'm realizing we had before I messed everything up."

My breath was coming faster and faster as the tears started to spill out.

"I'm so sorry, Abby. You saw me, the real me, when no one else ever has, and it scared me that someone could randomly cut through all of the bullshit I'd thrown up. The challenges you threw my way terrified me because, even then, I knew that if I rose to them, I'd be someone that I wasn't ready to be. I'm ready now and I want — no, needed — you to know that."

"Matti, I don't know what to say," I finally choked out.

"Don't say anything. I'm not asking you for anything at all. I needed to tell you, finally, how I feel."

"Thanks, Matti."

"No, thank you, Abby. You've meant everything to me and I'm sorry I screwed everything up, the words I said, the way I wasn't there for you when all you did was support and care for me — trying to make me be the best person I could be. I regret my choices that led me here, but not the ones that brought us together."

"Oh, Matti —"

"No, please don't say anything. I needed you to know."

We were both silent and I heard the buzzing come to a halt again. This time the man said, "All done, buddy. Wanna take a look?"

"Abby? I've got to go, but can I call you again? I miss you."

"I don't know if that's such a good idea. This is hard."

"Hard things are the ones that are the most rewarding, no?"

Now I was laughing through my tears. "For sure, for sure. Yeah, you can call me."

"Good, gotta go, Stabby. Talk soon."

My concentration was shot after that call, even after I cleaned up my phone and my eyes stopped leaking. Slowly, I drove home, back to my little guest house, where I immediately poured myself a very healthy glass of wine and unloaded everything on my unsuspecting cat.

"And then he told me he missed me. Can you believe that, Spock? Oh, and he says hi to you too."

"Meep."

"That's not even a real cat noise, Spock. What the hell?"

"Merow."

"Good, that's better."

Spock leaped into my lap and circled a few times, kneading my quads and purring. I stroked him as I recounted Matti's words. He was sorry. He missed me. He realized he'd done wrong. Lots of words, but no action. It was easy to be sorry when you were still rich as hell and playing the game you loved.

The wine must have soured on me and I balanced the glass on Spock's purring back while I pulled out my phone to masochistically go through Matti's social media, idly thinking he'd show off the new tattoo, but all was quiet on that front. *Hmph.* I was in a mood, becoming more and more irritated that he'd call, say all those lovely things then go. That was so his way, though. Lots of talk, no action.

I gave up and tossed the rest of the wine down the sink and trudged back to my bedroom after making sure the doors were all locked. I had a game to coach in two days that was more important than almost anything I'd ever suited up for. This was my opportunity to make a name for myself in a new way.

Spock was waiting on my bed for me when I came back out of the bathroom wearing one of Matti's old practice jerseys with clean teeth and smooth hair. "Shove over, dude," I muttered to the little guy, who promptly rolled onto his back begging for belly rubs. A notification lit up my phone and I reached over to the nightstand to pull it over.

It was a text from Matti and my heart started to beat harder as I slowly opened it. A mirror shot at a tattoo studio, my former fake fiancé in his S-brand Adidas track pants, one hand holding his shirt up to show off the freaking enormous design on his side, the other hand holding his phone as he winced. I zoomed in on the new tat. A knife? With a banner above it?

I squinted and zoomed closer. It was an old-school dagger with a ribbon wrapping around it that had two words printed on it. A-B-B-Y S-U-E. My name—plus the fake middle name Sylvie had called me on our first day in Chicago. That asshole had put my name on himself, in one of the most painful places to get a tattoo. I could practically hear him whisper the short message that accompanied the image in my ear.

Like what you see, Stabby?

I did like it. I liked it a lot. Too much, and my eyes brimmed over. I sent back a heart, not having the words for anything else. He quickly responded with a whole string of emojis and a GIF of Renee Zellweger from *Jerry Maguire*. "You complete me," she blinked over and over at me from the text string. I closed out and set the phone aside after making sure that my alarm was set, resolutely not thinking about him anymore. I'd cried entirely too much over Matti Shellenberg today, but that didn't stop the tears from continuing to drench my pillow.

* * * *

After the Conference Championship, I'd learned a few things. Namely, that winning as a coach was more rewarding than winning as a player. When you played, the high from a win wore off faster than you'd expect, but coaching? That high never wore off, and I was rolling on it all the way into the National Championship tournament.

Our team was young, mostly freshmen and sophomores, with a handful of juniors and only two seniors. None of whom had ever played at this level before. Williams and I were giving them the pep talk of a lifetime — it seriously belonged in like every cheesy sports movie ever. I could practically hear Tom Hanks spieling it as inspirational music swelled and actors in uniforms nodded solemnly. We led them out to line up in the tunnel and, when the stadium employees in headphones waved us out, we sprinted onto the field with them — my knee barely even twinged, the energy was infectious.

As we stood in the middle of the field for the anthem, I glanced around, all of the people and signs blurring together until I saw a huge clump of vaguely familiar figures right behind our bench. I squinted, unable to believe my eyes, but it looked like a guy with a bunch of kids around him were holding posters up with my name on it. I shook my head, trying to see more clearly. Nope, blurs and small blurs with blurry things in front of them.

Following the coin toss, Coach Williams and I headed to the bench with the subs and other staff members. One row above the bench was a man I would have recognized anywhere. Longish blond hair tied carelessly back, ruthlessly razored undercut looking sharp, vintage aviators pushed back on his head to show off his laughing eyes, wearing a white T-shirt, gray jeans and, I imagined, his own branded Adidas kicks on his feet. He was holding a sign that would have appeared to anyone else that it had been fingerpainted by a three-year-old, with shaky Sharpie'd lettering, "Go Coach Abby! We Love You!" I knew better. He'd written that himself.

To his left and right were little faces I recognized from months before—kids from the camps who'd meant something to both of us. Their families were right behind them, along with Tiana and Coach Sherman, Daniel and Mer Lopez too. And every one of them held a sign. "Forgiveness Is the Best Medicine!" "He Was an Asshole, but He's a Really Nice Guy...Usually." "Give Him a Second Chance!" "He's Sorry, Please Forgive Him!" And my personal favorite, "Make Him Beg!" held by Mer. I grinned at her and blew her a kiss.

Matti acted like I'd stabbed him as he clapped a hand to his chest and mimed reaching around to pull out a knife. I grinned and gestured to him to raise his shirt. He frowned for a second, unsure of what I was asking, and finally caught on. He bowed to me, handed off his sign to someone next to him and slowly lifted his shirt to show off the colorful dagger. Everyone around him laughed uproariously and he took a second bow. Then he put his hands into the corny heart shape that he'd always done at his games and pointed at me. For the first time ever, I did it back.

A whistle blew.

The game was back on.

* * * *

Unlike the day that I'd snagged my final victory as a player a little less than a year ago, the sun was shining brightly as air horns, screaming and confetti polluted the air above the field as the Northwestern men's soccer team accepted the trophy for the NCAA Division One Championship. People were hugging everywhere and I smiled that same smile. The smile that came from winning this beautiful, beautiful game. This time I wasn't one of the ones in uniform, I was on the sidelines in my school-issued warm-up, jumping up and down on the arm of Coach Williams, who was in tears.

We shook hands, hugged our players, dealt with the requisite Gatorade shower, headed to the locker room for the requisite fired-up, inspirational-sports-movie victory speech, then showered and changed. Williams and I handled the post-game press conference and he ushered me out a side door to the parking lot immediately afterward.

"But the team's bus is out in front?" I asked uncertainly.

"But your ride is right out there," he answered with a shit-eating grin and pointed to an enormous SUV with a blond in a white T-shirt leaning against the driver's side door, all cool and casual like a *GQ* ad. If a *GQ* ad could possibly be nervous, because that's what Matti looked like as he raised his left hand to his mouth to gnaw on a cuticle.

He did a half-wave around waist height and closed his eyes. The breath he blew out sent a loosened strand of hair straight into the air above him. I could practically see his thoughts. "Be cool, man. Christ, can you not be cool for like once in your life?"

This was another of life's little moments, the ones that you know ahead of time are going to be indelibly printed on your gray matter for years and years to come. The decision to be made hovered in the air above me. I stood immobile until Williams let out an amused grunt and gave me a shove out the door. It closed and clicked shut decisively. He'd locked it, the bastard.

"Abby?" Matti pushed off of the car and started toward me, a hand outstretched uncertainly in front of him.

His voice cracked a little as he said my name and it was enough to unlock my feet from their hold on the cement. I started moving toward him, picking up speed until I was sprinting. At the last second I leaped into the air, knowing that he would catch me.

"I missed you, you bastard," I whispered in his ear and felt my eyes start to leak all over the neck of his shirt.

"I missed you too, Stabby. So, so much. Can you ever forgive me?" He pulled back to stare earnestly into my eyes. "I screwed up so bad and I understand if you want me to go, never want to see me again, but I had to let you know. I've quit Tottenham when they wouldn't take me as I am and I'm moving back here."

"You are, really? Why here?"

His eyebrows quirked at me, like I was asking a very silly question. "You, Stabby. Because you're here. I love you and will do anything to prove it, even move to a place where the winter is worse than Russia. You mean everything to me. I'll get down on my knees if you want..." His eyes beseeched me as he held my biceps tightly. "Please, Abby, can we try this again?"

I stared deep into those baby blue eyes, and the tiny gold flecks began to twinkle in their depths as I slowly smiled at him. "Yes, Matti. Yes. We can try this again. I love you too."

"Oh, thank fucking god. I really wasn't sure. Sylvie didn't think this would work—did you know she'd basically been planning this all along? She thought we belonged together or whatever—"

"She what? You're kidding." I tried to play it off.

"No, no. She was playing a wicked game of matchmaker this entire time. We only gave her the weapons."

"Yeah, I found out too."

He swatted my arm. "Stinker. Give me that."

"What?"

"Your hand, hold it out."

I flattened my palm and extended it toward him as I imagined how our perfidious agent would react to this scene. She'd probably be cackling like a witch as she tangled her yarn and crunched nicotine gum like it was her job.

"There, what do you think?"

The sudden, familiar weight on the third finger of my left hand took me aback and I stared down at the ring, his grandmother's ring, sitting snugly beneath the second knuckle.

"Is it okay? Not too soon, I hope? Dammit, give it back. I'm sorry, I get ahead of myself, you know how I am… Let's pretend that didn't happen and go back to being happy that you're giving me a second chance. Engagements aren't necessary." He struggled to pull the ring back and I clenched my fist, trapping his fingers between my own.

"Nope, it's mine now, boy." I grinned at him through yet another haze of tears. "I love you too, you big jerk, but this time there's nothing fake about this, right? No contracts, no meddling agents, just us."

"Always us, Stabby. Always."

"And Spock. He misses his daddy."

Matti swept me tightly into his arms and kissed my forehead while I wrapped my legs around his waist. "I love you, Abigail McKinnon, and your little cat too. I'm gonna marry the shit out of you someday very soon," he whispered into my ear.

I pulled back and grinned, then booped his nose. "You sure are."

He kissed me hard and all of my plans for the future evaporated before recombining into the person who was holding me tightly, murmuring that he loved me, that he'd never let me go, that we were a team.

"Wanna get it on in the SUV for old times' sake? I got the one with the darkest tint possible," he mumbled against my lips.

"You say the sweetest things. Let's do it," I mumbled back as he fumbled open the door to toss me in the back seat.

He smiled down at me as I lay sprawled across the big bench, then swung himself up and shut the door gently behind him. "I've dreamed of this, of you, for so long. Thank you for taking me back."

There were no more words as I pulled him down to me. There was no point. Of course I'd take him back. He was part of me, my team, my best friend, my cheerleader, mediator, inspiration. Matti Shellenberg was everything.

Epilogue

Matti
One year later – Austria

"Where's Markus?" Abby asked as we stepped carefully around a stack of barrels that seemed like they were moments away from crashing down upon us. "And what's that smell?" Her nose wrinkled adorably as the smell of organic fertilizer – also known as manure – wafted through the hazy afternoon light.

"He must have gotten tied up somewhere." I waved vaguely at the vineyards and grinned.

Max and I had finally, finally beaten Markus in the prank war that had been brewing over the last few years among the three of us. It had started off so innocently, Markus posting a shot on his massive social media account of a sleeping Max with a hairy penis drawn on his face, then managing to snap me and Abby sneaking out of a bathroom in his house, her lipstick smeared all over my face and the collar of my shirt.

Both photos, I should add, were massive hits with his fans.

The joke was certainly on Markus now as we'd left him hog-tied in his underwear amidst the grapevines in the wee hours of the morning. Bless Max for his no-longer-secret BDSM tendencies and his ever-present supply of ropes, ties and ribbons. Alina had received our note and managed to untie him and get him back to their room, but not until copious photographs were taken to commemorate the occasion.

Ahh, the Brothers Shellenberg, up to their usual shenanigans. Sure, Alina was pissed, but nowhere near as pissed as Markus would be when he learned that we were going to hold those photos over his head, maybe put them on blankets, or china or something. His twin sons would think it was hilarious when they got old enough.

"Matti, are you sure this is okay?" Abby anxiously tugged on my sleeve and interrupted my daydream of Markus' mini-mes tormenting him with those photos. I'd make them baby T-shirts and they could wear them to Christmas dinner next year.

"What? Yeah, it's fine. Don't worry about it. Max and Charlotte are cool with it. Charlotte hates attention and you know I'm the ultimate distraction, especially since I'm in a tux. And you, my sweet, sweet lady with your beautiful beach ball trapped beneath that charming dress, are the perfect accompaniment to my gorgeousness — *ow*!"

Abby shook her hand out. She'd punched me with her thumb on the outside of her fist.

"I thought we talked about how to throw a punch, Stabby. Jesus, that had to hurt you more than it hurt me."

"Fuck you, Matti," she seethed and stopped abruptly to bend over and groan. "And fuck you for this too."

Abby was pregnant. So super, beautifully pregnant, and we were in Austria, slowly lumbering toward my brother's outdoor, vineyard wedding ceremony. Only it wasn't just his wedding ceremony — it was ours too, in a surprise for pretty much everyone.

Right after Abby took me back, which she definitely shouldn't have and I know I didn't deserve it in the slightest, Sylvie had found the two of us jobs in Los Angeles. I played for the United, while Abby had taken a job at UCLA coaching the women's team. We'd stuck with our engagement, but never planned a wedding. Neither of us had needed it. Until the baby news landed completely out of the blue and suddenly everyone and their mother — especially Abby's and my own — had had something to say about the absolute necessity of our getting hitched before the little striker hit the field.

We'd put them off long enough and Max and his soon-to-be-wife Charlotte had offered, no, *begged* us to join the nuptials since both of them hated the entire idea of weddings and being the center of attention. I, obviously, had no problem with that, and Abby had gone along with it too. So we'd snuck her family in and they'd be seated at the back. When she and I walked up the aisle as members of the wedding party, we'd stand next to Max and Charlotte and the officiant would marry us both — knock out four birds with one Bible verse.

Simple, right? Only, no one had counted on Abby being quite so pregnant by the time the wedding finally happened, since it had been pushed off for a few months due to weather or some nonsense. She was almost eight months along and so beautiful I wanted to scream every time I caught a glimpse of her. Still petite, no one could tell she was pregnant until she turned to the side and you saw her profile view. It was like someone stuck a cherry tomato on a toothpick.

"Oh god, the stench!" Abby cried out as we got closer to the pavilion amidst the vines. It really was awful — the winds were definitely coming from the wrong direction.

"Babe, it's gonna be okay. Get through this and we'll get to eat — "

She retched, dry heaving, and nothing came up, then looked at me with accusatory, streaming eyes. "Why'd you have to say 'eat'?" She was murderous.

"Aw, come here." I pulled her close and tried to pet her hair and rub her back.

"Stop petting me. Let's go get hitched. Quickly, before I hurl all over the place," she groused as we finally came to the site where everyone was impatiently waiting for us.

"Sorry, pregnant lady had to stop and puke."

"Oh, Abby! Are you okay?" Her mother came rushing up and suddenly everyone was staring at me in confusion and anger. Clearly this was all my fault. *Some things never change.*

"What is *she* doing here?" my mother hissed from the front row. There was little love lost between those two tiger moms.

"All right, all right. Places, everyone." Ella clapped and we all obediently fell into our positions, Abby pushing her mother to sit back down.

The music started, people stood, and first Ella and Martin, then Markus and Alina and finally Abby and I headed down the aisle to meet Max at the front.

Charlotte was escorted in by her grandfather, a genial farmer with a constant smile on his bright red face.

Clicking camera shutters and admiring murmurs rose and fell behind Charlotte in a wave. Like her grandfather, she was beet red by the time she popped up next to us, and Abby squeezed her arm in solidarity. Then it was go time, the officiant standing and explaining our sneaky surprise to the guests. A blur of saying yes to highly improbable things, then it was time for our vows to each other. I pulled a small piece of paper out of the pocket of my vest.

"I wrote my own, if that's okay."

Abby beamed and the officiant nodded at me. I heard Max snort softly and a rustle as Charlotte pinched him.

"Stabby Abby McKinnon," I began.

Abby rolled her eyes and cleared her throat. My mother hissed in disapproval from the front row. My nieces cheered.

"Kidding, sorry. Let me start over. Abigail McKinnon, I love you now, forever and always. You make me a better man, a better human, and I want to always be the best for you. I promise to love you through hard times and good, debilitating injuries and recovery and all the wins and losses that happen in a marriage. I promise to never leave you without saying goodbye and that I will always, always listen to you when you speak. Because of you, I am a stronger person, the person I've always been meant to be — yours and our baby's. Everything I do, I do it for you."

Ha. Markus might have his Phil Collins problem, but I had him beat with my Bryan Adams obsession.

Abby rolled her eyes and I could see her ears starting to turn red. I'd probably completely derailed her and now she was thinking of Kevin Costner in tights.

She cleared her throat again. "Matthias Shellenberg, I love you now, forever and always. Being with you has been the greatest of adventures and the most frightening journey."

Someone snickered behind us and I knew it was Markus.

"Together, we are better. Your sunshine makes my grump go into hiding and I need you to always be there for me like that—to remind me that not everything is life or death, that there will always be a tomorrow to work things out and that things always happen for a reason. Because of you I am a more complete person, someone I've always striven to be but would never have achieved if it weren't for you."

My eyes got all watery and started to leak all over the place like hers.

"I'm so pleased to marry you today. You are my greatest happiness."

We stood there, locked in the moment with the sun shining down on us, my grandmother's ring winking up at me, a few lazy kicks from our star striker rolling across my beautiful wife's belly, surrounded by all of our family. Finally, finally, we were where we were meant to be—and with who we were meant to be.

"You may now kiss your bride, and I believe I speak for everyone when I ask that you please attempt to keep it at a suitable heat level for children."

Everyone chuckled, but when I pulled Abby into my arms, the entire world disappeared and everything could have burned to a crisp around us.

Together, we were better.

Want to see more like this?
Here's a taster for you to enjoy!

Crashing the Net
Cheyenne Meadows

Excerpt

"What the hell are you talking about?" Ranger Deacon, the captain of the Denver Wolfpack, voiced the question probably every man in the room had on their mind.

"Piper Darrow is taking Gunderson's place. She'll be the number one goalie for the rest of the year."

"Holy shit," one of the guys in the corner muttered.

"We must be pretty damn awful to have to invite women to play with us," Adam Lancaster, seated behind Ranger, hollered out.

"Who came up with that fucking awful idea?" another asked.

A chorus followed, voices filled with exasperation.

Tommy Smith, the head coach, held up his hands. "It's a done deal. No use in getting all pissed off when we have to fill that crucial position. Besides, she's one hell of a goaltender."

"Let Rayovic play," Des Croft, one of the second line players, tossed out.

Smith pinned the guy with a firm stare. "I am letting Rayovic play. But he can't be expected to play every minute of every game for the next thirty games." His voice rose and turned hard as steel. "You know as well as I do one goalie can't do it all."

Ranger glanced across the room, noting the confusion and frustration painted on the guys' faces. They'd had a tough year thus far. The loss of their goalie had nearly proved to be the final nail in the coffin containing the men's morale. He knew many of them had voiced concerns, even whispering about finding a new home for the next season. As much as he hated to break up a team who'd previously gotten along so well, Ranger understood their sentiment. He couldn't claim to be happy right now either.

But a woman?

He pulled up what he knew about Piper Darrow. Certainly, the last name rang clear as a bell. Her Canadian father had been one of the game's best scorers in the almost twenty years that he'd played. Big, fierce, he had a talent for attacking the goal, combined with stamina, durability and a hell of a backhand shot. The name alone invoked reverence and legendary awe. At least to Ranger.

He'd seen Piper play a couple of times. Quick of hand. Fearless. She defended her goal like a momma grizzly defended her cubs.

Still, she wasn't big or bulky. The nature of the women's game protected her smaller frame from hard collisions commonly found with men. She'd have to be one tough woman to hold up physically for the rest of the season. As a goalie, she had a shot. As a forward, like her father, she'd be likely be out before the week was done from teeth-jarring checks meant to crush her against the boards.

Uncertainly flared. Again.

"She just won the women's league championship and was named MVP," Tommy added.

"Whoopee." Anthony Hillman twirled his finger in the air.

"Big fucking deal," Riley Dickenson snarled.

Ranger swung around to glare at Dickenson for that comment. "I don't care what sport or what gender plays that sport, being the best there is demands respect."

"The decision is final. So if anyone still has an issue, there's the door." Tommy bit out every word and pointed toward the exit. He would have made a drill sergeant proud.

Murmurs answered.

Sometimes being captain sucks.

Ranger stood up and moved to the front of the meeting room. "It boils down to this. We have to have a goalie. As hard as Rayovic tries, he can't do it all." Ranger nodded toward the young rookie, who dipped his head in acknowledgement.

Time to think outside the box and get this motley crew on board. "Think of it this way, you all know who her father is, right?"

A chorus of "yeah" followed.

"Well, who do you think she faced all those years in practice?"

A few laughed. Others began to smile.

"If nothing else, it should prove to be an interesting rest of the season." Tommy grinned encouragingly.

The men agreed. Ranger eyed each one, saw the various reactions, and knew Piper faced a formidable challenge before even meeting their first opponent. She had to earn these men's trust and belief. Hard enough for any new player. Let alone for one who started with predisposed attitudes against them. He had no doubt most men would consider her gender a handicap.

"Get geared up. Practice starts in fifteen." Tommy waved them toward the door. "No cheap shots. The first man who lays a hand on our new goalie will answer to me."

The stern tone told Ranger all he needed to know. The head coach already saw Piper as a daughter figure. To cross him would earn his wrath.

Good. That just might keep Piper standing after today's practice.

Heaven knew she needed all the help she could get.

A few minutes later, Ranger ambled up to the ice, his eyes drawn to the woman with the long blonde hair streaming behind her as she zipped from end to end, chasing a puck with decent skill. She ducked, dodged and finally flipped the puck on edge, pulled back her stick, and let loose. The wobbly shot hit the upper right corner of the net.

"She's the goalie?" Rocky, the left winger on Ranger's line, asked.

"Looks like more of a forward to me," Sven, his linemate and the right winger, pointed out.

Ranger watched the gliding motions, the power contained in a small body. As he stared at her, she stopped on a dime, lifted her chin and turned to face the lot of them. He caught a glimpse of narrowed deep blue eyes, a short sigh and a furrowing of her forehead. Defensive mechanisms if ever he'd seen any. She stood up straight, then rested her hands on the stick before looking back at the guys. Her body language spoke of irritation from having her playtime interrupted along with bracing herself for the impact of dealing with twenty men, all new to the idea of playing with a woman. On the ice. Ranger had no doubt the guys had spent many hours playing with a woman in bed. Including himself.

She checked them all out, sizing them up. As a group or individually, he didn't know. The second her focus landed on him, his breath caught as an electric zing carried through his body. Intelligence showed in her features, along with classic beauty tempered by fitness and strength.

Interest piqued, he skated out on the ice toward her. "You must be Piper."

"Yep." She tilted her head and raked him from top to bottom and back again. Cautious appreciation flared in her eyes. "You must be Ranger." She pointed at the big C on his jersey.

"That's me." He noted the others closing around them.

"She's not dressed for practice," Hillman, another forward pointed out.

Piper cut him a glare. "First of all, I was told practice started at three. It's only two-fifteen now. Plenty of time to put the pads on. Secondly, since I don't have a Wolfpack jersey, the best you're gonna get is my Bobcats one until someone provides me with a uniform." She shifted her gaze to Tommy.

"The order's in already." He offered up a small smile. "Since that's taken care of, do you think you can get into gear so we can get to work?"

Piper grinned at him and saluted. "Yes, sir." She kicked the puck at her feet into motion. In a flash, she flew to the other net, spun and fired.

Another strike.

"Damn." Ranger couldn't take his eyes off her. Beauty. Talent. All with a fiery attitude. Impressed, he found himself staring at his new teammate with avid interest and more than a hint of desire.

"Shit, she's good," Adam remarked.

"Don't start handing out line places yet, Adam." Anthony rubbed his forehead. "Scoring is easy when there's no one in your way."

Ranger had played hockey most of his life, starting on the frozen ponds of Minnesota as a small child. He'd seen a girl occasionally play with the boys during pickup games, but never one in organized play. He didn't doubt Piper had plenty of skills. What he did question was whether she could be the answer they needed and hold up under the pressure of the big leagues.

Time will tell.

* * * *

Piper watched one of the forwards approach, pass the puck off to another guy, then swing his stick as it sailed back to him on the ice. Instinctively, she did the splits, preventing it from sliding under her and across the goal line. Her glove came down fast, covering the puck before anyone could smack at it on a rebound try.

The whistle blew. None too soon, as the two huge men crowded her space just in front of the net.

Tommy skated over. "Nice save."

"Thanks." Piper regained her feet and tossed the puck back out and into play. She'd spent the past hour fending off pucks sailing her direction. None of them had gotten by. A pretty snazzy showing, if she said so herself. Of course, she'd carry a few marks tomorrow morning for her efforts. She'd thought some of the women had powerful line drives. The men had them beat easily. One puck to her chest had stolen her breath and nearly put her down for a good couple of minutes. Sheer pride and determination had forced her back to her feet as if nothing had happened. Good thing she had years of practice with that particular move. Her father had taught her toughness above all else.

Gunther Darrow, her father, could be considered a hockey legend. He'd taken her to the rink with him one day while her mother was away. Piper had been six at the time. He'd strapped hockey skates to her feet as well as those of her brother, Darius, and let them loose. Piper had never once looked back. The ice offered her more than a chance at playtime and exercise. It gave her an outlet.

"Change lines." Tommy waited a beat before tossing the puck toward the middle of the ice.

Piper resumed her butterfly position, her focus completely on the small piece of black rubber zipping across the ice. As the other team brought it over the blue line, a tall, solidly built man took up position three inches from her crease, the blue area directly in front of the net. She craned her neck, shifted back and forth, and struggled to keep her eye on the puck with such a big man right in her way. Tempted to give him a shove, she maintained her composure instead, knowing she'd face this situation over and over again in the near future. Screens weren't limited to the men's game. Women had also developed the practice. Although none were built like the moose presently blocking her view. She'd seen enough of that from peewee games all through college. With no women's leagues at that time except for the professional level, she'd had no choice but to play with the boys. Hadn't bothered her. She had still kicked their butts at every given opportunity.

"Hey, Moose. You might have one fine ass, but I really don't need a bird's-eye view, all the same. So move it."

Ranger turned around and flashed a quirky grin.

She poked him with her stick while keeping a close eye on the puck. A player took it down the middle, then cut across near the face-off circle. He pulled back, then lined up for a shot.

The slash of a hockey stick caught her across the shoulder, the force spinning her around. She maintained her balance, found the puck in her peripheral vision, and grabbed it with her glove at the last second.

After a moment to suck in air, she dropped it in front of her and stared back at the men gaping in her direction.

Aha. There it is. The look of amazement and shock she'd been waiting to see since the rest of the team had stepped on the ice that afternoon.

Hiding a smile, she used her stick to nudge the puck back toward the tall man with black hair and green eyes. Ranger. Ranger Deacon. The team's captain and one of the best power forwards in the league. Built like a true position guy, Ranger towered over her and could easily outweigh her twice. Just now in his prime, he'd played with the team for a couple of years after doing his time in the minors. Skill, talent and plain old hard work had carried him to the pros and landed him a spot on the team. Attitude, people skills and leadership had netted him the captain position as well.

Rumor had it he didn't take crap off anyone. Normally laid-back, he was slow to rile, but once there, he made sure his opponent never trod down the same path again. Big and strong, the guy could generate speed as well as send another player flying when checked.

Piper liked that in a man.

Too bad most of the guys carried a chip on their shoulder and attitudes that belonged in the caveman days. Just another reason she didn't date hockey players. Hell, lately she hadn't dated anyone, athlete or not. She'd lost interest after finding too many toads and none that turned into a prince with a mere kiss.

The couple of men that she had dated hadn't ended up working out, either. Mostly, they'd had sex on their minds. Typical for guys that age, she figured, especially athletes who lacked shyness and had primed bodies to show off. The difference between men and women. Intimacy ranked low on her totem pole behind companionship, friendship and romance. A traumatic childhood had made trust difficult, pushing that level of closeness way down the line. Only time, familiarity and love could motivate her to sleep with a man. Her beaus, on the other hand, had made it known that getting hot and heavy in the sack hovered around the top of their list of goals. At an impasse, they had each gone their separate ways. Since she refused to be a trophy put on display, she'd turned her interests to other, more meaningful activities. Until a man wanted her for her, she wouldn't bother to give them more than a fleeting look.

When and if that happened, she'd reconsider her take on men. In the meantime, she focused on making a place in the world for herself and trying to do a bit of good along the way.

"Penalty shots, then we'll call it a day," Tommy hollered from the nearest blue line. He moved to the edge of the rink and watched them all with a critical eye.

Piper perked up. *Time to shine.*

She banged her stick on the side bars and resumed her stance. The past couple of days she'd spent hours watching video on these guys, in preparation for this very moment. She'd learned their preferences, their tendencies. All that studying would pay off. It always did.

Skater after skater approached her with speed, snaking their way toward her before taking their shot. She rejected each one in turn. Until Rocky flew past her, caught her going low, and shot a nice top-shelf laser that streaked by her before she could do more than blink.

He waved his stick in celebration.

She flipped up her goalie mask and smiled at the team's leading scorer. Since creating masks took time and precision, she'd kept her old one. While the bobcat painted on the side might not match up well with a wolf for a mascot, she didn't really care. As long as it fit well and worked, she would hang onto it. "Good shot. Guess that's why you're the sniper on the team."

"Yeah. You could say that." He grinned at her before tipping his head. "You're not so bad yourself."

She accepted the compliment with a quick grin.

"Nice job." Rayovic skated to a stop in front of her. "You've sure got the fast glove."

"Thanks. You've got some guts standing there with the whole team crashing the net."

Rayovic smiled proudly. "That happened a lot on the ice when I was a kid." His Czech accent came through well, though his words weren't hard to understand, testament to his time and practice speaking English.

"You've got a bright future." She sobered. "I'm sorry it had to happen like this. I feel like you've been given the stick."

Surprisingly, Rayovic offered up a sly grin. "It is okay. I'm not one of those men who have a problem with women playing the game. You play great and the team needs someone like you."

"Thank you." Piper smiled softly. "How do you say thank you in Czech?"

"*Děkuju.*"

"*Děkuju.*" She stumbled over the word the first time, earning a chuckle from the other goalie. "*Děkuju.*" Her second try earned her a nod of approval.

"With your size you have to focus more. If the other team realizes this weakness, they'll take advantage big time."

Piper's grin faded with the heavily accented words. "Stanza. I was wondering when you'd appear." The old Swede had written the record books on goaltending back in his day. He'd turned coach a couple of decades ago and passed his nuggets of advice to his players. *More like beat it into their heads.* Stanza believed in a hardline approach and in-your-face challenges rather than praise and uplifting inspiration.

He snorted and skated closer. "You want to play men's game, you have to think like a man."

Piper rolled her eyes. "That might be a problem. I'm not one to ogle boobs and think with a dick that I don't happen to have. Guess that leaves out scratching the balls as well."

Rayovic laughed openly.

Stanza stared at her for a long moment before his lips twitched. "You're going to be difficult."

"Who? Me? Difficult?" She shrugged. "I'm not the one trying to turn me into a man."

Stanza's lips curled up into a reluctant grin. "Point taken. Now, we still have some work to do."

Piper caught a glimpse of the rest of the team leaving the ice for the day. She had a momentary longing before shaking it off. The ice had become her home away from home years before. With a non-existent social life and the decided lack of hobbies, she had nothing waiting for her at the house anyway.

"When you see the shooter coming…" Stanza rattled on.

She tuned into him completely, needing to get her head on straight before the first game, when she faced opposition in the form of a rival team. Filled with men. Who probably didn't want a woman invading their territory.

The story of my life.

About the Author

Amanda (A.B.) Wilson is the pen name for a heat-seeking librarian from the upper Midwest. Long after her sassy five year old and long-suffering husband go to bed, she writes steamy, escapist contemporary romances about celebrities, athletes, and billionaires — with a twist.

Amanda loves to hear from readers. You can find her contact information, website details and author profile page at https://www.totallybound.com

Home of Erotic Romance

Sign up for our newsletter and find out about all our romance book releases, eBook sales and promotions, sneak peeks and FREE romance books!